# Target: Bragg

"Bragg!" cried Benny, staring over my shoulder.

I spun around. A figure loomed in the darkness just outside Benny's shattered window. Whoever it was carried something in a two-handed grip. I gave Benny a hard shove against the wall. "Everybody duck!" I yelled.

The man outside began shooting as we dove through the door. He fired in quick succession. The shots sounded as if they were large caliber. Zither screamed as a bullet smacked into the outer wall of the studio. I pushed Benny and Zither inside.

"Call the cops!" I yelled again, running down the hallway after the fleeing gunman.

Some private dick I'd turned out to be. Flirting with Zither, the sexy painter lady, while the attempted murder of my old buddy Benny Bartlett was in progress downstairs. Well, I'll pay for it now, I thought, as I ran outside to retrieve my gun and give chase to the would-be assassin.

Also by Jack Lynch

*SAUSALITO*
*SAN QUENTIN*
*MONTEREY*

Published by
WARNER BOOKS

# JACK LYNCH

## A BRAGG NOVEL

# SEATTLE

**WARNER BOOKS**

A Warner Communications Company

Warner Books, Inc.
75 Rockefeller Plaza
New York, N.Y. 10019

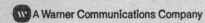 A Warner Communications Company

Printed in the United States of America

First Printing: October, 1985

10  9  8  7  6  5  4  3  2  1

# Chapter 1 —————————

Benny Bartlett called me long distance that Saturday and said he needed help. He said he was in all kinds of trouble, but he didn't want to tell me about it over the phone. The tone of his voice said all that I needed to know. He was scared. I asked him the number he was calling from and told him I'd get back to him.

Benny was special. He was the funny little sort of man who could restore my faith in people whenever I got fed up with the tribe of whackos, con men, and bad guys I'd met over the years, first as a newspaper reporter and now as a private investigator. Benny had been my pal since those awful adolescent years, when life at times could make a guy want to scream in the night. About his only shortcoming, so far as I could figure, was that he loved Seattle and wouldn't think of living anywhere else.

We'd both been born and raised, gone to school, and gotten married in that town. But I hadn't really grown

1

up, I realized years later, until I'd moved away from there. I decided I hadn't really known what sort of town it was until I'd been to a few other places and had something to compare it with. Much the same might be said of my ex-wife.

I phoned a travel agent and was booked onto a flight out of San Francisco International the next afternoon. Then I phoned Benny back and told him when I'd be arriving. He asked if I wanted him to pick me up at the airport, but I told him I'd rather rent a car of my own. It turned out he was under some kind of deadline pressure so he'd be working that Sunday at his office in one of the old buildings down near the waterfront. He gave me the address. I told him to hang in there. He made a gusty sigh and said he'd been doing that for several days now.

I left my Sausalito apartment and drove on over the Golden Gate Bridge and into San Francisco, to the offices on Market Street I share with a couple of attorneys. I didn't know how long Benny's problems might keep me out of town, and I had a little paperwork to clean up. It took me longer to do than it normally would because Benny's call kept my mind drifting to thoughts of the old hometown.

I felt really ambivalent about Seattle these days. It's the home of the University of Washington, which has a top-flight medical school, a fine drama department, routinely awesome eight-oar rowing crews, and football teams erratic enough to make a bookie weep. It's also home of the Boeing Aircraft Company, which had given the world among other things the B-17 Flying Fortress and the 707 jetliner. And it's a pretty city if you can ignore the months of drear and drizzle. It has an hourglass shape, a deep water port, and mile-high ranges of mountains to both east and west. Its citizens radiate an open, outdoor demeanor, and the place had gotten a lot of favorable national press in recent years.

But I felt I knew a little different sort of a city underneath all that.

Seattle had been a frontier town, make no mistake about it. Early settlers had killed off a number of the local Salish Indians and stolen their land. They'd sloughed off the hilltops to make them easier to build on and they'd run off the Chinese, who'd laid track over the mountains for their railroads. And the early locals had coined a term that's identified today with flophouses and squalor—Skid Road. The original Skid Road had been a broad, muddy track used by ox teams to drag the great logs of Douglas fir and western cedar down from surrounding hills to the steam-operated sawmill that Henry Yesler had built where the Duwamish River empties into Elliott Bay. South of Skid Road, in the early days, was where you'd find the saloons and dance halls and theaters and whorehouses.

And then, as the place grew and the railroad came and more women settled there and churches were built, the town from time to time would experience a cramp of high morality and shut down all those bawdy houses south of Skid Road. At least for a while. And Seattle today, it seemed to me, still had this awkward mix of puritanism, rawness, hooray outdoorness and small-town venality I'd also witnessed unthinkingly during my own formative years. The damn town just couldn't make up its mind about things, was the way I saw it.

I left a note for Ceejay, our secretary, receptionist and all-around troubleshooter, to let her know I'd be gone for a few days. Then I went home and packed a bag and thought about things, and what I finally decided was to include a couple of handguns along with the shirts and shorts.

The plane touched down on the slick runway of Seattle-Tacoma International Airport the next day at a little after 4 P.M. About the time we'd flown into cloud cover over Eugene, Oregon, the captain had come on the speaker and told us it was fifty-eight degrees and drizzling in Seattle. The captain had been wrong. It wasn't drizzling, it was out and out raining. I picked up a small rental car and drove north. Approaching downtown Seattle, I had another sharp sense of wrongness. I didn't recognize the skyline any longer. They'd thrown up a bunch more high-rise buildings. The times I'd been to New York the tall buildings had seemed in natural place there, on that long, flat island of Manhattan. But Seattle was hilly and wasp-waisted, and those huge blocks of marble and stone and glass looked all out of whack. When I'd been growing up, the tallest building in town had been the forty-two-story Smith Tower, a venerable old thing of gray stone with a pointed crown. These days I couldn't even find it amid the towers and spires. I passed a billboard that urged people to CAST YOUR BREAD ON POTLATCH BAY. I didn't know what that meant. What I felt like doing was casting a stick of dynamite or two at some of those high-rises.

Benny's office turned out to be in a great old warehouse of a building down below the Pike Place Market. It had been a veteran structure before Benny and I had been born, even, but it still stood solid and dependable right next to the Burlington Northern railroad tracks. The building was one of those red brick treasures that today attracted artists and craftsmen and other odd sorts who needed a lot of space for modest rent. It was red brick because that's what they used to rebuild the town after the terrible fire of 1889 started when a pot of glue boiled over on a gasoline stove in a basement paint store and cabinet shop on Front Street. Before the day was over, flames had devoured the heart of downtown Seattle—twenty-five city blocks of it. So they rebuilt with bricks. Bricks don't burn. They do, however, crumble when a sharp earthquake rattles through town, and I'd been in more and stronger and scarier earthquakes while growing up in Seattle than I had in all the years I'd lived and worked in San Francisco.

From the sound of things inside the building, Benny wasn't the only one working that Sunday. There was laughter from the floor above and a couple of radios were playing. A lobby directory told me Benny's office was up at the north end of the ground floor. The hallway was dim, and its wooden floor was worn and warped. Just outside the door to Benny's office I heard the clickety-clack of a typewriter. Benny was a free-lance writer, and he'd managed for the past twenty years to support himself and his wife and a couple of kids by clickety-clacking the hell out of that old manual typewriter. I rapped on the speckled glass pane in the door and went inside.

Benny kept on typing for a moment, his thin shoulders hunched over the machine, a cigarette in his mouth, thick-lensed eyeglasses giving him his view of the world. I noticed the view through the window over his desk wasn't of a particularly attractive part of the world. Crumbled foundations in the lot across the street indicated there had been a building standing there once. Now it was a weedy lot that was home to rusty tin cans, old wine bottles, and probably some other things I wouldn't want to get close enough to identify.

Benny slapped the carriage return bar and swiveled around in his chair.

"Thank God, safe at last," he cried, coming out of the chair to grab my hand. "Though, frankly, I don't know if I'm a victim of my own imagination or a case of the crazies or what. I almost phoned you back this morning to tell you to forget it. I thought I'd try to adopt the old wait-and-see attitude. But then I thought, Well, if I waited and saw until I was dead and buried, then what would Dolly and Timothy and Al have to say about that, huh? 'Boy, Pop, you really blew it this time,' they'd say, standing over my lonely rain-soaked grave. 'Why didn't you let your old pal Peter Bragg in on things soon enough to save your ass, instead of us now having to go fatherless to the workhouse for the rest of our lives?'"

"Al? What happened to Fred?"

"His given name is Alfred. We called him Fred until he started speaking in complete sentences in much the way I just mimicked. He's too much of a smartass for a Fred. Al it is."

"Maybe I've been away for too long."

"Five years, pal."

"Actually, I did pass through town a year or so ago, but I was working and didn't have time to look up anybody."

"We're not anybody, Pete, we're family. You're missing a sensational show not being around while the kids are growing up. Timmy's thirteen, plays piano and drums, is noticing girls for the first time in his life, and is beginning to get a squeak to his voice."

"That makes Fred, or Al rather, eleven?"

"That's right. He doesn't do much yet, though, except lip-off."

"How's Dolly?"

"Just great. A little more fleshy than you'll remember her. She'll swoon when I bring you in and tell her to set another place for dinner."

"Hey, if she's not expecting me, I'll just . . ."

"Don't be silly. She shines in such moments of crisis. And I didn't know until the last moment if I was really going to ask you to do this. I haven't gotten around to telling her about it yet. Your being here, I mean."

"You were a little vague on the phone about what the problem is. What's going on?"

"Ah Christ," he sighed, motioning me to a chair and sinking back behind the typewriter. "The thing is, there's this ugly-sounding guy who phoned me and told me I'd better leave town or I was going to be killed."

He blinked rapidly a time or two and began to straighten things on his desk. I leaned back and waited for him to gather his thoughts. It wasn't the sort of trouble a man like Benny was supposed to encounter. He wasn't an investigative reporter, he was just an article writer who once in a while would score with a well-paying piece in *Playboy* or *Esquire*. What put the bread and butter on the dinner table year in and year out were the dozens of stories he wrote for various trade journals and specialty publications most of us have never heard of. He sometimes would mail me copies of articles he was especially proud of. The last one he'd sent was about how to rid your lawn of gophers. He wrote about Puget Sound fisheries and new timber products, office management techniques and disc sanders. He had written about a new steel bearing developed at the University of Washington school of mechanical engineering and about the effect of tidal flow on clam beds. He was not a man to write his way into trouble.

"You're sure it's not somebody's idea of a practical joke?" I asked him.

"No way, Billie Mae. They've already tried it, I'm convinced. Tried it even before I got the phone call. Only the cops don't see it that way. I don't know how it is with you, but I don't have much rapport with cops. Never. Other people can go to them with a problem and they're courteous and attentive and capably efficient. With me it's like they were watching seven years of bad luck coming through the door. They turn sullen and bitchy and rude. I complained to the uniformed officers so much they finally gave me the name of a detective I should go talk to. Hamilton, his name was. I said, 'Detective Hamilton, somebody just tried to kill me.' Hamilton yawned and told me I was imagining things. But finally he agreed to look at the car along with somebody from the police garage, but they said there was no way of telling."

"The car?"

"Yeah, the car. Old Bronco Billy, my trusty Olds. I had some errands to run around town. I found a parking place down hill on Madison Street. You remember Madison Street, Pete? I mean I know you think you have hills in San Francisco, but have you ever tried climbing up Madison Street with a hangover? Anyway, once done with the errands, I'm planning to come back here. I climb into Bronco Billy, crank over the motor, release the handbrake and turn the wheels away from the curb, and WHEEEEEEEE, discover to my horror as I began to speed down Madison Street that the brakes have failed. I mean, talk about sweaty palms time. Kids were screaming and women were fainting along the sidewalks. I nearly dropped the gear box trying to shift down, and finally killed the motor altogether. By the time I tried to stop it with the hand brake, I was going too fast for that to work. Went two and a half blocks, swerving back and forth, scaring all the other traffic to a standstill.

"At the intersection of Second Avenue, I blew right through a red light, missing the front end of a Diesel bus by about eighteen inches and giving the driver a near coronary. I finally, as my entire life was passing before my eyes for the third time, managed with a little help from the hand brake to sideswipe three parked cars and a Dempster Dumpster trash receptacle and bring Bronco Billy to a halt up on the sidewalk. I swear to God, I was so shaken up it was twenty minutes before I could speak."

He sat hunched over, reliving it. There was sweat on his brow. I waited.

"Brakes failed, did I say?" he asked. "Not quite. What had happened, see, was that somebody hacked or sawed through the little copper lines that carry the brake fluid to the brake drums. All four! But Hamilton said so far as the guy from the police garage could tell, I probably broke the copper lines crashing into things on the way down the hill and jumping the curb. It's plain bullshit, of course, but try telling that to the cops. They gave me a ticket for defective equipment, and my insurance company already has heard from the owner of one of the three parked cars I slam-bammed against to save my scrawny neck."

"When did you get the phone call?"

"That night. I answered the phone and this voice coming from what sounds like the bottom of a rain barrel says, 'What happened today was no accident. Pack up. Leave town. Or you're a dead man.' Click went the phone."

"Did you tell the cops about the phone call?"

"Of course. They looked at me as if I were making it all up. I mean, they asked me a bunch of questions about what I do and any enemies I might have and stuff like that. The problem, of course, is that there's no reason for anybody—I mean anybody—to want me out of town. I'm not a threat to anybody. I know that and now the cops know that, so they figure I've been working too hard or something."

"Forgetting the phone call for a minute, could it have been an accident? Could some other part of the brake system have failed and the lines been broken off, like the cops suggested?"

"No, Pete, no way. I'd had the car greased and the oil changed just two days before, at my friendly neighborhood garage and service station. Been going there for years. Buzz does a thorough job. He knows I'm a mechanical illiterate. I mean, I can write about this and that if somebody else explains it to me first, but when it comes to just looking at a piece of machinery and seeing what's there in front of my eyes, I'm no good.

Buzz knows this and looks after the car real well for me. I asked him if he'd checked the brakes and things when he serviced the car. He said sure he had. Everything was in good shape."

"Still . . ."

"Still nothing. Let me tell you about the day before yesterday, Friday. I was out at Woodland Park, researching a piece on a new feed grain they're using in zoos. Has some kind of property that repels mites and gives the animals' coats a glossy sheen. Real space-age stuff they developed down at the University of California at Davis, not far from your neck of the woods. I'm leaving the park and starting to get into this loaner Buzz is letting me use while the guys in the body shop are trying to get Bronco Billy back on his feet. Anyway, I'm climbing into the front seat when I hear these two BLAMS! And this tear of metal. Somebody was shooting at me. *Me!* One of the shots put a crease in the roof of the loaner."

"Did you call the cops?"

"Not imemdiately. First thing I did was hunker down and take off out of there like a flying saucer was after me. About six blocks away from there, I pulled over to the curb and sat there trembling for a while. Then I found a pay phone and called the cops. A patrol car picked me up and we went back to the parking lot, but guess what—they couldn't find anything."

"Did you show them the crease on the car roof?"

"Certainly. They said it was inconclusive. And they looked around the area where I'd been parked, but they didn't find anything they said looked like a bullet."

"Did Hamilton get in on this?"

"Yes. I told the patrol officers about the earlier incident, so they got in touch with Hamilton and he drove out and poked around some. I must say I had the feeling he tended to believe me more about the shooting than he did about the brakes. He even went across

Phinney Avenue and asked questions at a couple of buildings over there, but he didn't turn up anything."

"Was that where the shots seem to come from, across the street from the parking lot?"

"Yeah, that's what it sounded like, at least. There's an old folks' home or something over there. I guess most everybody over there's half deaf. Nobody could tell Hamilton anything, at least. Hamilton even went up on the building roof with another cop to look around for spent shell casings or something. Came up with zip. He finally shrugged and suggested I hook up a tape recorder to my phone in case Deep Throat phones again. Said to let him know if anything else untoward happens. That's the word he used. *Untoward.* He said the only other thing he could suggest until they got more to go on would be for me to hire myself a bodyguard or a private investigator or something. That rang a bell, of course. That's when I thought of calling you."

# Chapter 2

Benny grabbed his cigarette pack off the desk.

"You've already got one going in the ashtray behind you," I told him.

"Oh yeah, thanks."

"It sounds scary, Benny."

"Believe it. I feel like I'm walking around with a blown-up balloon in my chest."

"You said you almost changed your mind this morning and called to tell me not to come up. What prompted that?"

He made a face and rolled his shoulders. "Whadaya suppose? I feel like a jerk. There is no way on God's earth this really can be happening to me."

"But it is."

"Yeah," he said quietly. "But it is." He looked up at me. "Christ, Pete, it ain't fair. I've worked my butt off for what I've got, and I haven't got all that much. A fine wife, two grand kids, a modest roof over my head, and Bronco Billy, but damn little else. Why is somebody trying to scare me out of here? I can't just pick up and leave. I've got contacts here—out at the university, at Boeing, a few other places around town. They help me research. They answer questions and give me leads. There's three or four ad agencies in town I can go to sometimes when I'm a little on the shorts. They'll take me on as a temporary copywriter. There's a zillion other reasons why I can't just pack up and leave Seattle. My whole life is here."

"Take it easy, Benny. We'll find out what's behind it and put a stop to it, but don't let yourself get all rattled. What does Dolly say about it? Does she have any ideas?"

"Naw. She's more puzzled over it than I am. I suggested after the shooting Friday that maybe she and the kids should take off. Go up to her folks' place in Sequim or something. She flat out refused. Can't jerk the kids out of school like that, she told me. If it were summer, she said, she'd think about shipping out with them. Not now. Not yet."

"Do Timmy and Al know what's going on?"

"Christ, no. They have overactive imaginations enough."

"You'd better tell them."

"They'd just blab it around school."

"Fine. The more people who know about it, the better. People you work with, neighbors. Anybody who might be able to notice something or somebody out of the ordinary. Get yourself an early-warning network. Get all the help you can—for yourself, for Dolly, and for the boys."

"You don't think anybody'd try something with the boys..."

"Just let's not be careless about any of this. Has anything else funny happened recently?"

"No, not really. Well..."

"Come on, Benny, has it or hasn't it?"

"I don't know. It's just that maybe somebody has been

going through my desk and things here. Only I'm not sure."

"What makes you wonder?"

He nodded toward the door. "Mary Ellen Cutler, across the hall. She makes these weird mobiles and jewelry and a bunch of different stuff. Her studio's been broken into a time or two. She's been looking around for some sort of safe she can have installed. In the meantime, once last week she had a little box of gemstones she was planning to use on some piece. She asked me to stash them in here until she was ready to use them. I mean, who would ever toss a writer's office, huh? Nothing much in here but a bunch of books and a feeble idea or two, right? So I stashed this box for her. I could swear I put it under some folders in that tub file over in the corner. Mary Ellen came over a couple of days ago and said she was ready for the stones. I went to the tub file and they weren't there."

"How big was the box?"

"Small, about the size a pair of earrings would come in. They were small stones. Anyway, when she asks for them back, I empty out that tub file and lo and behold, no little box, with Mary Ellen standing there in the doorway with this impatient look on her face. I mean, it was embarrassing. I felt about the way I did when the little buckles on my cowboy boots triggered the metal detector at state prison over in Walla Walla. So anyway. About forty minutes later, after Mary Ellen has gone back to her studio convinced I've hocked her gemstones, I found the little box in a lower drawer of my desk here."

"You're sure you put it originally in the tub file."

"No, damnit, I'm not sure of anything these days. I thought I put them in the tub file. But wherever I put it, I first did some thinking about where a good hiding place would be."

His eyes darted over the cluttered bookcase and file

cabinets lining the walls. "I could have changed my mind and switched the hiding place while thoroughly distracted, thinking about whatever magnificent story I might have been working on at the time. Sorry, Pete, I'm just not sure. But on the other hand, while feverishly searching for the stones, I came across a couple of other things here and there which I thought I'd stored someplace else. Maybe I'm just going nuts."

"Or maybe somebody's just trying to make you think so."

"Same difference, ain't it?"

We talked some more. I asked him what sort of articles he'd been working on in recent months, about business dealings he might have had or any run-ins of any kind with people, no matter how minor they seemed. Benny was a fairly competent photographer as well, so he could illustrate the various trade stories that might call for that. I asked him about the photos he'd been taking lately. And as we talked, I could understand how the cops must have felt about things. Benny just wasn't the sort of fellow who stepped on people's toes. The stories he'd been working on were the same sort of obscure writing he'd been doing for two decades. His only business dealings, aside from paying the bills that came regularly in the mail, was to send off queries to editors of various journals suggesting stories he could do for them.

"I did disappoint the editor of *Concrete Today*," he told me. "Went up to a place just outside of Vancouver, B.C., to do a yarn about an outfit fixing to build a bunch of elegant houseboats on ferroconcrete hulls, but they went bankrupt at the last minute so there was no story there after all. But that's hardly enough to kill over."

I asked embarrassing questions Benny swore not even the cops had asked, like was he running around on the side with somebody else's wife? Did he have a homosexual lover? Did he have any other secret passions or vices nobody was supposed to know about? He just sat at his desk and giggled at all these things.

"Okay, I give up. For tonight, anyway," I told him. "We'll go at it again tomorrow."

Before he closed up the office, Benny called home to tell his wife he was running a little late. He still didn't tell her I was in town. I complained about that after he hung up.

"Hey, not to worry. Look, some guys once in a while bring home flowers. I sometimes bring home a tall drink of water from the past. It'll floor her."

He turned out the lights and closed and locked the door. People were talking in the studio across the hall and the door was partly open. Benny rapped on it and stepped inside. It was twice the size of Benny's office, filled with glass display cases, work tables, and benches. A woman in her mid-forties, stout, with gray-streaked bangs hanging limply across a broad forehead, was sitting in an overstuffed chair. A younger woman, tall, pale-skinned and thin as a rail, sat on a nearby sofa that was losing some of the stuffing out of one of the cushions.

"Hi, Mary Ellen, hello, Zither," said Benny. "Want you to meet a friend of mine."

"Come on in, Benny," said the older woman, getting to her feet. "Have a glass of wine?"

"No thanks, Mary Ellen, we're just on our way home."

"Nonsense," said Mary Ellen, crossing to a loudly humming refrigerator. "Won't take a minute to toss back a glass of jug Chablis. Bring your friend in."

We crossed the studio while she poured wine into a couple of jelly glasses.

"This is Peter Bragg from San Francisco," Benny said. "And these two sexy broads," he told me, "are Mary Ellen Cutler, who makes exotic jewelry down here, and Zither Lawrence, who paints exotic paintings upstairs."

We exchanged hellos. "Bragg's a former ace newspaperman turned private investigator. He's come back to his old hometown to try to save the spindly body of yours truly. I've had some strange things happening to me lately. Like getting death threats."

Mary Ellen gasped. Zither sipped her wine. After a brief glance at Benny, she looked back toward me. It seemed she'd been staring at me since we came through the door.

"Am I doing all right?" Benny asked me.

"You're doing swell," I told him. "Rally the troops. Put out the pickets."

Benny briefly recounted the perils that had befallen him. Mary Ellen Cutler listened with rapt expression. Zither's eyes stayed with me. It was a kid's game she was playing. I glanced at her, smiled, then looked away and sipped my wine. Zither reminded me of a woman who'd caused a mild sensation on late night television years earlier on the West Coast. She'd hosted old movies, as I recall, and presented a stark appearance under the stage name Vampira. The woman on the couch might have been her daughter. She had long, lank black hair. She was wearing black slacks and a white silk blouse. She highlighted her pale skin with scarlet lipstick on her thin mouth and matching polish on her long fingernails. When I looked back at her, she was still staring at me. I went over and sat down beside her.

"When I was growing up here, the girls weren't this forward," I told her.

"Is that what I'm being?" she asked in a quiet voice.

"Aren't you?"

She tilted her head. "I'm not sure. You have an interesting face. And body, for that matter. I was thinking I might like to paint you sometime."

"Oh."

Put properly in my place, I turned back to listen to Benny telling Mary Ellen about the hair-raising ride down the hill in old Bronco Billy. A moment later Zither reached out and touched my arm. I looked across at her.

"I said I wasn't sure," she told me. "Maybe I was being a little forward, as well. I have small breasts and a skinny frame. A girl has to compensate."

We just looked at each other for a moment. She looked as if she'd be fun to flirt with. There was a look about her eyes that suggested she might feel the same about me.

I turned my attention back to Benny. When he'd finished his tale, Mary Ellen asked him a lot of the same questions I'd asked him, trying to help figure out who might be coming after him and why.

Zither touched my arm again. "Are you married?"

"No."

"Mmmmmmm. Steady girl?"

"One who's kind of special."

"Where is she?"

"In a little town down in California."

"A long way from here."

"You're right, it is. Quite a coincidence about you two."

"What is?"

"She's a painter, too. A pretty good one."

"What sort of work does she do?"

"She used to do a lot of seascapes, with fishing boats and docks and scattered tackle and gear in them. She lives right on the coast. Lately, though, she's been branching out, doing less representational pieces. I don't know what you'd call it, really. She uses a lot of spirals and different gewgaws. But she puts it all together in an interesting way. I don't understand what it's supposed to mean, but I find myself sort of transfixed by some of it."

"Has she ever done you?"

"Painted me, you mean? No. Figure painting doesn't interest her. Is that what you do?"

"Uh-huh. Most people find them quite sensual. Maybe you'd like to look at some of them sometime."

"Maybe so. When are you there?"

"Most all of the time. I live in a corner of the studio. It has everything I need. Bathroom. Hot plate and refrigerator. Bed."

"Sounds comfortable."

"It is. And with all those sexy paintings on the walls. Benny said you're on the way to his place now?"

"That's right."

"Too bad."

She finished her wine and got up and crossed over to Mary Ellen. She bent to give the older woman a quick kiss on her cheek.

"Thanks for everything, love," she told Mary Ellen. "I have to get out of here before I do something really embarrassing."

"Oh yeah, like what?" asked Benny.

"Like whatever turns you on," she replied. She gave me a little wave of her hand and left the studio.

"Wow," said Mary Ellen. "What were you two talking about?"

I cleared my throat. "Benny, we'd better get on the road."

I'd made a reservation at a motel out on Aurora Avenue, north of the downtown area. Benny followed along and went up with me while I hung some things in the closet. He whistled when he saw the revolver and pistol I'd packed.

"You really use those things?"

"When it's necessary. Other people have them too, you know."

"Yeah. I found that out."

I considered leaving the handguns locked in the

suitcase in the motel room. I didn't want to be packing them around inside Benny's place, in case I got into any horseplay with his two boys. I decided to take along the .38 revolver and leave it locked in the rental car's glove compartment.

Benny lived out further north of the motel, in a pleasant neighborhood of split-level homes on gently rolling terrain with enough pine trees and foliage around to give you a sense of privacy and rural spaciousness. Benny had phoned home again from the motel to let Dolly know he had a dinner guest in tow. From his end of the conversation you could tell his wife didn't mind having a dinner guest, but she tried to find out who it was. Benny wouldn't tell her and hung up chuckling to himself.

Benny parked in his driveway and I left the rental car on the street out front. I followed him into a dim living room. Stairs to the left led to an upper hallway with the sound of a television set coming down it. Women's voices came from through the dining room to our right from a kitchen beyond. I trailed Benny through the dining area and nearly bumped into his back when he stopped abruptly.

"Oh boy," he said in a troubled tone.

There was a woman standing with her back to us in the kitchen doorway talking to a voice I recognized as Dolly's. The woman in the doorway was wearing a soft gray sheath that emphasized her neat, slender figure. I couldn't make out the color of her hair in the backlighting from the kitchen, but there was something familiar about her stance in the doorway. I was trying to remember when she turned in response to what Benny had said.

Her jaw dropped and so did mine. It was Lorna, my ex-wife. The last time I'd seen her was a dozen years earlier, on the morning of the day she had left San Francisco on the arm of a trumpet player with the Stan

Kenton band. The last time I'd spoken to her had been later that same day, when she'd phoned me at the *Chronicle* to tell me she'd decided we'd outgrown each other and had wished me a happy life. Now, standing in the doorway to Benny's kitchen, a puzzled Dolly Bartlett appeared behind her and said what the rest of us were thinking.

"Oh my God!"

# Chapter 3

There followed one of the most confusing evenings of my life.

Dolly pushed past Lorna into the room and turned on the overhead light. She turned and gave me a hug and a kiss. Benny was right—she'd put on a little weight, but she carried it well and she looked matronly and motherly and just fine.

"You idiot!" she told Benny. "Why *didn't* you tell me you were bringing him home? Or that he was in town, even?"

Benny threw up his hands. "How'd I know she'd be here?"

Lorna and I were still too surprised to say anything. Dolly took both Lorna and me by the hand. "Look, you two, this is really inexcusable. If this is awkward or embarrassing, we can forget about dinner and just make some other arrangements." She turned to Benny.

"I asked Lorna to stay for dinner before you told me you were bringing anybody home, you knucklehead."

"Hells bells, I thought it'd be a pleasant surprise," Benny complained.

"No," Lorna said finally, a blush rising from her long neck. "It's perfectly all right, with me at least. I have to get over the shock of it is all. I'm not—I mean, it won't bother me to sit down at the dinner table with Peter if it won't bother him. But I don't know. We haven't spoken since, since I left San Francisco. Pete?"

She looked at me in a way that told me she remembered the circumstances of that day just as clearly as I did. She was embarrassed. I felt she had every right to be. But I spoke what I felt.

"No, that's okay with me. It's been a long time. I've gotten over all that."

"If you haven't," Benny said brightly, "you can always go back to Zither."

"Uncle Pete!" cried a boy's voice behind me.

It was Timmy. He bounded into the room and tried to bring me down with a tackle. I ruffled his head, and now the younger boy I'd known as Fred, who now was Al, joined us as well.

"What's all the racket in here?" he asked. "Hi, Pete."

"Uncle Pete to you, buster," said Benny.

"Who's Zither?" Lorna asked.

"Just somebody he met at the office," Benny told her, rubbing his hands together. "Well, everybody, what the hell you say we all have a drink and make ourselves comfortable?"

"Sounds like a good idea to me," Lorna told him.

"I could use one," I added. "A martini, maybe, if you have a large glass. With ice."

"I think we could all use one," said Dolly, raising her eyes to the ceiling.

"Hot dog," said Al. "I'll have a lemon twist with mine, please."

"You'll have a soda pop and consider yourself lucky," Dolly told him.

I looked away from Lorna long enough to grapple with the boys some. Although he was two years older, Timmy was only a couple of inches taller than his brother. He was thin and wore glasses, like his dad. He had a serious look about him even now. Al was a little chunkier, and when he wasn't doing anything else, the younger boy stood around with his hands on his hips. He looked as if he should have had a cigar in his mouth and a derby hat on his head. Benny had been right. The boy definitely was an Al.

When Benny went into the kitchen to fix drinks, the boys went back to their room to watch television and Lorna and Dolly and I went into the living room. Dolly turned on lamps, and then the three of us stood around awkwardly until Benny returned with the martinis. He passed out glasses the size of coffee mugs, filled with ice and gin. We all clinked glass and had a toasting sip. Just before I took a seat on the sofa, Lorna raised a tentative hand and touched my cheek.

"You've aged," she said quietly. "I didn't remember your face being so craggy."

"Haggard," I told her. "I've been through some haggard times. Sure, I've aged. But it doesn't look as if you have, even a bit."

She blushed again and turned to sit in an easy chair. I looked at her closely. She really hadn't aged, not noticeably. She had the same slender figure and unlined skin. Her light auburn hair fell just shy of her shoulders, shaped on the sides to show off that long patrician neck and unusual face. There was no single remarkable feature about it, but her nose and mouth and chin all just seemed perfectly proportioned for her. It was a face men spent a lot of time studying.

When Lorna noticed that I was staring at her, she lowered her eyes and sipped at her martini. I felt a sigh coming on and tried to keep it subdued. She looked just about the same as she had on that miserable, black Sunday when she'd left town with the horn player. I thought I'd put that all behind me years ago, but seeing her there across from me in the sheath that flattered her figure, her face flushed, as pretty and as desirable as I'd ever remembered her, it all came flooding back. Maybe I hadn't still been in love with her the day she left, but it had been a terrible experience nonetheless.

I remembered saying to myself over and over at the time, a trumpet player, for God's sake. A lousy goddamn traveling trumpet player. The fact that he had a respected position in a big-name orchestra didn't matter at all. It could have been the angel Gabriel and I'd have felt the same way. It led to my quitting my job at the *Chronicle*. I found an apartment in Sausalito and spent a time wallowing in self-pity. But I'd put that behind me long ago, I told myself now.

"Bragg, you're staring," Benny chided me.

I shifted my eyes away from Lorna and realized I hadn't heard any of the conversation that had been going on around me. I knew Lorna hadn't been saying anything. I'd been watching those lips along with the rest of her. She'd hardly glanced at me since we sat down. Benny and his wife must have been trying to carry on a conversation by themselves. I noticed my martini was drained. So was Lorna's.

"Benny, Dolly, I apologize," I told them. "This is just a surprise I wasn't ready for." I glanced across the room. "Lorna, how have you been?"

"Oh fine, just fine, Peter," she said, blinking and looking at me with a brief smile. "And you? Are you still with the *Chronicle*?"

"God, no. I quit the paper a long time ago."

"That's too bad," she said sincerely. "You were a good newspaperman."

"Let's hope he's as good at what he does now," said

Benny, circling the room with a tray and carrying empty glasses back to the kitchen.

"What's that?" Lorna asked.

"I do investigative work," I told her.

"He's a private eye," said Dolly with a wink.

"Oh golly," said Lorna. "Are you serious?"

"Serious as all get-out when I'm working," I told her. "What about yourself? You still with the horn player?"

The blush started up from her throat again. "No, that didn't last hardly any time at all. I—I live alone these days. I'm partner in a restaurant and catering business downtown."

"Restaurant?" I shook my head. "Sounds unusual for you, somehow."

"Oh I don't do the cooking, silly. I've been back to school since we knew each other. I'm into the business end of things. There's a lot more to a restaurant and catering business than just putting food on the table. But it's all pretty boring. It pays well, but it's boring."

"How long have you been back in Seattle?"

Lorna looked across at Dolly. "Five years? Six?"

"About that," Dolly agreed.

Benny was back handing out fresh drinks.

"You never mentioned her," I told him.

"Didn't figure it was anything you'd be interested in," he replied. "I mean, ahem, I know things were a little rocky there for you for a while..."

He mercifully dropped it, but Lorna's head snapped up, all interest. "Rocky? When was that?" she asked.

"It's nothing," I told her, giving Benny a look. "He's just rattling on over things he doesn't know anything about."

We made it through dinner in a yaw and jerk sort of fashion, the conversation taking odd circles and turns, but you had to expect that under the circumstances. Dolly might recall something the four of us had done together when we all were still living in Seattle, and that might prompt Lorna to relate it to something that happened to an ex-husband post-Bragg, which would cause an awkward pause in the conversation that I might try to varnish over with an amusing incident that occurred when I was a bartender in Sausalito, or maybe something out of my present tradecraft.

We were back in the living room having coffee when Benny's troubles and the reason I was back in town came up. We'd waited until the boys were back in their room. Benny promised to tell them about his woes in the morning. Benny then told Lorna about things, and during the retelling Dolly stared at the carpet, opening and closing one hand. Benny's account was straightforward enough, more somber than the version he'd given me. Lorna listened intently. I closed my eyes, listening for something he might have left out in the earlier version. I didn't find anything.

"But what will you do about it?" Lorna asked. "Peter?"

I opened my eyes.

"I put you to sleep, for Christ's sake?" asked Benny.

"No, I was just trying to concentrate on what you were saying, trying to find something new." I turned back to Lorna and opened my mouth to answer her, but words didn't come right then. She was sitting with her back slightly arched, her coffee cup and saucer held in both hands in front of her. The hem of her straight, unbelted dress was hiked slightly above her knees. She was wearing light tinted hosiery, but it didn't conceal the quality of her knees. Lorna would see to that. She had about the finest looking knees of any woman I'd ever known. But then she'd had about the finest looking legs, from thigh to toe. I made myself speak.

"What I'll do is beat up on Benny until he tells me something he doesn't even know he knows. That'll give me an idea to pursue and eventually will lead to whoever it is who thinks it's important to get Benny out of the way."

"What could I know I haven't already told you?"

"Somewhere in your files or your head or somewhere there's probably a story you've done, something or somebody you've written about in the past. And it might not have meant much then, but maybe it's taken on a new dimension and poses some sort of threat to somebody now. That's probably where the answer is."

"But I don't write that sort of stuff."

"You don't understand, Benny. Things and people change. What might have appeared innocent at one time can take on a whole different perspective at another time, depending on other circumstances."

"That makes sense," said Dolly, taking a sip of her coffee.

"Am I that dumb?" Benny complained. "It still doesn't make sense to me. Does it to you, Lorna?"

"I don't know," she said slowly. "Not on the face of it maybe, but Peter always did have a way of seeing things a little differently from the rest of us. That's why he always was so good at what he did."

She had her head cocked slightly to one side. She was putting some of the same moves on me that she'd used, consciously or not, in the days leading up to the one on which I'd asked her to marry me. A lifetime ago. With a conscious effort, probably not lost on anybody in the room, I turned back to Benny.

"For instance, you said something in your office about visiting the prison over at Walla Walla. What was that all about?"

"When I zinged out the metal detector, right. That was to interview an old con named—Horgan? Hogan? Something like that. Well, he wasn't an old con, really. He'd been serving his first prison term ever, but he had a pretty heavy background in what is loosely referred to as organized crime. The old *Seattle Magazine*, since folded, shudder, wanted me to do a piece on his return to society, et cetera. I actually made him sound like a rather lovable old scalawag. Surely he wouldn't wish me any harm."

"Things change. Do you have a copy of the story you did down at the office?"

"I should have."

"I'd like to look at it tomorrow. But first I'd like to meet you at Woodland Park on your way downtown. I want you to show me where the shooting occurred."

"I could gladly go the rest of my days without returning to that particular site."

"I'll have my hardware with me."

Lorna had been sipping her coffee. She lowered the cup. "Hardware? What hardware?"

"His gats," Benny told her. "One of 'em's a big ugly sucker. Looks like it could stop an elephant."

"It's a .45-caliber automatic pistol," I told them, "which really is a misnomer since its operation is only semi-automatic and it couldn't stop an elephant, probably, but it'll stop most men I can think of."

Lorna put the cup and saucer on a little table beside her and leaned forward slightly. It hiked up the sheath a little further above her knees. "You really carry a gun, Peter?"

"I really do. Other people carry them. Some of them try to use theirs on me or on people I'm out there to protect. A person does what has to be done."

"Have you been shot at?"

"I sure have."

"Have you shot other people?"

"A fair number of them."

She seemed to grow conscious of the skirt. Her eyes never left mine, but she lifted herself just enough to tug down her hemline. "It sounds like a pretty dangerous way for a man to make a living," she said with a little smile.

"It keeps a guy on his toes."

"Do you really run into that many rough people?" Dolly asked.

"No, not really. But the ones you do run into can be pretty bad actors."

Benny cleared his throat. "The .45's back at his motel. But he's carrying a smaller gat out in the glove compartment of his car. A revolver."

"Oh God, really?" asked Lorna. "Could I see it?"

"Not in this house," said Dolly, glancing up the stairs.

"Dolly's right," I told them. "That's why it's out in the car."

It was a little after nine o'clock when Dolly began to stifle yawns. "I've put in a long day," she announced, "and now I'm going to chase you people out of here. Why don't you give your ex a ride home, Bragg. Save Benny a trip."

"Sure, if it's all right with Lorna."

"Of course it is," she told me, while I thought about the trumpet player.

I made plans to meet Benny the next morning and we said good night. When we were sitting out front warming the car engine, Lorna asked to see the revolver. I opened the glove compartment, broke open the cylinder, and showed it to her. She didn't want to touch it, but just stared at it a moment, then lifted her eyes.

"It seems to fit," she told me.

"Fit what?"

"How your face has changed. The look about your eyes."

I put away the gun and backed around into Benny's driveway. "Don't you have a car?"

"I do," Lorna told me, "but I helped stage a wedding party out near Kenmore this afternoon. Instead of going back to town in the company wagon, Dolly and I met to do some shopping."

"Where do you live?"

"Actually, not far from where I guess somebody shot at Benny. I have a condo on the west side of Phinney Ridge."

I started in that direction. Without the presence of Dolly and Benny, our conversation tended to lag. There was both too much and not enough for us to talk about by ourselves. I should have left well enough alone probably, but that isn't my style. I was driving south along Greenwood Avenue, starting up the north end of the ridge just past 85th Street, which in my youth had been the old city limits.

"Those were a couple of pretty kind things you said about me back there," I told her. "About the newspapering and all."

She took a deep breath and let it out again, not replying right away, then she turned sideways in the seat toward me. "I could have said a whole lot more. I've been married to two other men since you, Peter. I see things—you—in a far different light these days than I did in San Francisco."

"Don't make too much of that," I told her. "I'm different from the man you knew in San Francisco. There are parts to me now that you probably would dislike even more than whatever you disliked back then."

Her hand touched my arm. "I never disliked you. I just grew bored with my life. I've always been like that. I'm bored with my life right now. I'm making quite a lot of money and I tell myself, Well, there is that, at least. But there's no spark to my life these days. No fire."

She gave my arm a little squeeze before taking her hand away. "Would you give me a call sometime tomorrow? Whenever you're not hard at work trying to save Benny's skinny bottom?"

"Sure. Give me something with your number on it. Maybe we could even have dinner together or something."

"That's what I was thinking," she told me, groping in her handbag.

I reached back and turned on the dome light so she could see better. She took out a notepad, wrote on it, tore out a page, and reached across to tuck it into my shirt pocket. Then she squirmed back around to turn off the dome light. She always had done her share of the dozens of little daily chores that needed doing.

She gave me directions to a recently built, two-story condominium complex a couple of blocks down from Phinney Avenue. I parked in front of the building and left the engine running. I put my hand on the door catch, planning to see her to the building entrance, but she opened the door on her own side.

"Don't get out, Peter, I can manage." But she hesitated still. Neither one of us wanted to end it just then.

"You're funny some ways," I told her.

"Like how?"

"You're the only woman I know these days who would refer to my trying to save Benny's skinny bottom. Anybody else would call it his ass. You still don't ever speak in vulgarities."

"That's not quite true, Peter," she told me, dropping her eyes.

"Oh? You let slip a cuss word now and then, do you?"

"Not that, exactly. But I do, as you put it, speak in vulgarities on occasion. When I'm in bed. With a friend."

She looked back up at me then, without a trace of excuse or embarrassment. I whistled lightly.

"Well, that's something," I told her. "You never used to."

"I know." She reached out, repeating the gesture she'd made when we first met back in Benny's dining room. She touched me along one cheekbone and let her fingers tail down to alongside my jaw. "You're not the only one who's changed some."

And then she was out of the car and tripping quickly

up the front walk. She let herself in with a key and disappeared from view without a backward glance. I reached into my pocket and brought out the slip of paper she'd put there. Lorna had written down both her work and home telephone numbers, along with something else. I took a breath and wondered if I really knew what I was letting myself in for. Below the numbers, she'd drawn a single *X* and signed her initial, *L*. The *X* was a throwback to our earlier life. It signatured a kiss. She used a rising scale of them, to show her degree of fondness and passion. A single *X* didn't promise a guy the whole world, but it did suggest things between us this time around had gotten off to a rousing start.

# Chapter 4

It wasn't raining the next morning, just threatening to. The west gate parking lot at Woodlawn Park was a long paved area between Phinney Avenue and the perimeter fence of the park and zoo itself. It hadn't been a parking lot when I lived around there. But then the park hadn't had a fence or charged an admission fee back then, either. What now was the parking lot had been just a tree-lined field of grass where neighborhood kids would gather to play touch football, keeping one eye out for the park cop, who would come by from time to time to chase us off and urge us to use the playing fields up at the north end of the park. But I guess we were too lazy a gang of kids to go all that way to play touch football. We were all from the southern end of the park, near Phinney and North 50th Street. We didn't want to make the walk up to the other end. Besides that, the grass was a classier playing surface than the dirt and hammered-down turf of the fields up north. None of that mattered now. Now it was just a parking lot. I met Benny there at a little after ten o'clock.

"As near as I can remember, I was parked where that green VW is," Benny told me. His shoulders were hunched, and he glanced regularly behind him toward the buildings across the street. "It was either there or in the slot next to it. I remember that bent area in the fence."

"How about moving your car up to the empty space where it might have been that day?" I asked him.

He looked at me with a little frown, but then went down to where he'd parked the loaner car and drove it up next to the VW. I asked him to position it as near as he could remember to the way it had been on the day of the shooting. He got back out of the car while I studied the sharp crease near the front of the car roof. It was about midway between the middle of the roof and the driver's side. I walked around to in front of the hood and studied the angle of the crease. I could see how the cops figured the trajectory was from the roof of a building across the street that Benny had said was some sort of retirement home.

"Show me where you were when the shots were fired," I told him.

Benny opened the driver's side door and started to get into the car. He made a false start or two, then slid in behind the wheel. "No, damnit," he said, getting back out again. "I can't do it. I was just in the act of getting behind the wheel. I can't stop action like that. I was a moving target. It's probably what saved my ass."

It made me think of Lorna and her telling me of the vulgarities she sometimes mouthed these days when she was in bed with a friend. It was a little erotic, thinking of those sweet lips talking dirty.

"Hey, you doping off again?" Benny asked.

"No, just thinking about things." I went over to stare at the fence, then went across to the VW and estimated where the slugs might have hit if Benny's car had been in that slot. "Did the cops do any poking around inside the park?"

"No. The shooting was out here, not in there."

"I don't mean that far in. I mean just beyond the fence here. Did they go through the gate and search the area just beyond the fence?"

"I don't think so. They kept talking about ricochet tracks."

I tore a couple of sheets out of my notepad, tore the pages into strips, studied the crease in the car roof again, then went to the fence and folded the strips of paper near the outer limits of where I figured the slugs might have gone through. I did the same to the section of fence in front of the VW.

"Okay, Benny, thanks for the help. You can go on into town now. I'll finish up here by myself. I don't know how much work you've got piled up, but it would be a help if you could take some time and go through your files and look for anything out of the ordinary. Like we were talking about last night."

Benny sighed. "Okay, but I keep telling you, I don't do that sort of stuff. How far back do I go?"

"When did you do the Walla Walla story?"

"Couple of years ago."

"Okay, go back that far, at least, for a start. And keep in mind, what we're looking for isn't necessarily what you're going to see on the written page in front of you. It's the potential of a thing we're after, in a subject, an idea, or an individual. Use your brains and intuition. I'll be along later."

"What're you going to do?"

"I'm going to search inside the fence." Benny grunted and climbed into the car.

He drove off and I stared after him. I paid my

admission and walked back along the inside of the fence along the parking area and searched the earth and scruffy grass for about forty-five minutes. At the end of that time, I had two chunks of lead in my pocket that looked as if they could have been from the bullets that were fired that day at my friend Benny. One of them was skinned along one side. It could have been the one that nicked the car top. The other was in nearly perfect shape, which meant it had all the funny little individualistic marks and scratches that would be made on a slug traveling down just one gun barrel in this wide, wide land of ours. It was the sort of hard evidence I figured a police lab would like to get its hands on.

I considered taking a stroll through the rest of the park to see what it looked like these days, but the skies looked as if they were going to open up again at any minute, so I went back out to the car and drove downtown. There, at the Public Safety Building on Fourth Avenue, I raised about the same interest and enthusiasm with the cops that Benny had.

Hamilton was a cadaverous-looking detective lieutenant with a prominent Adam's apple who told me Benny's complaints weren't receiving a very high priority because there just wasn't enough to go on. "We don't even have any real evidence that a crime has been committed yet," he told me.

I took out the two slugs I'd found at the zoo and put them on the desk in front of him and told him how and where I'd found them. He turned them over with his fingers, then gave me a so-what expression.

"What the hell do these prove?" he asked. "Maybe they're what you think they are, maybe they're not."

We chatted for another ten minutes or so, his Adam's apple bobbing and weaving. But his position to do with

Benny remained basically the same. If you work as a private investigator in one town long enough, usually you develop some contacts with the police and can have a decent working relationship with them. But in a strange town, forget it. You couldn't blame them, really. Just because you carried the license, it didn't mean you weren't a jerk. I finally put the slugs back into my pocket and left.

At a stationery store I bought a small box and some wrapping material. I packed the slugs into the box and addressed it to a private criminalistics lab down in Berkeley. I mailed it at a postal substation in one of the department stores, then phoned down to the lab and told a man I knew there what I'd put into the mail. Then I drove on down to Benny's building by the Burlington Northern railroad tracks.

Benny had copies of four published articles to show me what he felt might have fallen into the category of things I'd told him to look for.

"Except I really don't put Bomber Hogan in that category," he told me, pointing out the story he'd done about the mobster who had served time at Walla Walla. "He's really a sweet old guy. Lives in a posh sort of place over on Mercer Island, right on the lake. I think he's retired. Grows roses or something."

"They call him Bomber?"

"Yeah, everybody does. Even the warden referred to him that way. His real name's Julius."

"Why does everybody call him Bomber?"

"I don't know. When I asked him, he just chuckled and shook his head. Said it was something that happened a long time ago back in New Jersey."

I skimmed through the article and had to agree with Benny. It seemed unlikely the piece would raise anybody's wrath. The tone of it was one of respect and good humor for one of the community's elder statesmen. Every profession has to have elder statesmen,

Benny's article implied, even racketeering, which happened to have been Bomber Hogan's vineyard. Still, I set it aside. If a man has received death threats, you can't just ignore somebody he's met who spent more than four decades in the crime business.

Another of the articles had appeared in an electrical journal and detailed the problems that had developed in a line of industrial motors manufactured locally. It turned out the trouble had been caused by faulty switches supplied by a subcontractor. There hadn't been any serious fires or injuries caused by the bum equipment, but there had been costly, time-consuming problems in a lot of plants. The experts Benny interviewed indicated a combination of bad original design and a certain amount of cost cutting in the manufacturing process had been responsible.

Another article, published a year earlier in the magazine section of the Sunday newspaper, had probed the causes of earth slippage on Queen Anne Hill. Some structures had been lost, and the story suggested they shouldn't have been built there in the first place, but too many parties had been involved—city engineers, realtors, builders, and architects—to neatly put the blame at the doorstep of any one of them.

The fourth article, for a local weekly newspaper, was a comprehensive look at Seattle's busy drama scene. In it, Benny mentioned a theatrical agency whose operators had dropped out of sight owing a lot of people money.

"Did these people ever turn up again?" I asked him.

"Not that I know of."

"Well, you're right," I told him, putting the stories aside. "I don't see much in any of this to bring somebody out of the woodwork after you."

I sat back in a chair alongside his desk and stared at

the dim ceiling. Benny rested his chin on his hands at his typewriter and stared out at the vacant lot across the street.

"Benny, have you ever had anybody—I mean *anybody*—make any kind of a threat to you before? I mean, go back ten years or more. Anyone at all?"

"As a matter of fact, there were a couple of chaps who told me to lay off certain of their affairs or they'd do something dreadful to me. A month or two ago, it was."

I sat up straight. "How come you didn't tell me before now?"

"Well, they were kidding, is how come. At least I think they were. They were smiling when they said it."

"Who was it?"

"Strange coincidence, this, but it was a couple of guys from a local private detective agency, Tom and Wally Jackson. They're sons of one of the founders, old Grady Jackson."

"Tell me the rest of it."

"Pete, it's no big deal."

"Tell me."

"Well, I wrote this piece on private eye agencies in the Pacific Northwest. You ever hear of these guys, by the way? The Jackson Detective Agency?"

"No."

"Well, I hadn't before either, but their name came up during interviews with people at some of the other agencies. They seem to have kind of a tough reputation. They've had their license temporarily suspended a couple of times over the years. And there was a hearing down in Olympia just last year over whether it should be suspended again. It wasn't a big deal, just some accusations of padding the old expense account. One of their former clients squawked, but the former client never showed up for the hearing, so the thing was canceled. But I figured these guys might add a little color to the story. Most of you PIs are a pretty dull lot, I learned. So I phoned for an appointment with old Grady Jackson himself. He thought I was a potential client. When I went in to talk to him and told him what I was writing, you'd have thought he'd just been brushed by the man who turns faces to stone. A flintier pair of cold gray eyes I have never seen. All in all, the man isn't too sinister-looking himself. He's maybe six feet tall, but he must be pushing seventy or thereabouts, so to make an impression on me he called in his boys, who were both in the office at the time, Tom and Wally. Now they look sinister, make no mistake about it. Both big, beefy guys full of hard looks and growls. Then, with Tom and Wally standing on either side of me with their arms folded, old Grady tells me he doesn't want a word about them to appear in the story I'm doing. I argued myself blue in the face. I said theirs was the only agency that had been called before the state licensing body in the recent past, and I wanted to mention the occasion just to illustrate the appeal process when a beef is brought. I told him I'd emphasize that since the complainant didn't show up, it was assumed in the eyes of the state they were as pure as the driven snow."

"What was the threat?"

"Well, near the end of our conversation, Wally Jackson cleared his throat, a noise that resembles the cannon they fire off at the conclusion of the 1812 Overture, and he told me if I wrote one word they didn't like, they wouldn't bother with any libel suits or anything, they'd just come after me with an axe and cut off my left leg."

I leaned back and thought about it.

"Pete, he was kidding. I think."

"When did the article run?"

"It hasn't yet. It's due out this week. Running in a

new regional publication called *Sound Sounds*. That's for Puget Sound, get it?"

"I get it. I'm going to have to go see those guys, you know."

Benny fidgeted in his chair. "Boy, I wish you wouldn't. It might just get them all pissed off at me again. I mean, these are pretty hard guys. If you do go see them, I sure as hell hope you carry your hat in your hand and call them sir."

"Leave it to me."

"Yeah, well I guess I have to do that, but, boy..." He shook his head and stared at the typewriter.

I picked through the four articles again. "And I'll try to go see this guy Bomber Hogan. Have you checked in with Dolly lately to see that everything's all right around home?"

"I spoke to her an hour or so ago. Things were fine."

"No more threatening phone calls?"

"Naw." He chuckled. "Timmy picked up an odd one, though."

"When?"

"Last night. Just after you and Lorna left."

"Who was it?"

"Didn't say. Wrong number, probably. Tim was out in the kitchen getting a snack when the phone on the wall rang. He picked up the receiver and said hello. Then he heard this guy's voice say, 'It's nine o'clock...' Timmy said the guy hesitated a moment, then hung up."

I glanced at my watch. It was almost three o'clock. "Benny, what time do the boys get out of school?"

"About now, I guess. Why?"

"Do they take a school bus?"

"No, it's not that far from home. They walk most of the time."

He had a street map of Seattle taped up on a wall to one side of his desk. "Show me where the school is."

He got up and pointed it out. "What is this, Pete?"

"I'm not sure. Maybe nothing. But call the school. Tell them if the boys are still there, to hold them until I show up." I headed for the door.

"Hey, what is this, Pete? You don't think..."

"I don't know, Benny. I just don't want to take any chances. I'll be in touch with you later."

## Chapter 5

I could have been all cockeyed. Maybe the phone call to Benny's home the evening before had been an innocent mistake or some sort of Pacific Northwest prank I couldn't relate to. But some months earlier, the television stations in the San Francisco area had run a series of public service messages suggesting that parents be a little more concerned about their children out on the streets as the evening wore on. As I recalled it, the message had been: *It's ten o'clock. Do you know where your children are?"*

Granted, an anonymous voice on the phone saying that it was nine o'clock wasn't necessarily the same thing. But it was close enough to bother me. It could have been a warning to do with the Bartlett youngsters. It could have been meant as a warning, only the caller might have been thrown off his stride when he realized it was one of the boys who had answered the phone rather than one of the parents. Maybe it was all in my

44

imagination and I was the one being thrown off his stride. It didn't matter right then. I just wanted to assure myself about Timmy and Al.

Once you get onto the Interstate 5 freeway, it's a fast shot to the north end of town, where Benny lived. It took me five minutes to get from Benny's office to the freeway, and about seven minutes later I was back off the freeway, a mile from the school where the boys went. One thing I'd forgotten to ask Benny was what route the boys took going to and from school. But chances were he wouldn't have known anyway. Chances were the boys themselves wouldn't have known until they sniffed the air leaving the school grounds and let the zephyr breezes point their toes. I sped along a road running west of the freeway. When I got to the vicinity of the Bartlett home, I drove in a ragged northwesterly direction toward the school, a mile further. I didn't see the boys.

At the school, a sprawling brick and pastel paneled building, I parked on the street and trotted inside and found the principal's office. There still were kids around in the halls and out on the grounds, and classes had let out just twenty minutes earlier, I was told. They'd received the phone call from Benny a few moments later, but the Bartlett kids had already left the grounds. Nobody knew which way the boys walked home. Was there anything wrong at home, I was asked. No, ma'am. Nothing wrong at home. Not that I knew about. I used the office phone to call Dolly. I didn't want to alarm her, but it turned out that Benny had called her a few minutes before, asking if the boys were home yet, and she already was suspiciously upset.

"Pete, what is it? I knew there was something about that telephone call last night. What did it mean?"

"Probably nothing, Dolly. Now, just stay calm. Do you know which way the boys walk home?"

She wasn't sure, but she was able to tell me the route

she used on the days it rained hard enough for the boys
to talk her into giving them a ride, provided Benny
hadn't already taken the car into work. It was close to
but not exactly the same as the way I'd traveled up to
the school. I told her I'd be calling again and went back
out to the car.

I was halfway back to the Bartlett house when I
spotted them. They were a couple of blocks ahead of
me, on a residential street of neatly tended homes on
widely spaced lots. The boys had stopped to talk to a
man in pale slacks and a brown sports jacket, who was
standing with his back to me beside a large sedan with
both right-hand-side doors open. The man had one
hand on Timmy's shoulder. Al, the younger boy, was
standing nearby with his hands on his hips staring at
the man grasping his brother.

I sped up and began honking the horn. The man
and both boys turned to stare in my direction. I kept
hitting the horn button in short honks. The man turned
and slid into the front passenger seat and closed the
door. As the car pulled away from the curb, he reached
back and pulled shut the rear door. I wasn't able to get
much of a look at him. I screeched to a stop beside the
boys.

"Uncle Pete!" cried an astonished Timmy.

"What was that all about? What did the people in the
car want?"

"They wanted us to go with them," said Timmy.

"I think they were going to try a snatch," said Al.

"Okay, get in, boys. Let's go see if we can catch up
with them."

"Wow," said Timmy, climbing into the front seat
beside me.

"Hot dog," said Al, pushing the back of his brother's
seat forward so he could scramble into the back.

"What did they say?" I asked.

"They said Mom had sent them," Timmy told me.

"Said I'd won a new set of drums in a contest she'd entered without telling me about it. I was supposed to go pick out the outfit I wanted in some store in West Seattle. I figured, boy, what a crock."

The large sedan was moving in a hurry, about two blocks ahead of me. I kept after it until we both were headed south on 1st Avenue Northeast. It was a well-traveled thoroughfare but only had one lane of traffic in each direction. When I started closing the gap between us, the sedan began taking some chances passing other vehicles. They were chances I felt I couldn't take with the boys in the car.

"Don't you have a siren?" asked Al from in back.

"I'm not that sort of detective," I told him. "Who all was in the car?"

"The guy who put the arm on Timmy and a wheelman," said Al.

"Would you recognize them again?"

"I don't know."

"I'd recognize the man who got out," said Timmy, "but I didn't pay any attention to the driver. I was trying to figure out this drums business the guy was talking about."

I had a chance to go around a couple of cars and began moving up behind the target car again. It whistled through a green traffic light ahead. I went through the light as it was turning red.

"What kind of voice did the man on the walk have?" Timmy shrugged. "Normal."

"I think he was trying to disguise it," said Al.

"How do you mean?"

"It seemed a little high for such a tall dude. I think he was faking it."

"Any kind of accent?"

"Not that I noticed," said Timmy.

"Were they waiting for you there at the corner?"

"They were tailing us from school," said Al. "I spotted them a block in back of us."

"What made you spot them?"

Al didn't say anything right away. So his brother told me.

"Jellyroll Hansen said he was going to beat the stuffing out of Al after school."

"Why would he say something like that?"

"Because Al lipped off to him at the end of lunch period."

"I didn't lip off. I just made a joke," Al complained.

"You're always lipping off. And Jellyroll didn't think it was funny. So Al kept looking over his shoulder."

"And spotted the getaway car," said Al.

"What getaway car?" asked Timmy.

"You know what I mean. You think they were trying to put the snatch on us, Pete?"

"I don't know."

"Mom says to call him Uncle Pete," Timmy chided his brother.

"Did your mom or dad tell you about the threats your dad's been getting?"

"Yeah, but that's crazy," said Timmy. "Everybody likes Dad."

"Can't you rev up this old bucket anymore?" Al asked.

"I'm doing the best I can."

The sedan went around a couple of more cars and began to widen the distance between us, then at 130th Street it braked and made a left turn. Another car pulled out of a parking space a half block ahead of me and I had to slow, and by the time I got to 130th and turned the corner, the sedan was out of sight. I muttered a curse under my breath.

"It probably went onto the freeway," said Timmy.

"Where's the on ramp?"

"Down another block," said Timmy.

I slowed as we went past it. There was no hope of finding the sedan again if it was headed south on I-5. I went over a block but had trouble trying to circle around back to the west side of the freeway.

"You have to use 130th or go a little ways north or south," said Timmy helpfully.

"They sure screwed up the streets when they put that thing in," I complained.

"Wasn't it here when you lived up here?" Al asked.

"No it wasn't."

"Wow," said Al softly. "It's been here since before I was born, even."

I started to say something, but dummied up. What can you expect kids to know? I wondered about what the boys had just experienced. Was it a kidnap attempt by the people trying to run Benny out of town? Some sort of mistake? Or, nearly as bad as a kidnap attempt, an approach by men who just liked the physical company of young boys? Whatever, it was the sort of thing that could give you sleepless nights. I'm sure it would with Dolly and Benny. I slowed, then pulled over to the parking lot of a small market.

"You know what we need, gang?"

Timmy blinked at me from behind his large-lensed glasses and shook his head.

"Sure," said Al from the back seat. "Faster horses, older whiskey, younger women, and more money."

I turned around to look at him.

"Well, that's what Pop is always saying."

"Okay. But one more thing we need is a code. One we can use between us in case we're ever separated, so we can speak to each other without anybody else knowing what we're saying."

"Wow," said Al. "You mean a secret code?"

"That's what I mean."

"Maybe we could all learn some obscure language," said Timmy.

"That would take too long," I told him. "Don't you have something like that you can talk to your buddies at school with so the teachers can't understand you?"

"They can't understand us when we speak English," said Al.

"What do we need this for, Uncle Pete?" asked Timmy, a gleam of suspicion building behind the goggle glasses.

"Emergencies," I told him. "In case World War Three starts or something." I thought a minute. "Pig Latin."

Timmy's eyebrows went up again.

"What?" asked Al.

"Don't you guys know how to speak Pig Latin?"

"Never heard of it," said Timmy.

"Perfect," I said. "Just maybe it's been out of vogue long enough. Want to learn it?"

"Is it complicated?" asked Timmy.

"Not at all, if I can remember. *Ooey-phay oo-tay ou-yay.* Guess what that means."

"You're kidding," said Al.

Timmy just shook his head.

"Phooey to you, is what I just said. You take the first letter of a word, provided it's a consonant, and move it to the end of the word and add the sound *ay.* So 'you' becomes *ou-yay.* Timmy becomes *immy-tay.*"

"What does Al become?" asked Al.

"I don't know. I forget what happens if the word begins with a vowel. You just have to improvise, fellows. You don't speak in complete sentences in Pig Latin. It's code, right? For emergency use only. Hopefully, you could give an important, short message without some grown-up standing around knowing what you're saying. But you guys should practice it between yourselves. What's my name in Pig Latin, Timmy?"

"*Cle-unpay Ete-pay?*"

"Good. Al?"

"*Ragg-bay.*"

"See? You got it already."

Timmy shook his head doubtfully.

*"Ooey-phay oo-tay ou-yay,"* said Al with a whoop.

I put the car back in gear and drove the boys home. Benny and Dolly came to the front door when they saw us drive up. Benny had left work early. They sent the boys down the hall while we talked about the phone call and the two men in the sedan who had followed Timmy and Al from school.

"The contest story is ridiculous," said Dolly.

"But it tells us they know Timmy plays drums," I told them. "That bothers me some. Somebody's been doing some homework on you people."

"You think it was a genuine kidnap try?" Benny asked, lighting his third cigarette since we'd sat down.

"I don't know. But I'd take precautions if I were you. Either arrange for rides for the boys between here and school or keep them home for the next couple of days."

"You figure you can get to the bottom of things by then?" Benny wanted to know.

I threw up my hands. "I don't know. But these odd doings seem to be occurring more frequently. If it keeps up, there's bound to be something I can go after."

Dolly took a deep breath and looked across at her husband. "What are we going to do?"

Benny stared at her a moment, then lowered his eyes and shook his head.

"Maybe you should do what they want," I suggested. "Or at least give the appearance of it. Leave town for a few days. Take some time off. Get out of the way."

"No," Benny said sharply. "This is my town. I'm not going to let some slob chase me out of it, or even think he has. Dolly and the kids, maybe." He looked across at his wife. "Hon?"

"I don't want to do that any more than you do," Dolly told him. "Let's give it a little more time. If anything more happens to do with the boys, I'll take them out of school and send them off somewhere."

Benny looked up at me. "Sound right to you?"

I shook my head. "Can't answer that for you. I guess take it a day at a time. But get on the phone to Hamilton. Tell him what happened this afternoon. Maybe it'll finally get him off his tail. Maybe he'll start to take you seriously. I'll be in touch."

I drove back to the motel, not particularly happy with myself. I should have had brains enough to ask Benny earlier if there'd been any funny telephone calls. I might even have been able to set up something so I could have grabbed the two men who followed the boys from school. I might have had things all wrapped up by now and been on my way back to San Francisco. I thought about that some and told myself, No, I might have had things wrapped up, but I wouldn't have been on my way back to San Francisco.

From the motel I tried to phone Lorna, but she'd already left work for the day. I called down to my office and chatted with Ceejay for a few minutes. Nothing had come up that couldn't wait.

"How does it go up there?" she wanted to know.

"Not well. I missed a good opportunity to clear up things today."

"Hmmmm. Are you charging your friend the usual rates for what you're doing?"

"Of course not."

"I thought not. Maybe you should. Maybe it'd help keep your mind on business."

That was the problem with Ceejay. You had to take the sharp mouth along with the keen brain. After we hung up, I tried phoning Lorna at home. She answered on the second ring.

"Hi, it's Pete."

"Oh hi. Gee, I was hoping it would be you. I came

home a little early to freshen up in case I got that dinner invitation."

"Yeah well, the reason I'm calling is I'm not sure I can make it. Something more happened involving Benny today. I probably should spend the evening working. I have to make a couple of calls, at least. There's somebody I want to see, and if he's available tonight, I think I'll just drive on over to see him."

"Something happened to Benny?"

"Not directly. I'll tell you about it another time."

"Well, I guess if you have to go see a man, you have to go see a man. Where does he live?"

"Mercer Island, Benny said."

"And where are you now?"

"At my motel, out on Aurora."

"Well gee, why not stop by and make your phone calls from here? It's not far out of the way. At least we can have a drink together."

I hesitated. My brain shrugged. "Okay. Why not? I want to clean up first. In about forty minutes?"

"Oh grand, Pete. Thank you. I'll expect you."

I hung up and stared at the phone. She had that same half-out-of-breath tone she'd had the night before, when we'd first met at Benny's place. She never used to sound that way talking to me. But then I'd only been her husband back then.

I took a quick shower and shave, then sat on the edge of the bed trying to decide something. I still had the .38 in the glove compartment of the rental car, but I wondered if I should be carrying the .45 as well. The hesitation turned into a couple of minutes of changing my mind back and forth. I stared out the window. It was starting to get dark out there. The pavement was dry, but more clouds had been scudding low overhead. More rain on the way, probably. I went to the closet and got my black raincoat off its hanger. I stared down at the suitcase with the .45 in it. The town had me off balance. The buildings that didn't belong there, the freeway that screwed up driving the streets I used to drive, and the weather you could never depend on. And on top of all that, I really didn't know what the hell I was doing fooling around with Lorna again. I'd been through all that once; it should have been enough. And still...

I finally left the .45 in the suitcase. Maybe with my scrambled frame of mind I shouldn't be packing that much gun. Seattle could be the death of you.

## Chapter 6

Lorna greeted me with a little squeeze of the arm when she opened the door. Her place wasn't really spacious, but it was comfortable enough for one person. The main living area was a large, airy room of blond wood paneling, mission white walls, and big sheets of glass looking out over Ballard and the government locks a couple of miles away. Off one side of the room was a small breakfast bar and kitchen beyond. A short hall-way to the rear of the place had deep closets on one side and a small bedroom off the other. She didn't use the bedroom to sleep in but as a dressing room. She slept in a bed up on a balcony over the main living room.

"It's like sleeping in a loft," she told me. "Always wanted a sleeping loft."

She was wearing a straight black skirt. Like the sheath that she'd been wearing the night before, it showed off her slim waist to good advantage. She also wore a white cotton blouse with long sleeves and a high collar with a thin black string tie around it. She looked like a fresh-faced college girl. Her hair this night was wrapped atop her head in casual looking swirls, but it was kept firmly in place with clips and other whatnots.

"If we do go out to dinner, people will think you're my daughter."

"Let them think what they like. What can I get you to drink?"

"I'd better stay away from the martinis tonight. Maybe a gin and tonic if you have it."

"I have it," she said with a wink. "The phone's on the stand at the end of the sofa."

She'd gotten over the fluster I thought I'd heard earlier. Maybe she practiced yoga or something. She went briskly to the kitchen while I crossed to the phone. It was a little before six o'clock, about the time the man I was going to call would be sitting down with his wife and any of the grown children who might be there to have a glass of sherry before dinner. It was a good time to call him. Make it seem more like a social call. Although the man I was going to call and I had cooperated on matters of mutual interest in days gone by, I didn't care for anybody to get the idea we did business together, in the generally accepted meaning of the word. I looked up his number in the pocket address book I carried and used my credit card to place the call. A male voice answered.

"My name is Peter Bragg," I told him. "I'm a private investigator. Mr. Drocco and I have met in the past. I am phoning from out of town. If it wouldn't be an inconvenience, I would like to speak with him."

The man said he would tell Mr. Drocco. Lorna was looking over at me with a questioning expression. I gave her back the wink with a little smile. She brought over the gin and tonic for me and what looked like a martini on the rocks for herself. She sat in a nearby chair as Drocco came on the line.

"Mr. Peter Bragg, so nice to hear from you. How are you?"

"Pretty fair, Mr. Drocco. How about yourself and your lovely wife?"

"Both of us are excellent. She asked me to give you her regards."

"Please thank her for me, and give her my love in return."

"I will do that. My man told me you were calling from out of town."

"That's right. I'm up in Seattle for a few days, trying to help an old friend who seems to be having some problems. He's a writer named Benny Bartlett. Perhaps you've heard of him."

"No, it is not a name that I know."

"Well, he's been threatened by somebody. Was told over the phone to leave town. A couple of near-miss death attempts have been made on his life."

"Near-miss?"

"It would seem that way. As if somebody checked their swing at the last minute. Then just this afternoon it appears somebody tried to abduct his two young boys. And as near as I can find, there's no good reason behind it all. He doesn't write stories of a very sensational nature. He has a lot of friends and no known enemies. I'm trying to get to the bottom of it all for him."

"And from me you would like some sort of contact to query?"

"That's right, Mr. Drocco. A specific person, as a matter of fact. Benny interviewed a man named Julius Hogan some while back, just before Mr. Hogan was released from Walla Walla, the state prison up here. Benny said the two of them hit it off pretty well. I read the piece on Mr. Hogan that Benny wrote. It was warm and funny. I thought Mr. Hogan might be willing to discuss my friend's problems with me. Do you know him, sir?"

"Of course I know Bomber." He chuckled briefly. "We are a relatively small circle out here, Peter. When would you like to see him?"

"The sooner the better, under the circumstances. This evening, if possible. If not, tomorrow maybe."

Drocco said he'd phone Bomber and get right back to me. I hung up and had a sip of the gin and tonic.

"Drocco?" asked Lorna. "He sounds a little like an Italian hood."

"He's Sicilian," I told her. "At least that's what his antecedents were. And yes, I've been told he's Mafia, but you wouldn't call him a hood, or at least I wouldn't."

"You, Peter? Work with the Mafia? Old straight-arrow Peter Bragg?"

"No, it's not like that. I don't work with them. In fact I've gone up against some of those people on a couple of occasions. People from back East and the Midwest. But sometimes Drocco and I exchange bits of information or small favors, like the one I just asked of him. An introduction."

Lorna's look was dubious. "Sounds to me you're walking a pretty thin line there."

"Thin, but clearly delineated," I told her, having some more of the drink. "It's all in the way you express yourself. Like in the conversation we just had. I didn't hold back anything. And from Benny's standpoint, it was an affirmative development."

"How so?"

"Chances are Drocco's colleagues aren't at the root of Benny's problems. If they were, Drocco probably would know about it. That's why I mentioned Benny's name up front. If the mob was connected to whatever is going on, Drocco would have said something like, 'It is a name I have heard others speak.' Something like that.

That would have told me that if I didn't want to get into the gritty, tit-for-tat relationship I try to avoid..."

"Doing business with the mob, you mean."

"Okay, doing business with the mob, if I didn't want it to come to that, I would have said I was sorry to have bothered him and wished him a happy Halloween or something and hung up. But he gave me a green light, and he'll ask Hogan to talk to me."

Lorna took a sip of the martini and leaned back, her face taking on an expression I remembered from the past. It was a faintly amused look, the sort she'd give you when she thought you were full of hot air.

"How did you and this Drocco person come up with all this subterfuge? Just sit down together one afternoon like a couple of kids in the clubhouse to work out your signals?"

"No, it just sort of developed. I guess I have a feel for that sort of thing."

Lorna snorted.

"You're mocking me," I told her with a straight face. "You used to get on my nerves in a lot of ways, Lorna, but you never used to mock me."

She covered her eyes with one hand and laughed quietly. "I'm sorry," she told me, "but I think it's hilarious, this cautious, unsoiled relationship you have with a bunch of goons and killers."

"A lot of them have put that pretty much behind them," I told her. "They put their money into other things and play it pretty straight."

"Sure they do," she told me. "How did this whacky situation come about in the first place? Did you just look up Mafia in the Yellow Pages?"

"No, it just developed out of a job I had. His youngest daughter, a girl named Maria, was a pretty wild youngster when she was growing up. She'd gotten into some minor scrapes in the past, then one night found herself in a situation that could have sent her to prison. She wasn't really involved that much, it just looked that way."

"Involved in what?"

"A double homicide. She knew some people who knew some people, and unknowingly was in the wrong place at the wrong time. Witnesses later identified her, and the cops were able to build a pretty good case that she had motive and opportunity. I was hired by the family of her boyfriend, a kid with too much money to spend who had the same streak of wildness in him that Maria had. So for a period of time, my interests were the same as Drocco's. He had his own people working on the same thing, of course, but I was a little faster. I managed to show the boy and Maria just happened to be shacked up together at the same motel where the killings occurred at the same time they occurred. And just before she was released to her family, I had the opportunity to give Maria my lecture for wayward youth. It basically involves trying to scare the bejesus out of them to the extent they somewhat modify their future behavior. And apparently that, along with the time she had to spend in jail on suspicion of murder, did in fact tone down her act in the days that followed. Drocco appreciated that. He invited me to an afternoon lawn party one time to tell me so. We've been . . . acquaintances, I guess you could call it, ever since."

"God," Lorna drawled. "There he goes, my ex. Confidant to kings and crooks."

"Mock, mock, mock . . ."

She went to the kitchen and fixed fresh drinks. She'd just resumed her seat when the phone rang. I reached for it, then hesitated. "Maybe you'd better answer."

"Oh, go ahead."

"But it might be a boyfriend."

She waved a hand in dismissal, but then got up and answered it.

"Yes, he is," she said in a sultry tone she'd developed since the old days. "I'll ask him to put on his trousers and come to the phone."

"Thanks, Lorna," I said quietly with my hand over the receiver. "That really adds class to things."

She smirked, and I said hello.

"I have just spoken with Julius," Drocco told me. "He will be happy to meet with you, but it would not be convenient for him to see you this evening. He will see you tomorrow afternoon. After one o'clock, he said." He gave me Hogan's phone number and said I should phone Bomber in the morning to get directions to his home.

"Mr. Drocco, I appreciate this. Thank you very much."

"You are quite welcome. I hope you are able to solve your friend's problems. Uh, Peter?"

"Yes?"

"Who was that woman who answered the telephone just now?"

"Who answered the phone?" I repeated, looking over at Lorna. "It's a dame who's caused me a lot of grief over the years. Maybe I should have talked contract to do with her a long time ago..."

Lorna sat up with a stricken look, one hand to her throat.

"You are making a joke," said Drocco in all seriousness.

"Yeah, I am. Actually, she's my ex-wife. We split up before you and I met. She's living here in Seattle now. She's a friend of my friend."

Drocco chortled. "Of course. Well, have a good evening, my friend." He was still chuckling when he hung up.

"You bastard!" Lorna cried when I put down the phone. "That was a ghastly thing to say."

"Back at 'cha," I told her.

She swallowed the rest of her drink and got to her feet. Her long legs switched and her round rump rolled as she crossed to the kitchen and poured gin into her glass. "I don't think I should go out with you now whether you're free or not," she told me.

I got to my feet with a shrug. She came back from the kitchen with a little pout on her face. She put down her drink beside the telephone and took hold of the lapels of my jacket.

"I don't mean that," she said. "But that was a terrible thing you said to that man. What if you'd had a heart attack right then and died before you were able to tell him it was a bad joke. He might have sent somebody after me."

"No worry. He wouldn't hurt a pretty thing like you."

A slight blush rose from her throat again. She had always liked men to flatter her. "Well, what about this evening," she said. "Are you free now?"

"I'm free."

"Then let's finish our drinks and go into town. I want you to see my restaurant."

Scandia Farms was on Pine Street, just off Fifth Avenue. We parked in a basement garage and took an elevator up to the restaurant level. The place had a well-scrubbed, Scandinavian flavor to it, with gleaming blue and white walls, bright lighting, white tile floors, and pretty waitresses in milkmaid costumes. She took me through the place, introducing me to people as her ex-husband, the private detective from San Francisco. I asked her not to do that.

"Why not? You're getting a free dinner out of it. And you have a lot to make up for with the contract remark to Mr. Drocco. The least you can do is let me flaunt you a little."

When we settled down to eat, she ordered salmon and I had some sort of chicken dish. She showed a take-charge side to her when dealing with the help, but on a couple of instances when our conversation touched on things of a more personal nature, she would revert to the awkward girl she'd been the day before, hesitant in speech and manner.

She did something else as well. Our original waitress was a tall, dark-eyed brunette whose gaze and smile would linger over me whenever she came to the table. Partway through the meal, Lorna excused herself and went over to say something to the hostess who had seated us. From that moment on we had a different waitress, one who devoted full-time attention to Lorna.

"What did you do, fire the first one?" I asked her.

"Who?" Lorna asked. All innocence.

"The brunette waitress who had eyes for me."

"No, I didn't fire her. I just asked that somebody else wait on us. I didn't bring you in here to flirt with other women."

"I wasn't flirting."

"But you wanted to."

"What if I did?"

"Oh, stop it. Forget you're my ex-husband and try to pretend you're my date."

"Okay." I put one hand under the table and squeezed her knee. She gave a little jump and moved her legs.

"Oh stop it. You're acting like some teenage geek."

I had to laugh, but right then her face took on a troubled expression at something she saw in back of me.

"Damn it, she breathed, but then assumed a dazzling smile.

A couple of men stopped by the table to say hello. One of them was a tall, small-headed, balding man with thick lips. A pair of rimless glasses had slid a little ways down his nose. He was wearing a knockout of a green and white plaid sports jacket. The other was a short, compact man with a lazy smile dressed sanely in a dark suit.

"Lorna, my dear," said the tall, older gent. "I thought you'd left for the day."

"I came back to show off the place to an old friend from San Francisco. Peter, this is Gene Olson. He's senior partner in our firm."

I stood up and shook hands. The man had a friendly grip and he sounded affable enough, but it was a shame that with his looks he didn't at least have somebody to pick out his clothes for him.

"I'm happy to meet you, sir," said Olson. "And I'd like you to meet Brad Thackery. He's with the Seahawks organization. They're looking for somebody to cater the big post-season party. Victory party, we're hoping this year, and I've been giving him the old Scandia Farms pitch."

I shook hands with the younger man. He met my eyes just long enough to be polite, before turning his attention to Lorna.

"And it's nice to see you again, Miss Bragg," said Thackery.

I looked at Lorna and blinked.

"It's nice to see you again, Mr. Thackery. All I can add to what Gene has told you is I think it would be a thrill to accommodate your team and friends."

I raised an eyebrow, but I seemed to be the only one there who thought that an odd turn of phrase to use regarding a small herd of hardy jocks.

"As I told Gene, you're one of the front-runners," Thackery told her.

They chatted a little more, Thackery staring at Lorna with his little smile, Olson beaming, Lorna's eyes darting between the Seahawks man and her partner.

When the two men made their farewell and left us, I sat back down and looked across at my ex-wife. She lowered her eyes and fiddled with the napkin in her lap. A moment later she looked up to catch the eye of our waitress and point at her coffee cup. I waited until the woman had brought our coffee, poured, and left again before I cleared my throat. When I did that, Lorna dropped the spoon she'd had in her hand.

"That guy from the Seahawks, Thackery. I thought I heard him call you Miss Bragg."

"That's right," she said quietly, still avoiding my eyes.

"You told me you'd had two husbands since me."

She nodded, then looked up with a fleeting smile. "I hope you don't mind."

"No, I don't mind. I just don't get it."

She made a little shrug. Maybe it was my imagination, but she seemed to have wilted some since the men had visited our table. She looked a little defensive and vulnerable. It's the sort of look that can bring out the baser instincts in a man. At least in this man. Time, I told myself, to keep my wits about me and my hands at home, although I noted that Lorna had launched one of her own toward my side of the table.

"I took your name again after my last marriage," she told me. "Of all the men—I mean, of all the names I've had, I liked yours best of all."

"Why didn't you revert to your maiden name?"

She looked up at me then. "Lorna Wilks? You've got to be kidding. No, Lorna Bragg sounds just fine to me, thank you."

She'd turned her head partly to one side and withdrew her hand from no man's land. Then she did the one thing that always leaves me mute and feeling shabby. She began to cry.

# Chapter 7 ——————

We didn't spend much more time at Scandia Farms. Lorna couldn't compose herself and we left soon after she'd started weeping. We went down to the car and I asked her if there was anyplace she wanted to go. She shook her head.

"I'm sorry, Peter. I'm afraid the evening is ruined for me, through no fault of your own. Please take me home."

So I took her home. I walked her to the building's front door and waited while she unlocked and opened it. I hung back, expecting her to want to work through whatever misery she had on her own, but she reached out and tugged my sleeve.

"Please come up for a bit. I don't want to be alone just now."

It didn't make a lot of sense to me, but then neither did anything else that had happened since I hit town. I followed her up the stairs and into her place. She turned on some dim overhead track lighting and hung her coat in a closet. She moved like a sleepwalker. She stood at the closet door a moment, then crossed to sit on the sofa. She sat on its edge, her chin in her hands, staring out the plate-glass windows at the twinkling lights of Ballard. Even a rowdy place like Ballard can look romantic at night from a couple of miles away. Of course I'd been out of touch long enough, so I didn't even know if Ballard was still a rowdy place, with its blue-collar mill industries and fishing fleets, pool halls and beer taverns and auto wrecking yards.

I turned back to stare at Lorna. I didn't really know her any longer either. She'd never been a woman to cry, the wife I'd known. She could be bitchy and steely cold and even throw things in anger, but I'd never seen her cry. It seemed all a part of that vulnerability I'd noticed back in the restaurant. Maybe it was the flip side of a strong-willed woman who trades in her failed marriages for a business career.

I went out to the kitchen and poked through cupboards until I found the liquor supply. I found a bottle of Rémy Martin I took out, then looked some more until I found a couple of balloon glasses. I turned on the warm water tap and let it run for a bit, then filled both glasses with hot water and let them sit. I tried not to stare at Lorna. She was slumped back in a corner of the sofa now with her face in her hands. I poured out the water and put a generous splash of Rémy into both glasses. I switched off the kitchen light and went in and sat down next to my ex. I put my own snifter down on the rug nearby.

"Here," I told her, taking her hand and placing the other snifter in it.

She opened her eyes and took the brandy with a little nod of thanks. Then I did one of those things that are common with me from time to time when in situations of stress and ambiguity. I kicked over the other snifter of cognac on the rug where I'd left it so as to have both hands free to pass the ammunition to Lorna.

"Shit," I murmured.

Lorna giggled.

I went out into the kitchen to wet a sponge. I carried it back and mopped the rug. I made a couple more trips to the kitchen to rewet the sponge. I was going to do it another time, but Lorna stopped me.

"Never mind, darling, that's good enough. Stay here and hug me and tell me things are going to be all right."

I stood there a little dumbfounded. We'd never been ones to use that sort of endearment. I think she'd called me darling maybe twice in our entire married career. She took my hand and tugged me down on the sofa beside her and put her arms around me. I hugged her in return. It wasn't a passionate embrace. It was the sort of reassuring homecoming type of hug a couple would give each other if they'd been married the way we had and parted amicably and a little sadly, instead of one of them having run off with a horn player in the Stan Kenton band. We broke it off mutually after several seconds.

"Thanks," she said, reaching over to get her brandy snifter. "I needed that."

"Okay," I told her. "Now what's the trouble?"

She made a little moan and shook her head, then sipped at the brandy and handed the snifter to me. I sipped in turn while she told me about things.

"It's just the very old story of a woman trying to make it in the professional world being expected to throw her body into the bargain."

"Who expects it?"

"Everybody," she said, looking up at me. "Well, not everybody maybe, but enough of them. Clients. Suppliers. My boss."

"Your boss? I thought you were a partner."

"I am. A junior partner. Enough of a junior partner so whenever Gene Olson gets stubborn about things, I pretty much feel I have to go along with whatever it is he wants."

"Even to going to bed with people?"

"Oh, he doesn't say it in so many words. But he says an attractive woman is an asset to any business venture and that all of a firm's assets should be used to best advantage. It doesn't take too much reading between the lines to know what that sort of pep talk is all about."

"Is this Seahawks guy one of the ones he has in mind?"

"Very much so. He says I should cruise by their office some day. Show the flag." She reached for the brandy snifter. "Show my legs, is what he means."

"What's Thackery's position in the organization?"

"I don't know. He's a former player. Now a front office man of some sort. He arranges the team parties, among other things."

"What about Olson himself? Does he feel the firm's assets should be available to him as well?"

"No. I've been able to evade that little scene so far." She gave a little shudder and sipped at the brandy. "We'd skirted around some of these things just this afternoon," she continued. "I hadn't expected him to be at the restaurant this evening or I wouldn't have taken you there. And when they came over to the table, well, you were there. You heard the conversation."

"I wasn't paying all that much attention. What was said?"

"God, what kind of a detective are you? Gene practically came out and told him I'd be available for some extra innings if we got the catering contract."

"Overtime," I told her.

"What?"

"In football it's overtime they go into if the regular game ends in a tie. Baseball goes extra innings."

"It means the same thing."

"I admit I was a little startled when you told Thackery you wanted to accommodate his football team. In some circles that would mean..."

"I know exactly what that would mean in some circles. Gene suggested I try to work something like that into the conversation the next time I encountered Brad. God, I could learn to hate men."

I grunted and got up and took the snifter out to the kitchen and poured a little more brandy into it. I didn't bother refilling the snifter I'd knocked over. I preferred drinking out of the same glass Lorna used. Her lipstick was imprinted on the rim. It had a nice flavor to it. Better than the brandy, I thought. I went back in and handed her the glass.

"So, Mr. Bragg. How does a girl handle this sort of problem?"

"I'm not sure. One thing, though. I think maybe before going into a business venture with somebody of the opposite sex, I'd make up my mind as to whether I'd be willing to do that sort of thing or not. And if not, I'd make that emphatically clear from the start."

"Well yes, that's a slick idea, except this isn't the start. We've been in business for nearly four years now. It didn't come up at the start."

"When did it come up?"

"Oh I don't know. I even sometimes wonder if I'm only imagining all this. If I'm reading something into our conversations that isn't really there. But we're getting ready for a major expansion. We're going to open a branch of Scandia Farms and eventually move our catering operation to a new commercial center going in right down there in Ballard, out near the locks. It's a place called Potlatch Bay."

"So that's what that's all about."

"What?"

"Potlatch Bay. I've seen some billboards around town touting it."

"Oh yes. It's going to be Seattle's newest razzmatazz development. Nearly everyone in town wants in on it. Anyway, we're going to be a part of it. They're having a luncheon next week to celebrate the lease-signing with everybody. They're just starting construction, but you'd think it was going to open next month from the publicity it's getting. And when we open down there, we're anticipating business to really take off. Well, that's not quite accurate. What we're anticipating is a need for business to really take off to pay for all the additional help we'll need to hire and operational costs. And Gene has sort of hinted I might be better equipped than he is to bring in that new business."

"But you say this is still all kind of vague."

"Yes, that's exactly what it is, kind of vague, and I don't really know how to cope with it. And all of this came flooding back when the two of them came over to the table, and I already was in a nervous state being out with you, so I just began to bawl and..."

She bit off the statement and drank at the brandy. When she lowered the glass, she stared at me and blinked her eyes a couple of times. "So there. Now you know."

"Know what?"

"How I feel about you after all these years. The last thing in the world I ever expected. I'd grown just plain tired of you down in San Francisco, but when you came into Dolly and Benny's home last night, I turned absolutely sappy. You've matured in a way I'd never thought possible. You're like a different man, almost. Tougher, sexier... If you'd told me when you brought me home last night that you wanted to make love to me, I couldn't have refused you to save my soul."

My mouth fell open and I probably gaped.

"Don't get me wrong, Peter. Tonight's not last night. I've thought about it some since then and I don't know if that would be such a good idea. And after the evening I've had, it just wouldn't work tonight anyhow. But you might as well be forewarned. I might wake up in the morning feeling that same sappy way and come chasing after you with all colors flying. You deserve to be aware of this. You might have feelings one way or the other about it yourself. You might not want to see me anymore. I do remember, after all, the circumstances under which I left San Francisco."

I sat stock still, studying her in the room's dim light. She gave a little sigh, and before I knew what was going on, any resolve or willpower I might have had just turned to tapioca pudding. I put my arms around her again and she came into them with an eagerness that nearly belied what she'd said about what would or wouldn't work out that night. We clung that way for a long time. This wasn't homecoming; this was holding on for dear life in the haunted house that stores all the emotions we aren't sure of. It wasn't until I lowered my head and brushed a kiss against her ear that she pushed me back.

"No, Peter. I meant what I said. I think you should go now."

She got up and led me to the door. I straightened my jacket and smiled at her. She opened the door, but turned back with one hand on my chest to keep me a moment longer.

"What do you feel about all this?" she asked. "Think we should see any more of each other?"

"Lorna, I don't know what to think. No, that's not right either. Look, I think I'd like to see more of you. If nothing else, I'd like to try to think of some way to get things back on a businesslike basis between you and old Gene."

"If that's what's needed," she told me. "But I'd just die if you or I or anybody else brought it up and it turned out I was all wrong about things, that I'd just been reading things into his remarks. That's what makes it so difficult. I just don't know."

# Chapter 8 ———————————

The Jackson Detective Agency was on the upper floor of a two-story brick building down on lower Second Avenue. It wasn't a smart part of town. The neighborhood had pawn shops, camping goods stores, small secondhand merchandise marts, and more than a few abandoned storefronts. The air in the building was musty, and the wooden stairs I climbed had the worn grooves made by heavily shod men going up and down them over several decades. The agency office itself had the same old-time bare-knuckle feel to it as the streets outside. Just inside the outer door was a small reception area with a couple of straight-back chairs. A wooden slatted counter, waist high with a locked gate in it, separated the reception area from the main part of the office, which was about forty feet wide and twice that deep, with a walled-off inner office at the rear of the room. Scarred brown linoleum covered the floor and bare light bulbs screwed into green metal shades hung from the plaster ceiling. There were several banks of file cabinets and a number of desks spotted here and there.

A tall hatchet-faced man with straight black hair slicked back on his head was banging his way through file drawers, looking for something. Another man, built like a fireplug with gray crewcut hair, was at one of the desks talking on a telephone. Both of those men had their coats off and their sleeves rolled up. Both of them wore shoulder holsters that had handguns in them.

A third man, younger than the others but just as raw-looking, also was on the phone at a desk a little ways beyond the counter and gate. An ashtray to one side of his desk was overflowing with old butts and he had a cigarette going in his mouth. He also was in shirt-sleeves, but he wasn't wearing a shoulder holster with a gun in it. That was on the desk next to the ashtray. He looked me over thoroughly while he finished his conversation, then he got up and came over to the counter with a raised eyebrow. I gave him one of my business cards.

"The name's Bragg. I'd like to see Grady Jackson if he's available."

The guy nodded and whistled lightly through his teeth as he studied the card. He turned and went over to his desk, put the holster and gun inside one of the drawers and locked it, then walked back to the office in the rear of the room. He went through a door with a pane of translucent glass in it and was in there maybe a couple of minutes before he came out again. During the couple of minutes, the other two guys were committing me to memory. The guy who'd been banging through the file cabinets was at a desk and on the telephone now. The older fellow was off the phone and rubbing one hand across his blunt jaw. He picked up a file folder on the desk in front of him and began paging through it. It was about as no-nonsense a place as I'd ever seen.

The younger fellow came back up front and pushed a button on his desk that buzzed open the gate in the counter. "Go on back," he told me. I did as he said.

Grady Jackson's office was a little less utilitarian than the outer office. He had carpeting on the floor, a couple of comfortable-looking leather padded chairs with armrests—one for him, one for visitors—and a dark wooden desk. A Tiffany-style glass lamp hung over the desk, which had piles of papers scattered across it. Open shelves to one side held an array of folders, road maps, and telephone books. A window in the wall behind the desk looked out at the back of another brick building across an alley.

The man studying me from behind the desk was in his late sixties. He sat tall and erect but had slack facial muscles that gave his wide mouth a rubbery look. Like the fellows out front, he worked in his shirt-sleeves. A gray suit jacket hung from a coat tree in the corner. He had on a white shirt and a wide blue-and-white striped cravat that had been made about the year the Japanese bombed Pearl Harbor. His eyes were the color of his suit and they stared at me noncommittally. He stood and leaned across the desk with a bony hand extended.

"Welcome to Seattle, Bragg."

He had a quick way of speaking, as if he didn't like much to do it.

"Thanks. Actually, I grew up in this town," I told him, sitting in the leather chair he waved me to.

"What made you set up shop down in that land of queers?" he asked, looking at my business card.

I smiled patiently. "They don't bother a person much. There probably aren't as many of them there as people other places think. Outside of a couple of areas in town where they live and caper, you hardly notice them. I used to work for one of the newspapers in San Francisco. That's how I opened my office there."

The older man grunted. "Shoulda seen the newspaper picture they ran here a while back. Taken in San Francisco on—what is it they call it? Fag Freedom Day?"

"Gay Freedom Day."

"Anyways, there musta been thousands of 'em, barechested and smooching all over the goddamn place. Jesus Christ, was enough to make a man puke. You're not one of 'em, are you? You don't look it."

"No, sir. I've preferred girls my whole life. And the photo you saw probably was a little misleading. That annual celebration they have with a parade and all attracts people from all over the West. If it was like that there all the time, I'd probably move."

That seemed to satisfy him. He looked at my card again. "You working or just bumming around the old hometown?"

"A little of both. Actually, what brought me up here, and eventually to see you, is a problem an old school chum who lives here has been having."

"What kind of problem?"

"Somebody wants to get him out of town. He's had some phone threats. Somebody took a couple of shots at him up by Woodland Park one day—monkeyed with his car brakes. Things like that. I thought maybe I could try to get to the bottom of it for him. I haven't done so well up to now. The only reason I came to see you is that by now I'm really clutching at straws."

He didn't make a move, but something in his face made me feel he was putting a little distance between us. "What sort of a straw am I?"

"He said he had a talk with you a while back. And I'm to the point where I'm checking in with anybody he's had contact with lately. I can't find any obvious reason for the things that have been going on."

"What's this fellow's name?"

"Benny Bartlett. He writes free-lance articles. Said he did a piece on detective agencies in the Pacific Northwest that's due to run soon."

"Oh yeah yeah yeah, I remember that fellow. Owly-looking little man. Wears glasses and squints a lot."

"That's the one."

Jackson chuckled. "You figure maybe we're trying to stifle the press, something like that?"

I smiled back at him. "Not really. I wouldn't just come dancing on in here and lay it all out for you if I really believed that. Benny said when he told you why he needed to mention your agency—to show how things work in Olympia and what he intended to write—that you were reasonable enough about it. I just want to hear you say the same thing. Maybe ask if you have any ideas on the matter. See if you've heard of anything similar happening around town recently."

He scratched his chin and stared at the ceiling. "No," he said after a minute. "Doesn't sound like anything I'd know about. Somebody just called him up and told him to get out of town? That it?"

"About that."

"Huh. A strange one, for sure. And yeah, he pretty well described the talk we had. I naturally didn't want him to slander the agency. When's that story coming out, you know?"

"He said any day now. In something called *Sound Sounds.*"

He grunted again and picked up an old-fashioned fountain pen to jot a note on a pad beside him. "Like to see that when it comes out." When he had finished making the note, he looked up at me. "That it?"

"Yes, sir, I guess it is," I told him, getting out of the chair.

"Sorry I couldn't be more help," he told me, coming around from behind the desk and putting one hand on my shoulder as he opened the door. "Where are you staying, in case I hear something?"

I told him and gave him Benny's office number as well.

"Okay. And you steer clear of them queers, you hear?"

He stood in the office doorway cackling behind me as I made my way back up front with a friendly smile for all the hired help. The fellow with gray hair was cursing at somebody over the telephone. He seemed to be discussing a bill. The younger man up front buzzed me back through the gate. His holster and gun was back out alongside his ashtray. At least the old man back in the rear office hadn't been wearing a holster. Probably kept a sawed-off shotgun in his desk.

My first look at Julius "Bomber" Hogan that afternoon was of his sitting behind the wheel of a fourteen-foot power boat towing a young woman on water skis out on Lake Washington. From what I could see of him, Hogan had a tanned round face and seemed to be grinning around the corners of a cigar he had in his mouth. He was wearing a dark blue skipper's cap and a black turtleneck sweater beneath a blue jacket. The girl on water skis behind the boat appeared to be in her twenties. She had a full-bodied figure encased in a white one-piece swimsuit. Long blond hair hung in a braid down her back. She was grinning too as they zipped past out beyond the small dock down where the back lawn of Hogan's home met the lake. It wasn't sunny and warm out there on the water, but it wasn't raining either, and the sky was only partly overcast and in Seattle you take what the Good Lord gives you.

I stood beside a dark-complexioned man in his mid-forties wearing a chauffeur's uniform. He'd been polishing a Lincoln Continental parked in a driveway off to one side of the house when I'd driven up. The two-story

Colonial-style home was set on a half-acre lot of lush lawn. On one side of the house was a swimming pool, on the other a rose garden. When I'd rung the front door chimes, a woman wearing a maid's uniform had answered. For a man who'd done time in the state pen at Walla Walla, Hogan led a comfortable life.

He spotted us standing there at the top of the lawn and waved, then made a final loop out into the lake and swung in past shore. The woman skied up onto where the lawn met the water. Hogan throttled back and pulled into the dock. The chauffeur went on down to secure the boat.

The girl was toweling off at the lake's edge. Hogan climbed stiffly out of the boat. He had a short, squat figure and he walked with a rolling gait over to the blonde. He said something that made her laugh, then gave her a pat on the fanny and made his way up to where I stood. He had an affable grin and a firm handshake.

"You Bragg?"

"That's right, and you must be Mr. Hogan."

"Call me Bomber. Let's go up to the house and get comfortable."

Getting comfortable involved sinking down into a pair of dark leather chairs in a large study that had a roaring fire in a fireplace and a full bottle of just about every kind of liquor that's made on a nearby side table. A servant came in and Hogan asked him to fix a Dewar's White Label on the rocks.

"You, Bragg?"

"No thanks. It's a little early for me."

"Oh have a drink, for Christ's sake. Unbend."

I asked for a tall bourbon and water, short on the bourbon. The manservant poured, then went out of the room and closed a pair of tall wood-paneled doors behind him. Hogan and I raised our glasses to each other and drank.

I looked around me some. "Nice place."

Hogan shrugged. "Yeah well...forty years in the business, you know. You either end up like this or at the bottom of the river." He laughed loudly. I joined in politely.

"But you didn't come here to bullshit about old times, most of which I wouldn't tell you about anyhow. I've got the advantage of you. Drocco gave me a pretty thorough rundown on you. Your rep and all. What you did for his daughter. And you don't know beans about me except I been an active man who's done all right for himself."

"And served a little time in Walla Walla."

"Yeah, but that was nothing. A political thing more than much else. Two years is all. A lot of people owed me favors. They went out of their way to make my stay as comfortable as they could."

"I didn't know Walla Walla could be comfortable for anybody."

He shrugged and gestured around the room. "I gave a lot of books to the prison library. They let me work there. I had a cell to myself and certain commissary privileges. I said 'yes, sir' and 'no, sir' to the guards and there wasn't anybody in the population there foolish enough to try laying a number on me. It was like two years in the army, only I didn't have to worry about anybody shooting at me. And I knew when I got out, I'd be going into more or less retirement and had this waiting for me."

"A guy could do worse. Is that where you're at now, in more or less retirement?"

He nodded and sipped his Scotch. "I'm not active in any of the enterprises. People come out to visit from time to time. I'm sort of a consultant, and not just to people I used to work with. Cops come visit—sometimes just to get a general drift of things if they're having problems. But mostly I just fart around the place here.

Do a little traveling with Kathy. We just got back from Puerta Vallarta. Kathy, that's the blonde you saw on water skis, and no, she isn't my daughter."

He was grinning. I gave my head a brief shake of admiration and sipped the bourbon.

"Now what's this about problems this writer fellow is having? He visited me in the joint, you know. A funny little man. I liked him."

"That's good. He'll be mighty pleased to hear it."

And then I laid out the troubles Benny had been having—all of it, including the suspected abduction try on his kids. I told him about Benny's background and the sort of stuff he wrote, and when I'd finished, Hogan sat staring into the flames, then got up and went over to pour some more Scotch into his glass.

"That doesn't make much sense, does it?"

"Not to me it doesn't, so far."

"Well, you don't have to ask if anybody I know could be involved. They're not. In fact, if it should turn out in the course of all this that you need a little help, I can give you the names of a couple of good men in the area."

"Thanks, but I'd like to avoid that if I can."

"Yeah, Drocco said you were a little skittish. But that's how I feel about the funny little man. We had a good visit, and I liked the story he wrote. He made me sound even friendlier than I really am. I mean, jeez, after all, you don't get a name like Bomber for nothing, right?"

He laughed again and I laughed right along with him.

"Tell you what," he said. "You just wait here and make yourself comfortable. Help yourself to anything you want. I'll go make some phone calls, see if I can come up with anything."

"I appreciate your taking the time."

He waved a hand in dismissal and left the room. He

was gone for more than twenty minutes, and when he came back into the room he was thoughtful.

"Well, I didn't come up with a whole helluva lot," he told me, settling back into the chair. "Nobody I talked to has ever heard of your friend. They don't know of any scam of this kind. In fact, the only funny sort of thing going on around town wouldn't have any connection at all with Bartlett near as I can make out."

"Can you tell me about it?"

"No. Not now, anyhow. It isn't all that firm. I just have some friends who are very sharp when it comes to matters of commerce. They've been mildly curious about some little patterns they've noticed recently. Nothing involving us—my former colleagues, that is—but there might be something just a little funny going on. Involves some foreigners, they said."

"I've heard there's a lot of Japanese money coming into town. Could it be them?"

"I don't know. I told them to try looking at it a little closer, see what more they can find out. Where can I reach you if I get anything?"

I took out one of my cards and wrote a bunch of numbers on it. My motel, Benny's office and home, and Lorna's. "If I'm not at one of these places, you can leave a message and I'll get back to you."

"Fine. And don't forget about the men I mentioned. You wouldn't have to look at it as a favor. I'd be doing it for the funny little man. I put his story in my scrapbook."

# Chapter 9 ————————————

I phoned Benny's office to see how things were going.

"Nobody's shot at me today, anyhow," he told me. "I've got Bronco Billy back out of the shop and Dolly borrowed the neighbors' car to drive the boys to school this morning. She's picking them up in, oh, about forty minutes. And you were right about the cops. When I told Hamilton about the move on the boys, he took a new and sudden interest."

"What'd he do "

"He had me drive them into town last night. He had a guy waiting with one of those kits with different kinds of facial features in it, noses and eyes and things. They had Timmy and Al come up with a likeness of the man who got out of the car and told Timmy he'd won the drums. Oh, and Hamilton wants to talk to you, too."

"What about?"

"Get your description of the car you tried to chase."

I decided to get that out of the way and told Benny

I'd stop by his office later. The sun had come out to tease everybody for a while. I parked down the street from the Public Safety Building and went up to Hamilton's office only to be told he was out for the rest of the day. I asked if Hamilton had run off reproductions of the face Timmy and Al and the police identification man had come up with. They said he had, but nobody knew where he'd put them. I drove on over to Benny's office.

"You're too early," he told me, turning briefly from the typewriter. "I want to get this piece into the mail tonight. Go do something for an hour or so." He started to turn back to his work, but then called me again on my way out the door.

"Go upstairs and visit with Zither. She's been asking about you. She wants to show you her etchings or something."

What he suggested wasn't a bad idea. I was feeling all mixed up about my ex-wife. Maybe a little companionship with somebody else could put things in perspective for me. Maybe. I went back down the hall and up to the second floor.

Zither's studio was in the middle of the building, on the side looking out over the nearby waterfront. Her door was open and I just stood there a moment looking over the place. The light in there wouldn't have been too good even on a sunny day. It was blocked by an overhead viaduct that had been built to speed traffic from the residential north end of the city to the more industrial south end, back before I-5 had been built. So somebody had installed long banks of fluorescent tubes that made it as bright in there as a photo studio. It was a big place, as large as Mary Ellen Cutler's studio downstairs.

Zither was at an easel over by the tall windows. I couldn't see what she was working on, but I looked around at some of the other work she had hanging from the walls and propped up here and there on workbenches and chairs. Some of them were portraits. She showed an obvious talent, but there was something about those renderings that put me on edge. They had a starkness that reminded me of the painter's own features. Then I saw what it was. She had a way of emphasizing the facial bone structures. These people all looked as if they'd been on starvation diets or had just come out of an internment camp.

Her other work didn't make any sense at all to me. I could pick out a human figure or two, but what they were doing was a puzzle. Zither herself was wearing a pair of blue denim jeans and an old white shirt with its sleeves rolled up. Over that, she had on a paint-smeared oilcloth apron that carried a big red and white advertisement for Beefeater gin on the front of it.

She stepped back from her work to study it. When I cleared my throat, she turned and stared quietly at me.

"So there you are," she said finally.

"Hi. Benny chased me out. He has something he wants to get finished. If this is a bad time . . ."

"No, this is a fine time. I was just about ready to wrap it up." She spent a few minutes tidying up her paints and pots and brushes, then took off the apron. "Come on in. Shut the door behind you."

I did as she asked and stared around some more. "I'm impressed," I told her.

"I make a living," she said. "At long last. Would you like some wine?"

"Sure. Sounds good."

She went through a beaded curtain off to the left. When she came back, she was carrying two huge glasses of white wine. They were schooner-sized beer glasses. She must have kept them in the refrigerator, because they were chilled.

"When the lady pours a glass of wine, the lady pours a glass of wine," I observed.

"I like to get a little swizzled when I finish for the day," she told me. "And I don't like to have to keep going back and forth to the refrigerator." We touched glasses and sipped. She turned and indicated the work around her. "Do you get it?"

"I'm not sure I'm seeing everything there is to see."

"Then you obviously don't get it. I mean, can you see what's going on in it?"

"The portraits are straightforward enough, although the people in them look a little bony."

"Most of my clients want them that way. Who wants to look fleshy?"

"Those are all commissioned works?"

"Most of them. I have them back on loan from the clients just now for a show I'm having at one of the local galleries next week. But the portraits aren't what I meant. I meant can you tell what's going on in the other works."

I walked over to study one of them, a somber-toned painting. I could make out a bare-chested man whose face had an odd expression on it, one of intense surprise, almost bordering on shock. He might have been a man astounded at having just been shot. The rest of it was all kind of indistinct.

I turned back to Zither. Her expression and thin smile were anticipatory. "Not really," I told her. "Why don't you explain a couple of them?"

She shook her head. Her long brunette hair was hanging loosely down her back. It shimmered gently when she shook her head. "Not just yet. Let's have a little wine first. Then I'll tell you about them."

She crossed to a panel of switches on the wall and turned off the overhead lights. She left on a floor lamp to one side and went around to turn on several small spotlights mounted to illuminate several of the paintings. She crossed to the beaded curtain and held it open. "We can sit in here."

I went into her living quarters. She had them behind the windows with the best view. They looked out over a gap in the warehouses and terminals along the waterfront onto Elliott Bay. As I stood looking out, a huge auto ferry slid into view, lights ablazing. In front of the window was a low round table with several big floor cushions scattered around it. There was a sofa placed with its back to the beaded curtain, and on the wall opposite were a sink counter, small stove, and refrigerator. A door beyond led to her bathroom. At the back of the enclosure, opposite the windows, was a wide, foot-high platform where she had a queen-size bed with a shelf to one side filled with books and magazines, a box of tissues, a radio, and other things a person might find convenient to have handy beside the bed. A small TV set on a portable stand was tucked away in a back corner. The floor felt as if it had a couple of layers of carpeting on it. It was a cozy place.

Zither settled gracefully on one of the cushions beside the low table, moving like a ballet dancer, and patted a cushion beside her. I joined her there, not nearly as gracefully.

"Tell me about yourself."

I laughed. "That's a tough order."

"I'm not a native of here," she told me. "Tell me what it was like growing up in Seattle."

"God." I shook my head. "I was quite a different person then."

"We all were, growing up." She reached across to touch my shoulder. "Tell me. Please?"

I sat and thought a moment with my chin on my fists, then began to ramble, telling her some of it. It was a strange experience. Nobody had ever asked me to give an accounting like that. As I got into the swing of it, I surprised myself with the things I remembered, going back all those years. Later, when I thought about it, I'd be amazed that I could rattle on like that to a woman who was little more than a stranger to me. Maybe the intensity with which she listened had something to do with it. She stared at me, hunched slightly forward, as if she were sitting on the edge of a chair, though we both were on floor cushions. She listened hard as I spooned it out, the daydreams along with the fistfights. Streetcars that used to rumble along Phinney Avenue, just a couple of blocks from where I grew up. The fire engines that would scream down the same avenue in the middle of the night, setting off a great wail and yelp from animals penned up at the zoo. Forest fires that could be seen across Puget Sound in the Olympic Mountains. The wintry displays of the northern lights, or aurora borealis, as we were taught to call them later. Pollywog ponds and hurt dogs and remembered deaths. The things that impress a boy strongly enough so he can recall them as a man and relate them to a narrow-faced oddly compelling woman sitting beside him in a darkened studio looking out over the Seattle waterfront. I must have run on for twenty minutes, what with the pauses to remember and the sips of white wine.

"You're either a good listener or asleep with your eyes open," I told her finally.

She smiled and reached out her hand again, this time to rest it on my shoulder. "No, not asleep. They're nice stories you tell. But you didn't mention any girls."

I shrugged. "I finally reached a certain age and began to notice them."

In another moment she took away her hand and finished her wine. She uncurled gracefully and got up and went over to the refrigerator. She brought over a jug of Chablis and refilled our glasses.

"You trying to get us drunk?"

"I don't know. A little, maybe." She returned the wine to the refrigerator, then came back to sit down beside me again, this time close enough so we were touching.

"Let me tell you about my paintings," she said after another sip of her wine. "None of the people in them are fully clothed. Most of the men figures are totally nude, because partially clad men, wearing contemporary clothing styles, look clumsy and awkward, but the naked male body itself is not clumsy and awkward, not by any stretch of the imagination. It is something I first noticed, I suspect, at an age somewhat younger than you were the day you blinked and realized there were little girls out there around you."

"Little girls beginning to grow into big girls."

"Of course. And while my male figures are nude, most of the female figures are at least partially clothed. And why should that be, Mr. Bragg?"

"Because a partially garbed female figure can be a whole lot more cha-cha-cha than a totally naked one. I've never understood why the people who put out those raw girlie magazines don't see that."

"You're right, of course. Anyway, that's what I allude to in my paintings. Boys and girls, and men and women, in various acts of eroticism. They are, for the most part, quite naughty. And that is why I now do a good business with my painting, but you have to know what to look for. Let me show you."

We went back out into the studio. She led me over to the spotlighted painting I'd noticed earlier, with the bare-chested man with the astonished look on his face.

"This is just a brief moment in time between a man and a woman," she told me. "Let me tell you what led up to this moment. They were caught in a thundershower while out walking in the fields. They have known each other only a short period of time. Caught in the rain, they have run hand in hand back to the small lodge where the woman is staying. They are both sopping wet when they gain the shelter of the lodge. He quickly stokes up the fire in the small fireplace. She brings him a large towel and urges him to strip off his wet clothes and dry himself. While he does this, she goes into a nearby room. When she comes to the doorway again, he is standing before the fire, naked except for the towel wrapped around his middle. She stands staring at his body in the firelight. He senses her and turns. She has changed into a dry russet skirt, but she is still wearing the blouse she wore when caught in the downpour. She has a hand on the top button of the blouse as if to change it, but now she crosses the room, slowly lowering her hand. She is wearing nothing beneath the blouse. Her neat breasts and nipples are clearly limned beneath the thin, wet material."

Zither turned to me. "What do you think he feels as he sees her thusly, Mr. Bragg?"

I cleared my throat. "I think he might feel a certain sense of arousal if he's hooked up right."

Zither smiled. "There you have it. And in this painting I have captured the instant in which this rather emboldened woman has slipped her hand beneath the towel and grasped that which betrays his arousal."

"Is that what happened there?"

She took a sip of her wine. "Yes, that is what happened there. Can you see it now?"

"No, but I sure wish I could."

"Study it some."

I backed off a ways and squinted. I was beginning to get hints and impressions, but it was nothing I could have thought of myself without her telling me. There was very little of the woman figure in the painting. In a lower corner I could just make out what might have been a thin white wrist crossing the top of what Zither said was the towel wrapped around the fellow's waist. The sneaky hand at the end of the wrist wasn't in the painting but below the field of vision. Out of sight and into mischief, from what she'd told me.

"He looks to me," I told her, "as if he's just been shot."

"You oaf," she said a little impatiently. "She's just caressed his you-know-what."

I grunted. "Is there any more to the story?"

"My God, yes. Wouldn't you suppose so? For starters, I'd suspect he takes her in his arms and kisses her rather roughly. But from this moment on, it is a tale for each individual to complete for himself."

"Well, if there are people who can see all this in these things, I can tell why you're making money at it."

She led me around the room and told a couple of more naughty tales leading up to the works she wanted me to be able to interpret. I wasn't any better at seeing what was going on in them than I had been with the one showing the man who looked as if he'd been shot. One concerned a woman equestrian with riding crop and one of her stable boys. Another was something about some twin sisters and their younger nephew in a wooded glade. Her stories were all right, but the paintings eluded me. And I told her so.

"Well, I don't suppose it matters greatly," she told me. "I was hoping, though, that they might titillate you a bit."

"Like the fellow who looks as if he's been shot?"

"Something like that. And I'd still like for you to pose for me before you leave town. It wouldn't take too much time. I'd want to make some preliminary sketches. Then I take photographs as well, to work from later on."

"Like these people you've described? In my birthday suit?"

She turned to me with a little smile. She took the goblet of wine from me and put it down along with her own on a nearby stand. She looped her arms around my neck and winked. "Who knows? You might even grow to like it, if you'll excuse the expression."

We might have gotten into a bit of mischief ourselves right then, Zither and me, and changed the whole direction of the rest of my stay in Seattle. Only we didn't, because right then some kind of explosion rocked the old building, knocking plaster from the walls and dust from the ceiling. It was from somewhere downstairs—up at the north end of the building, where Benny's office was.

# Chapter 10

I ran down the stairs with Zither right behind me. People stood out in the hallway gaping up toward Benny's end of the building, to where dust and smoke was curling around the corner. I got up there as fast as I could. I was relieved to find Benny and Mary Ellen Cutler standing just outside her studio, staring pop-eyed into Benny's office. The office door had been blown half off its hinges, and the pane of pebbled glass was shattered.

"What happened?" I asked them.

"A nasty suspicion just saved my life," Benny told me. "I had a phone call. When I answered, nobody said anything. They just hung up. With all the other funny stuff that's been happening, I decided to get the hell out of there. I crossed to Mary Ellen's to use the phone and call you upstairs. I'd just started dialing, when BLAM!"

His mouth twitched a couple of times. I stepped into

his office. The window in front of Benny's desk had been blown out as well. The desk itself looked as if it'd been cleared with an angry hand. Burned and curled papers and folders were strewn around the floor, along with shards of glass. His chair had been blown into kindling. The top of his desk was scorched black, desk drawers had been blown out of their tracks, and his typewriter was here and there all around the office.

"They did a real number this time, huh?" Benny asked.

"They did indeed. Okay, Benny, this is it. Call the cops, tell them what you can, then go get Dolly and the kids and get out of town. I mean tonight."

"But that's just what they've wanted all along."

"I know, and now you're going to do it—until the cops or I or somebody finds out what's going on. We can't . . ."

"Pete!" cried Benny, staring over my shoulder.

I spun around. A figure loomed in the darkness, just outside Benny's shattered window. Whoever it was carried something in a two-handed grip. I gave Benny a hard shove back into the hall. "Everybody duck!"

The person outside began shooting as we went through the doorway. The gunman fired in quick succession. The shots sounded as if they were large caliber. Zither screamed as a bullet smacked into the outer wall of Mary Ellen's studio. I slammed the sagging door to Benny's office. It didn't catch, and swung right back out again as I shoved everyone in sight into Mary Ellen's studio.

"Cops!" I yelled again as Benny slammed the door behind them.

I ran back down the hallway. Some private dick I'd turned out to be. Flirting around upstairs with the skinny painter lady while the attempted murder of my old buddy Benny Bartlett was in the process of execution. I ran outside to the rental car, unlocked the glove compartment, and got out the Smith & Wesson revolver. Combat Masterpiece, the S&W people had named it. Good name, good gun. Marines in Korea had given me this one on a bleak wintry day when I'd grown about twenty years older just like that. One minute I'd been a scared teenage kid, a navy aircrewman who'd been lucky enough to stumble onto a squad of marines after I'd had to bail out of a single-engine attack plane that crashed with a dead pilot in the cockpit. The marines had given me some rudimentary soldier training the first day I met up with them. They gave me a rifle and a hand grenade—just one—and told me how to use them. A few days later, we were crossing a rocky slope when an enemy machine gun above had opened fire on us, or rather on the rest of the withered squad. I'd fallen back to adjust a sock chafing me inside my boot. I was out of sight of the enemy gunners, but the rest of the squad wasn't. They were scrambling desperately for cover, but they were very exposed. And at that moment, with the machine gun firing at the people who'd taken me in, a cold emotional paralysis had gripped the scared teenage kid. Reason went out the window. I ran back a short distance, then sprinted up the slope, keeping low, moving as fast as I could, until I'd flanked the two men at the machine gun and shot and killed them both. Later I couldn't believe what I'd done. But the marines assured me that I had, and a scrawny sergeant from Brownesville, Texas, had given me the .38 revolver that had belonged to their lieutenant. He'd been killed two weeks earlier. There had been a lot of killing going on back then. There was apt to be more going on now. The .38 had spent its last moment joy-riding around in the glove compartment of the rental car.

I made it up to the corner of the building a lot quicker than I had made it that day to the high ground above the machine gun. It was dim up there. There

were streetlights up in the next block and over by
where the street crossed the railroad tracks, but they
didn't help matters much up at the end of Benny's
building. A ship out on the bay hooted. I squatted
down and took a peek around the corner of the building. The dim figure was still there. He'd moved up to
the window ledge and was looking around, as if he
couldn't make up his mind what to do next. A siren in
the distance made up his mind for him. He jumped
back from the window just as I yelled at him.

"Stop, or I'll shoot!" I cried.

He did what most people do when I yell something
like that. He spun and took a couple of wild shots in my
direction, then started running like hell up the block,
away from the waterfront. I fired a couple of times
myself to let him know I wasn't bluffing, then took off
after him. He did a little dodging from side to side as
he ran, then shouted something. Another figure stepped
out of a doorway near the corner. He raised his hands,
and I ducked and scrambled for the recessed entryway
to a nearby storefront as three or four more shots came
zinging in my direction. I tucked myself around and
got into a firing position as another slug made a tearing
sound in a wooden sill over my head. It looked as if
they were gutting the upper floors of a building behind
me. A huge metal trash container had been parked in
the street. I fired once up the street, then ran down
across the sidewalk and behind the trash bin. By the
time I'd worked to the upper end of it out in the street,
I couldn't see either of the gunmen. I started trotting
up the street again and paused beside a car parked at
the curb. I still didn't see them. I left the car and
started on up toward the street above me. That's when
car headlights came around the corner and pinned me
out in the middle of the street like a moth. I lunged
back behind the parked car and threw myself toward
the gutter, banging my knee on the pavement and my

head against the curb. Talk about being down and out in Seattle. At least I hadn't knocked myself brainless— and thank God for that, or it would have been the end of me and any future career as a hotshot detective. A single shot plinked the nearby pavement as the car sped past. Then I heard the screech of brakes, followed immediately by the low whine of the car engine. They were coming back for me.

I clambered out of the gutter and, by crouching low and moving nimbly, managed to keep the trash bin between me and the backing auto. Below the trash bin again, I darted across the street. The men in the car would have been looking for me over their shoulders.

The car braked again near where I'd been in the gutter. More sirens were approaching. The driver shifted gears again and started to make a U-turn, but the street wasn't wide enough for him to do it in one swing. He braked at the opposite curb and backed up. As the car began its turn to head back up the street, I shot at them twice more. No fool, I. I wanted them headed away from me before I revealed my position. I aimed for the dark figure in the passenger seat. What I hit was one of the rear windows. The car roared up to the end of the block and squealed around the corner. I dropped the revolver into my jacket pocket, dusted myself off, and went back to spend the next hour or so yammering with Benny and Mary Ellen and Zither and a bunch of cops.

The bomb-damaged office was the real thing. The attempts on Benny's life weren't just speculation any longer. Lieutenant Hamilton had come out on overtime to take a look at things for himself. His attitude, finally, was that of the concerned public safety officer.

"I want those two slugs you had at my office yester-day," he told me, his Adam's apple a-jiggle. "The ones you said you dug up out at Woodland Park."

"I didn't have to dig them up," I told him. "I just

went inside the fence and searched the ground some and found them lying right out there for anybody to see and pick up. And I can't give them to you now."

"Why not?"

"They're on their way to a first-rate criminalistics lab down in California. When they're finished going over them and have made their report, I'll ask them to mail them back to you."

Before I'd been a nuisance. Now, his expressive face told me, I was somebody he could actively dislike.

"At least," I told him, "you've got the fragments of the—what do you call it these days—explosive device? That should give your people something to sink their teeth into."

"Bragg, I want a copy of whatever the people in California have to say about those two slugs. I want it the same day you get it."

"I might be back down there by the time they're finished with them."

"Then you can pick up the goddamn telephone and read it to me."

"Yes, sir."

I turned and went into Mary Ellen's studio, to where Benny was flattened out in an easy chair. His head was tossed back and his arms and legs were flung wide. He looked like a pancake man somebody had dropped there.

"How are your nerves holding up?" I asked him.

"They aren't."

"Have you called Dolly?"

"Yeah. She's packing. For all of us. Don't know if we'll be able to catch the ferry out of Edmonds this time of night, but she's checking. And she's warning her parents we're all on our way. If we can't catch the ferry tonight, we'll just hole up somewhere until morning." He was silent a moment, staring straight ahead. Then the bitterness overcame his jitters.

"Goddamnit," he said bleakly.

I went over and gave his shoulder a squeeze. "I know what you're thinking, but it's for the best. And I'd like a key to your place. Out home."

He looked up. "Okay, but what for?"

"I don't know. If I run out of other things to do, I might just spend a little time hunkered down in there. Watch traffic go by. Things like that."

"You think they might be checking up on me?"

"I hope they do. I'd like just one clean crack at whoever these people are."

"What were you doing when you ran out of here earlier?"

"Chasing them. There were two of them, the man at the window, who must have tossed in the bomb, and another one up the street. We did some shooting at one another."

Benny sat up straight. "Jesus, Pete. You okay?"

"Aside from a scraped knee and a bang on the head."

"Hey, I'm sorry, man."

"Benny, it's what I do for a living."

"Think you hit one of them?"

"No. I didn't get a really good shot until the very end. Then I missed the guy I was shooting at by about two feet."

"You just said you did this sort of thing for a living."

"He was in a moving car. But it's nice to hear you're getting your spirits back."

After the cops left, I followed Benny home. I didn't bother to tell Hamilton about the exchange of gunfire I'd taken part in. I didn't see anybody well enough to identify him, and I didn't want to spend the next three hours looking at mug shots. And I didn't think the people I'd chased would go driving brazenly around with a bullet hole or two in their car window. Even if this was Seattle. They'd get it fixed.

When Benny and Dolly and Timmy and Al finally

turned out the lights and piled into old Bronco Billy, I trailed them in the rental car long enough to make sure there wasn't anybody following them. Then I drove back to my motel.

I felt as if I'd put in a day's work. I wasn't hungry, particularly, but there was a hot shower and a bottle of bourbon back there and I wanted some time to think about things.

At the motel I got out the gun cleaning gear and spent a few minutes reaming and swabbing and oiling the .38. Then I had the shower and drank some of the bourbon, and after stretching out atop the bed for an hour or so, I decided I wasn't hungry enough to go prowling up and down Aurora Avenue looking for a restaurant. With that decision under my belt I poured another stiff bourbon, propped up the pillows, and was about to spin the dial on the TV set when the phone rang on the stand beside the bed. I picked up the receiver and said hello.

"You're a dead man, Bragg. Bang-bang dead."

It was a male caller, and he had the voice Benny had described, as if it came from the bottom of a rain barrel. And then he hung up. I put the receiver back gently. My hand was still resting atop it when the phone rang again. I snatched it up.

"Look, asshole, I don't care if..."

"Peter?"

I exhaled slowly. It was Lorna.

"Sorry, I didn't know it was you."

"Who did you think it was?"

"Somebody who just called a minute or two ago. He didn't identify himself."

"What did he want?"

"He wanted to put a scare into me."

"Did he?"

"You heard how I answered the phone."

"I certainly did. How are you coming with Benny's problems?"

"I think I must be doing something right, or I wouldn't have had the phone call." I told her about the bombing of Benny's office. "He and Dolly and the kids threw some stuff in a suitcase and left town."

"For how long?"

"Long enough for me or the cops or somebody to find out what's behind all this."

"Do you have any idea how much longer it might be?"

"No, but I'm hoping the police technicians can make something of the bomb residue in Benny's office. God knows we're due for a break. These people have been taking awful chances, getting away with things without being tripped up. Nobody can stay that lucky."

She was quiet for a minute. "Peter?"

"Yeah?"

"If one of those people called you there at your motel, that must mean they know where you're staying."

I brooded for a moment, then cleared my throat. "You still do it."

"Do what?"

"Find the little chinks in my armor."

"I didn't mean anything like that. I'm just worried that..."

"No, it's okay, Lorna. I like to think I would have thought about that myself in the next ten minutes or so. These people have been lucky, but that doesn't mean they can't get away with something more. Damn it."

"What's wrong?"

"Oh, I've had some to drink, and I'd about given up on the idea of going out to get anything to eat because of the trouble, but now there's changing motels to think about..."

"You could come here."

And there it was, out there on the table for us all to think about.

"Just for tonight, I mean," she continued. "There's plenty of room. You've seen that. And it doesn't have to mean anything. Man-woman kind of anything. It could just be my night to be a good Samaritan."

"Is that what it could be?"

"Oh God. I don't know what it could be. Won't know until you get over here. But I could find you something to eat out in the kitchen. You wouldn't even have to pack now. Just bring stuff for the night. You can go back and check out of the motel tomorrow."

It was too good an offer to refuse, despite the horn player with Stan Kenton. "I'll be right over."

# Chapter 11

She stage-managed it pretty well, my ex-wife did. She met me at the door with a smile that spelled relief. "I'm so glad," she told me. "I was afraid you'd change your mind and be all macho and bull-headed about staying at the motel."

"I saw what they did to Benny's office," I told her. "Going out of a person's way for some of that action isn't macho, it's stupid."

She closed the door and led me into what originally had been intended as a bedroom, which she now used as a dressing room. But it did have a small bed in it, which she showed me she'd made up so I could spend the night in it, as if this were all businesslike and being done in the name of friendship to the bone. Then she led me out to the kitchen and poured me a large bourbon over ice, which I sat sipping at the breakfast bar while she made me a cheese omelet.

She was wearing what looked like one of those sweaters imported from England or Ireland, a lumpy white knitted thing a couple of sizes too large for her. She might have been a boy, for all the figure it revealed. The skirt she wore was something else. It reminded me of the straight black pleated uniform skirts the girls used to wear over at St. Benedict's parochial school when I was a boy. It might even have been an old school uniform, for all I knew. It barely came to her knees. She wasn't wearing any hosiery this time and the skirt showed off her fine bare calves. She wore a trace of eye shadow but no lipstick. She chattered aimlessly while she prepared the meal, then sat quietly sipping a glass of white wine while I ate.

When I'd finished she put things in a dishwasher, then poured a couple of snifters of brandy and turned out the lights in the kitchen. The only lights still on in the place were a couple of lamps up in her sleeping loft, but good old Ballard down below sent up enough light so a person could avoid cracking his shins on the furniture. We had settled down on the sofa in front of the tall windows, at a respectable distance from each other, when the telephone beside Lorna rang.

"Uh-oh," she said, putting down her brandy.

"Why uh-oh?"

"It's maybe something I should have told you about earlier." She picked up the receiver. "Hello?"

She listened a few moments, then laughed. "Gene, I do believe you've been drinking. Hold on one moment." She held one hand over the mouthpiece. "Would you do me a great favor, please? Just say hello and identify yourself."

"Who is it?"

"Gene Olson."

"The senior partner of Scandia Farms?"

"The very same."

"The fellow who thinks you should throw a little fleshy enthusiasm into your work."

"Now careful, Peter. The fellow whom I suspect thinks that."

I took the receiver. "Hello, this is Peter Bragg. What can we do for you this time of night?"

"Oh hey, I'm sorry," said Olson. "It is later than I realized. Tell Lorna we can talk about it later."

We said good night to each other and I hung up and handed the phone back to Lorna. "What was that all about?"

"I'm afraid I told a terrible fib today."

"What about?"

"About you. Us. Gene and I were talking this afternoon about Brad Thackery, the Seahawks fellow he was with the other evening. He said Brad had told him he'd found me to be a very attractive woman. But Gene also said the Seahawks organization still hasn't decided on the catering firm to stage their party. I couldn't quite tell whether or not he was making a connection between the two."

"Sounds a little vague," I said.

"Exactly. And then I had a naughty, whacky thought. I told Gene that I might consider trying to win over Thackery in my own way, except that you were my ex-husband and—well, that we were sleeping together again and you were very jealous of me. I think he didn't quite believe me, and I guess by now, tonight, he'd had enough to drink to phone here and ask me to prove it. Lucky for me you were here. I hope you don't mind."

"I don't mind. I've even been thinking about stopping by the office and telling him pretty much the same sort of story."

"It might even be sort of fun if it were true," she said quietly.

"Fun for you, maybe. But I'd like to think, Lorna, that I'd never be foolish enough to feel jealous of you again."

"Why not?"

"I've been through all the pain of that sort I'd ever want to experience."

"To do with me?"

"To do with you."

She took a sip of her brandy, then stared at the snifter. "Then what Benny said the other night was true."

"What was?"

"He said he hadn't told you I was back in Seattle because he knew things had been a little...rocky, I think he said. I assumed he meant after I left San Francisco."

"That's both when he meant and what he meant."

We were quiet for a little while, avoiding each other's eyes. "I didn't know," she said finally. "I thought we both were sort of tired of each other back then. That Sunday, when I phoned to tell you I was leaving, you sounded so matter-of-fact. So unsurprised. You sounded as if you'd been expecting it."

"No, Lorna. I hadn't been expecting it," I told her. "I put on a good act, was all. Oh I knew, or suspected at least, that you'd been doing a little slipping and sliding around with somebody else. But I thought it was just a passing fancy, something you had to get out of your system. I told myself things would sort themselves out, given time."

"Oh God." She lowered her head. Her eyes were squeezed shut. "You make me feel like a monster."

I put aside the brandy snifter—on an end table this time, not on the carpet. I scrunched over on the sofa and put my hands on her shoulders.

"Look, Lorna. It was an awful time for me, but that was back then and it happened to the guy I was back then. I've told you, I'm a different man now. I got over the pain in time, and in a way I guess you did me a big favor. After I got over the shock of it all, I did some serious thinking about myself, about who I was and where I was going. It completely changed my life. I'm more satisfied with myself now than I was back then. A lot more satisfied. And what the hell, you did leave me half the money in our savings account. Any other broad probably would have skipped town with the whole bankroll."

It brought a fleeting smile, but she was sniffing and wiping a hand across her eyes. She got up and excused herself and went down the hallway to the bathroom.

I got to my feet and stood by the window, staring down at Ballard, thinking about things. Everything I'd just told her was pretty true, I felt. But the memories were still there. I'd really felt back then as if I just wanted to crawl off someplace and die.

I didn't hear her come back into the room, but in a moment a vaguely familiar tune came softly from speakers she had connected to a tape deck.

"Do you still dance, Peter?"

I grunted. "No better than I ever did. That's one thing about me that never changed."

"Show me."

She came to me and stood close enough so I could tell she'd put on some sort of scent while she'd been in the bathroom.

"It's your feet," I warned her. I kicked off my shoes and we shuffled around the room in each other's arms.

"I think at heart I must be a very wicked woman," she said.

"Why's that?"

"I felt such remorse when you were telling me about the upheaval you went through. But then, while I was freshening myself in the bathroom, I had a different surge of emotion. To think that I could have caused anybody so much pain. It's a little heady. Does wonders for a girl's vanity, but at the same time I feel like such a heel."

She was grinning up at me. "It really hurt, huh?"

I had to laugh in spite of myself. "I don't know if hurt is quite the right word. Numbness and shock might better explain it. There are a lot of feelings involving ego that get all tangled up when something like that happens. Injured pride. You name it. But yes, it did hurt, too. I don't think I was in love with you still back then, at the time you left me. But you were a habit. And habits are hard critters to part with."

She stopped moving to the music then and just stood staring at me a moment with her arms looped around my neck, then she pulled my head down until our lips touched. It was a demure little thing when it started. I don't think either one of us knew just where we wanted to go with it. Or maybe we did. At least we found our way. And a couple of minutes later you would have thought we were a couple of teenagers experiencing the first joys of heavy necking.

You don't just stand idly by at a moment like that. You hug and grope and move around some. Before long, Lorna had lowered her hand to pull out my shirttail and ran her fingernails up across my back. It seemed to me that that sort of activity on the part of my ex-wife certainly entitled me in turn to pass a hand or two across her back under her sweater, and when I did that, I discovered she wasn't wearing anything beneath it. I made a little point of lightly tracing one fingertip up and down across where her bra strap would have been if she'd been wearing a bra.

She took a little pause in our kiss. "I shed my undies in the bathroom," she told me, "just in case it came to something like this."

And then we were smooching again, and it was plenty easy for me to slip my hands down inside the elastic band of her black schoolgirl's skirt and learn she spoke the truth. When I caressed her smooth, cool bottom she squirmed around a little. Finally, she broke off the kiss again. She opened her eyes and raised her hands alongside my face.

"Robert Louis Stevenson said it about as well as anybody," she whispered.

"What did he say?"

"*Home is the sailor, home from sea, And the hunter home from the hill...*'"

We made for the loft.

# Chapter 12

I don't know what time we finally went to sleep. Before daylight, anyhow. And while the sleep I had was shorter than I was used to, it was about as sound as a person gets. Lorna was still snoozing when I got up and padded downstairs and put on a pot of coffee. Then I went back down the hallway and had a shower and shave. The face in the mirror that morning could truly be described as haggard.

When I came out of the bathroom all fresh and clothed, Lorna was standing naked over at her tall windows, staring out at the rain drumming down. She still looked like a young sister of the woman I'd been married to.

"Aren't you afraid the neighbors will stare?"

She turned with a faint smile. "Let them stare. I have nothing to hide."

"That's not the Lorna of old speaking."

"No it's not. And it's all your fault, you know."

"No, I didn't know. What's my fault?"

She came over to put herself in my arms and clung to me tightly. "You turned me into an animal last night."

"It was mutual, or didn't you notice?"

"I noticed." She raised her face and kissed my cheek. "Damn office. I really don't want to go in there today, but I promised Gene I'd see the men from Potlatch Bay."

"Where's Gene going to be?"

"Out of town for the day. I'd much rather just spend the day in bed with you."

"Catching up on your sleep."

"No, not catching up on my sleep. Catching up on the years we've been apart. It was good last night, wasn't it?"

"You bet it was good. I might never leave town again."

"Oh God." She looked up at me. "It gives me goose bumps just thinking about us again. Things are better between us now than they ever were, don't you think?"

"What I think is that we just spent one wild night and didn't get enough sleep and maybe shouldn't try to make too much more out of it right now."

"You're wrong, Peter. Oh, you're so wrong. Listen, darling, go check out of your motel while I take a shower. Move in here. Forever, if you want."

"Now whoa, lady. Let's not move along so fast. I don't know where this is going, but I think we'd better slow down some."

She drew back from me. "You didn't seem to much want to slow down last night. In fact, I thought we'd set the sheets on fire."

She turned and walked down the hallway. She knew I was watching her. She was using the walk she used when she wanted to call people's attention to her hindside.

She paused at the bathroom doorway and looked back at me.

"Well if you won't move in, how about at least giving me a ride into work. I hate to drive in the rain."

"Sure. Why not?"

I drove on out to the motel where I'd been staying. My room didn't show any sign that somebody had been by to shoot me in the middle of the night. I packed up and checked out and told the clerk I'd be calling in from time to time for any phone messages I might get. I left a $10 tip to encourage him to hold on to the messages.

I went back and picked up Lorna and drove her into the city. She asked me to go up to the office with her.

"I want to see what you think of what they're bringing over this morning."

"What are they bringing over this morning?"

"Some renderings of what our new plant at Potlatch Bay will look like. Since Gene won't be here, I'd like another male opinion."

"I guess I can take a few minutes."

I parked in the basement garage and we took an elevator up to the Scandia Farms offices over the restaurant. The two men from Potlatch Bay were there waiting for us. Lorna introduced them as Marvin Winslow and Bruce Sherman. Winslow was a cheery-faced, rotund little fellow of sixty or so with thin gray hair combed straight back from a high forehead. He had a broad, scraggly moustache that looked just right for his happy demeanor.

Bruce Sherman was a younger man, in his forties, I guessed, with a long chin and sleepy-lidded eyes. They both wore neat dark three-piece suits and spoke with the sort of voices that suggested they might spell amaze with a zed.

"Bragg? Any relation to Miss Lorna here?" asked Sherman.

"He's my ex-husband," Lorna told them. "Just visiting for a few days."

"Dear me," said Winslow, beaming up at the two of us. "You two do make a striking pair together. Maybe you should rethink things," he said, nudging his partner. "What, Bruce?"

Sherman mumbled something indistinct with a shy smile.

"As a matter of fact," Lorna told them, "we've been doing just that."

I could have kicked her, but she probably had her reasons. Sherman's smile broke into a ragged grin beneath his droopy eyes, and Winslow looked as if he'd just won a bingo game.

"Now pull up chairs and show us what you have," Lorna told them.

The two developers unrolled several tubes of drawings. They were handsome enough, the way architectural projections of a project are apt to be more handsome than the finished project itself. They showed a stylish three-story frame building with a dramatic forward-soaring roof looking out over the Lake Washington Ship Canal. The structure had a lot of glass and gave an air of spaciousness. Lorna studied them critically but seemed favorably impressed as the two visitors pointed out this and that, chuckling proudly at the creation they'd ordered up.

"And the nice big parking area in back for your delivery vehicles and suppliers," bubbled Winslow. "Wide loading dock and integrated kitchen to serve the restaurant in front and caterer to the side. Storage here and main offices on the floor above, and then master offices for the company kingpins on the top level. Nice views in all directions. Blond wood furnishings. Smart, smart, smart."

"It's impressive," Lorna told them. "And when will it be ready for us to move in?"

"Lease signing and money package on Monday," said Bruce Sherman.

"Then we roll up our sleeves and spit on our hands and turn the crews loose," said Marvin Winslow. "Four months tops, I make it."

"We could move in by the spring, then," said Lorna.

"Looks like it," said Winslow. "May be a spot of work or two left on some of the other structures, but yours should be a cinch by then."

"Gene will be pleased," Lorna told them.

They carried on for another ten minutes or so. I edged around the desk, staring at the various drawings. They showed viewpoints of the building from all directions and overhead as well. I waited quietly as more pleasantries were exchanged and the two men finally rose to leave.

"Oh, but here, don't you need these?" Lorna asked, indicating the drawings.

"Oh, dear no," Winslow told her. "These are your copies. Pin them on the walls. Fill people with envy."

When they were gone, Lorna settled back into her chair with a little sigh. "Well, what did you think of them?"

"They seemed to be pleasant enough chaps."

"And the drawings?"

"They're pretty. But a little incomplete, aren't they?"

"How do you mean?"

"Aren't you supposed to get a look at the actual building plans or whatever they're called these days?"

"Why? I'm not going to be in there with hammer and saw and do the hard work. Maybe Gene will want to see them."

She made me promise to call her at home after work. I got my car and drove on down to the Public Safety Building. Hamilton was up in his office and seemed to be in a friendlier mood. I asked him what the technicians had to say about the explosive device that had rocked Benny's office.

"Probably dynamite," he told me. "At least it was some sort of low-order explosive. You know anything about bombs?"

"Not this sort."

"I don't either, but the techs said the device had what they call a pushing effect. The edges of cabinets, the typewriter remains, and other damaged items had a sort of mangled or bent edge to them. A high-order explosive, like plastic, they tell me, has more of a cutting effect, leaving sharp angles on whatever it tears through."

"Does all that mean anything to you?" I asked him.

"Not much. Except that if it was dynamite it would be pretty easy for somebody to put their hands on it and pretty hard for us to trace. Another thing, it had some crude gizmos on it to make it explode on contact with a solid surface. The techs say it went through the glass window without detonating and probably went off when it hit the desk. But even if it had exploded when it went through the glass, it would have done a job on anybody sitting just inside."

Hamilton also gave me a copy of the composite sketch that had been put together of the man who had tried to talk Timmy and Al into taking a ride on their way home from school two days earlier. I studied it some, but I've never been all that good at picking out the salient features in that sort of mockup and be able to pick them out on somebody I meet on the street.

"Would you recognize this man if you bumped into him on an elevator?" I asked.

Hamilton shrugged. "Maybe. Maybe not. Like a lot of other things, it's all a matter of percentages. I could spot a certain number of people who just might be the man in the composite. I could spot another certain number of people who probably could be dismissed. We're dealing with the memories of witnesses and the interpretive skills of an artist cop. Although in this case the witnesses were kids, whose memories generally are more accurate than those of most adults. How does it look to you? Didn't you see the man talking to them?"

"He was just a male-looking figure on a sidewalk, slightly bent over, talking to the boys. By the time I got close enough to have been able to tell anything more about him, he was in the car and the car was pulling away from the curb. I didn't even get close enough to get the license plate number."

"Well, take the composite with you anyhow. As long as you've got your nose into this thing, you might encounter the same man again. And if you live through the encounter, you might be able to help our artist modify the composite."

From a pay phone down in the lobby I called my office in San Francisco. "How's the weather?" I asked Ceejay.

"Clear and balmy. You know how the autumn can be down here. What's it like up there?"

"Threatening to rain. But then that's how the autumn is apt to be up here. Besides, it's almost winter. Any messages or cries for help?"

"Nothing from around here, but you got a message from up there. A Mary Ellen Cutler called. Know her?"

"Yes, she has a studio in the same building my friend is in."

"She wants you to get in touch with her. She said it was important. Not urgent, but important. She said you had checked out of your motel up there. Does that mean you're on your way home?"

"Not yet. I just wanted to resettle somewhere else. I'll let you know when I've found another place to stay."

Ten minutes later, I was sitting in Mary Ellen's studio with a mug of coffee in my hand. Mary Ellen was pacing around the studio, darting nervous glances at a frail figure with overly neat rust-colored hair and wispy chin whiskers who was hunched down in a chair across from me going through some manila file folders. The figure in the toupee and fake beard was Benny Bartlett.

# Chapter 13

"I heard noises from across the hall about an hour ago," Mary Ellen said. "When I went across to investigate, I found this one banging file drawers open and shut."

"Some of them stuck," said Benny, not looking up from the file folders. "Bomb damage, you know. Besides, I was mad. I've been mad since about an hour after me and Dolly and the kids fled home last night with our tails between our legs, headed for the Edmonds ferry slip."

"You had good cause to be fleeing."

"Did I, now? Maybe Dolly and the kids, but..." He looked up at me then, blinking at me from behind the thick lenses of his eyeglasses.

"You know, Pete, I'm not a big, rough tough guy like you. I don't carry guns and I can't fight my way out of a wet paper bag, but goddamnit, I still like to think of myself as a man. With honor and integrity and pride.

You know what pride is, buddy? Maybe you don't even think about it, because your brute force keeps you out of situations where you have to think about it. But with me, it's different. I guess you could say I've got a little man complex. My pride is important to me. Especially in front of Timmy and Al. How do you think it feels to be chased out of your own home under the watchful stares of a couple of your boys? And so I got mad and I started spouting off about it, and then when we got to Edmonds we'd just missed the ferry and I just said to hell with it and threw old Bronco Billy into reverse and drove back to the highway and found a motel where we could spend the night. And before we all settled in for the night, I told Dolly I was going to stay around here and fight this thing. I'd be sneaky about it if I had to. I'd get a disguise. But nobody's chasing me out of Seattle. Nobody."

"That toupee looks ridiculous," I told him. "Every hair in place. Somebody could spot it a block away."

"I wear a hat over it when I go out," he told me. "As a matter of fact, you sort of look like hell yourself this morning. What were you doing last night?"

I looked away and sipped the coffee.

"And something else we did last night," Benny continued. "We held a little family brainstorming session. The four of us. We hadn't done that before, to do with these threats and shooting and everything. Dolly and I would have whispered conversations from time to time, but last night we threw the floor open to free discussion. I told them what you'd said, Pete, about it probably being something connected with a story I'd written sometime in the past or something I'd been working on recently. And we're all of us batting it around here and there when out of the blue, Timmy, the genius of the family, said, 'How about the ones that didn't make, Pop?' And I smacked my forehead and said to myself, Jesus Christ, the kid's got something."

"What did he mean?"

"What do you mean, what did he mean? You used to work for a newspaper, for Christ's sake. He meant the stories I'd written or worked on over the years that never sold to anybody. And believe me, pal, I've had my share of those. You query an editor with a story idea and if he likes it he says, Sure, take a whack at it, but ninety-nine percent of the time that's done on speculation. There's no guarantee they'll like or buy or run the finished article.

"That's why I was banging through the file cabinets across the hall. Pulling out the limbo files. That's what these are. That's why I'm going through them right now. Searching for something I don't even know I'm looking for. Hunting for a clue. You know what that's like, don't you, pal? Looking for something that'll tell me who the sons of bitches are that are trying to run me out of my own hometown."

Mary Ellen made a curt "Oh!" that implied her biting impatience with the male mind and sank into a nearby chair, cupping her chin with one hand.

"What about Dolly and the kids?" she demanded. "Where are they?"

"I don't know," Benny said, his face back down among the papers and photos in the file folders. "There was a lot of back and forth discussion about that. I wanted them out of town at first, but then Dolly said something else that made sense. She said I'd gotten a new lead worth pursuing from Timmy when we tossed it all out for family discussion. She said that was one of our great strengths, the way we do things as a family. I know it isn't that way with everybody these days. But it works for us. We do things as a family. Through thick and thin, to dust off a creaky phrase."

He looked up at me again. "And Dolly said maybe

that was the way we should tackle this one as well. That if one of us was going to dig in his heels and refuse to run, then maybe that was best for all of us. And that's how we left it, kind of up in the air like that. I told Dolly to think it over and to do whatever she thought was best. I told her to go on back to the ferry slip if she decides to and head for the hills. I told her I'd be here at Mary Ellen's if she decides to stay."

"You could at least have sent the boys up to Dolly's parents," I suggested, "while you and Dolly snuck back into town."

"Not those two clowns, we couldn't," Benny told me. "They'd just sneak back on their own and put us under surveillance. I told you, Pete, you've been away for too long. You don't know how those scamps think. They'll go on up to Sequim with Dolly if she goes, but they won't be shot out of town on their own."

"How did you get back here?"

"Same as you. Had Dolly drive me to a rental car place."

Mary Ellen and I exchanged glances. She raised one shoulder in resignation. I sipped coffee and stared at the ceiling.

Benny continued his search through the files. A few minutes later, he looked up at me and blinked. "How come you checked out of your motel? I tried phoning you there earlier."

"I had a caller last night who sounded the same as the fellow who called you. As if he were talking from the bottom of a rain barrel."

"Oh yeah? What'd he want?"

"He didn't want anything that I could tell. He just said I was a dead man. 'Bang-bang dead,' is how he quaintly phrased it."

"What do you think that means?"

"I guess he wants me out of town, too."

"You changed motels last night?"

"I would have, but Lorna suggested I spend the night at her place."

He gave me a look.

"She has an extra bedroom," I said.

Benny just stared at me. Then he whistled one of those things they called a wolf whistle when I was growing up. The sort of whistle sailors and truck drivers would whistle when they saw a pretty girl.

"Don't be silly," I told him. "I said she has an extra bedroom."

"Sure."

Mary Ellen gave me a look that said I wasn't all that welcome around there any longer. Zither, of course. Zither would have told her what we were doing upstairs when the bomb had gone off. And I supposed there wasn't much sense trying to continue the charade with Benny, because the next time Lorna talked to Dolly, I was sure there would be a vivid description of the night I spent at her place and there wouldn't be any mention of an extra bedroom. It was the same sort of stupid predicament I used to get into in Seattle when I was growing up. Some things never change. Not in Seattle, at least.

It was twenty minutes later when Benny straightened, put down the file and checked through another, then said, "I think I've found something, Pete."

Mary Ellen looked up from a workbench where she'd been sorting out some metal clasps, the sort of work you do when you want to put distance between yourself and others nearby. I got up and went over to Benny.

"What is it?"

"No, it's not something I can show you, it's what I can't show you." He stared off into the distance. "You know when I told you about the stones Mary Ellen had me stash away for her and how I couldn't find them where I thought they should have been."

"Yes, I remember. You thought somebody might have been going through your files."

"That's right. And now I'm sure of it. Somebody's swiped some stuff."

"What sort of stuff?"

"Photos, and a partly written article. I noticed the photos were missing first. It was a family called— Barely? Bylie? Beyerly—that was it, with a 'wye.' I was working on what was to be one of a series of articles being run by one of the national mags. *People*, I think it was. About how the rich and influential live in different parts of the country. This man Beyerly lives, or at least used to live, up north, outside of Bellingham. He'd been a big banking muck-a-muck. He had an interesting family, a boy and a couple of daughters. Well, I noticed the photos of the family were missing. So I cross-checked the limbo writing file. All my notes and the partly written story are missing as well. If I were a detective, I'd find that very significant."

"And with good reason. How come the story didn't run? You sound as if you hadn't even finished writing it."

"That's right. There was a death in the family. One of the daughters. There was something funny about that, too. It was just called a sudden death, only the family wouldn't talk about it, and old man Beyerly packed enough clout in those parts so the coroner's people and cops wouldn't say zip about it either. But I don't think it was an accidental death."

"Wouldn't the cause of death be public record?"

"Ordinarily. And if anything good could have come from it, I would have gotten me a lawyer and made a stink about it. I was being given the triple runaround, though, and when I queried the magazine people, they scrubbed it. They wanted upbeat stories about the rich and spoiled, not the rich and tragic."

"When did this happen?"

"Couple of years ago. But when you stop to think about it, why the hell would anybody want to pinch that particular material? I told the family the story was being dropped. It never ran. So why should somebody get all excited about it at this late date?"

"I think those are questions that need to be answered," I told him. "These people live outside Bellingham? Do you have an address or phone number for them?"

"No, everything was in here together—raw notes and partial manuscript. But they're well enough known in the area. You could just drive up and ask most anyone in town. They live out east somewhere, on a horse ranch. I think I read since then, though, that the old man died. Maybe the family scattered. Hell, I could drive on up there and ask around myself."

"No, I'll go. You're in hiding, remember?"

"How could I forget it?" he asked, scratching the wig on his head. "These things aren't all that much fun."

"Do you have a pair of contact lenses?" I asked him.

"Yeah, I have a pair. I don't like them much."

"Do you have them with you?"

He nodded. "They're in my suitcase."

"Start wearing them whenever you go outside. Put away the glasses."

"Why?"

"They'll make you look ten years younger and go a lot further to change your appearance than the wig and fake beard will."

"Hmmmm. I'll give it a try."

"Is there anything else missing from your files you know about?"

"Yeah, there's another photo missing, but I figure that was taken inadvertantly, or by somebody who thought it was a part of the Beyerly story. I don't have these things in any particular order."

"What was it a photo of?"

"Just a mug shot of the guy I was talking to about ferroconcrete houseboats—before the project went bankrupt and the story went down the tubes."

"Do you still have your notes on that?"

"Yeah, they're all here," he said, holding up one of the folders. "That's why I figure the photo was lifted by mistake."

"Give me the name of the guy who was in the photo anyhow, will you?"

He checked through the folder. "Waldo Derington. He was the guy I was writing about."

"When was that?"

"Oh hell, three, maybe four years ago."

"Benny, you did good. It's the first thing that shows any real promise since I hit town."

Benny beamed. "Hey, great. The boys'll love it when I tell them you said that. Timmy especially. God, that kid's bright."

We were interrupted by a loud commotion out in the hall. Workmen had been by earlier to rehang Benny's office door and to replace the glass in the door and over his desk and to generally clean up the place. It sounded now as if somebody was trying to knock the door off its hinges again. Men's voices were shouting. Benny started for the door.

"Stay here," I told him. "You're out of town, remember?"

Mary Ellen joined me as I stepped out into the hall. The door to Benny's office must have been unlocked. It was wide open now, and the yelling men were standing just inside.

"Where is the little pimp?" one of them shouted.

"Come on, shithead, show your face," cried the other.

Building tenants were coming down the hall to see who was making all the noise. The men in Benny's office were big and beefy. Their faces were put together tough—wide-spaced eyes, heavy jaws, thick lips. One of them was as tall as I am, the other a couple of inches shorter. They wore dark topcoats and felt snap-brim hats. It was the way men in Seattle dressed when I was a boy.

"What's the problem?" I asked.

"You the manager?" demanded the taller of the two.

"Where's the little creep who wrote this garbage?" barked the other, holding what looked like a rolled up magazine in his fist.

"This office is leased by a chap named Benny Bartlett," I told them. "Is that who you mean?"

"That's him, that's the one. Little four-eyed shithead," said the shorter and more bellicose of the two.

"I hear he's gone out of town," I said. "The whole family has, I understand. Why? What's wrong?"

"We wanna smack him around some," said the shorter man. "Maybe break his typing fingers so he can't write filth like this anymore."

"Just who are you people?" Mary Ellen demanded. "What are you doing in here? Nobody invited you here."

"Nobody needed to, lady," said the taller man. "We pretty much go where we want to. Like right over the top of you if you don't dummy up."

"Okay, hold it, hold it," I told them, crossing my arms and leaning back against the doorjamb with a smile. "You are two big, tough hombres and you're irritated about something. Nobody's going to be able to help you unless you calm down and tell us what it's all about. If you have a beef with Benny, we'll spread the word around the building here. If he gets in touch with anybody here, we can tell him about it and ask him to give you a call. So what's the problem?"

"This is the problem," said the shorter man, shaking the rolled up publication. He didn't have a very tight grip on it and the magazine squirted out of his hand.

"Shit!" he cried, giving it a kick that sent it skidding across the floor. He crossed to it and picked it up, flattened it, and held it out to us. It was the publication Benny had told me about, *Sound Sounds.*

"He libeled us here," he told us. "We're from the Jackson Detective Agency. I'm Wally Jackson. He's my brother, Tom."

"Then you're Grady's boys. I was up to see him yesterday."

"You were up to see who?" demanded the shorter of the two, who'd said he was Wally.

"Your father. We probably were talking about whatever it is that has you two so upset. A story about Pacific Northwest investigators?"

"That's it," said Wally. "A piece of scum."

"Filth," said his brother. "A pack of lies."

"What were you up seeing the old man about?" Wally demanded.

I told them briefly why I'd been up there and what we'd talked about. "I know Benny from years ago," I told them. "Somebody's been trying to kill him. I'm in the same line of work you two are, down in California."

"Sure, that's right," said Wally. "Dad told us about you. You're from down fag city way."

I laughed.

"What's funny?" Tom demanded.

"Your brother has a colorful way of phrasing things."

"Well, if you're a buddy of this Bartlett," Wally broke in, "where is the lying little shithead?"

"I don't know. The pressure got too great. He and his family packed up and left town. I don't know where they've gone. He said something about putting his home on the market. I don't expect him back, frankly. But I'm surprised he wrote something that would bother you guys. He mentioned the story to me and said he bent over backward so as not to write anything that would offend you. Said he just needed to mention you to explain what happens when somebody complains to the state about a PI agency, whether the complaint is justified or not."

"Sure, that's the line he fed us," said Wally. "That's what he told Dad he was doing. But listen to this." He paged quickly through the publication until he found the part he wanted. "He says here about how the complainant didn't show up for the hearing in Olympia, and the state dropped the investigation without prejudice."

"Sounds innocent enough to me," I told them.

"Yeah, but then the little rat went on to say, 'But the Jackson agency still has a lingering, malodorous reputation among the Seattle investigatory community.' That's garbage!"

"Sheer libel," said his brother.

I raised my hands. "What can I say? Sounds like a cheap shot to me, and I've never known Benny to do things that way. Like I said. We'll spread the word around the building. If anyone hears from Benny, we'll ask him to call you guys and try to explain himself."

"Good," said Wally. "And you tell him if I ever get my hands on him, by the time I'm through with him he'll be doing any future explaining in a high, squeaky voice."

They gave us their best tough-guy looks and strode out into the hallway. Wally spun back around toward me. "You sure you don't know where the little creep is?"

"Honest. He's running scared. I doubt if he'll ever show up in these parts again. Somebody tossed a bomb into his office there last night. Wouldn't that be enough to scare you off?"

Wally chewed the inside of his mouth some. His brother stood there like a big stooge with his arms folded. Then Wally grunted and turned around and the two of them marched back down the hall and around the corner. They were talking loudly to each other again. Talking about the brutal things they'd do to my pal Benny Bartlett if he ever showed his face around town again.

# Chapter 14————————

Bellingham is about eighty miles north of Seattle. You can stop for coffee along the way and still make it in two hours these days. Before the interstate highway system was built, you could spend what seemed like half a day making the same trip, lurching and crawling in traffic along two-lane roads that went through places like Everett and Marysville and Mount Vernon and half a dozen smaller burgs. Bellingham had been a small town when I was growing up, but it was a city today, with a big oil refinery and a population of around 50,000. It's on a bay that was discovered in 1792 by an English explorer, Captain George Vancouver, ultimately much to the dismay of the Indians who had discovered it long before then.

I had left Benny shaken and fuming back in Mary Ellen's studio. He'd been standing behind her studio door and overheard the ranting and railing of the Jackson brothers.

"I never wrote that," he complained. '...lingering, malodorous reputation...' I've never used words like that in my life. It must have been that dizzy bitch Carlotta Pantree."

"Who's that?"

"Editor of *Sound Sounds*. When she first read the piece, she suggested I call around some of the other agencies and ask them what they thought of the Jacksons. Holy cow, I didn't have to call around. The Jackson agency had come up plenty of times while I was researching the article. I told her to forget it—to just stick with the bare-bone facts of the hearing in Olympia that never got off the ground. For God's sake, I knew what I was dealing with—sheer dynamite. So Pantree must have taken it upon herself to make a couple of calls and add that juicy bit. I'll murder the bitch."

Benny kept copies of all his work, so I suggested that instead of murdering Pantree, he just mail the Jacksons a photocopy of what he'd originally written. The Jacksons might or might not believe him, but he could enclose a note suggesting they phone or visit Carlotta Pantree and ask her who had written the offending passage. He said he'd give it a try.

Before leaving, I also put in a phone call to Turk Connell, head of the World Investigations office in San Francisco. World is a far-flung outfit that maintains a small force of investigators they bolster from time to time with free-lancers like myself. I asked Turk to call their office in Vancouver and see if they could provide any information on Waldo Derington, whose photo had been lifted from Benny's file along with those of the Beyerly family. As Benny suggested, the picture probably was taken inadvertently, but it's best to check on that sort of thing.

People at the *Bellingham Herald* told me I'd find the Beyerly place by driving out east of town on Whatcom County Route 542. They confirmed what Benny had remembered, that the family patriarch had died a couple of years earlier. They said his widow had moved up to British Columbia, where she had a sister. The Beyerly son, they said, taught at a small university somewhere in the Midwest, and the surviving daughter, Barbara, lived on the family ranch. But nobody would say much about the other daughter, whose death had prompted *People* magazine to scrub the story Benny had been working on about the rich and spoiled.

Skies were overcast and I drove through rain showers on my way to the ranch, which turned out to be about fifty acres nestled in a broad river valley. The ranch buildings were back a good mile from the county road. The ranch road leading back to them was straight as an arrow and out in the open, so that anybody at the ranch could have a good look at you coming.

The main house was a rambling sort of place made of Arizona sandstone and wood. It was two stories tall in the center, with a couple of single-story wings on either side of that. I suspected that if the remaining Beyerly daughter ever moved away, somebody would come by and transform the place into a ritzy bed-and-breakfast inn. The outbuildings were weathered, but both they and the horse pens and meandering rail fencing I could see were kept in good repair. You knew the person running things had enough money to provide good upkeep.

When I drove into the broad turnaround area in front of the house, an older fellow wearing Levi's and a plaid lumberjack shirt was standing waiting for me with his arms folded. I got out of the car, gave him a little wave, and crossed over to him. He had a face as weathered-looking as the outbuildings.

"My name is Bragg," I told him. "I'm from San Francisco. I'd like to see Miss Beyerly if she's home."

"She's home, but she doesn't much like dealing with strangers. What did you want to see her about?"

"It's a long enough story, so I'd rather not have to repeat it too many times. But you could tell her it involves a family down in Seattle. The father's been threatened. Attempts have been made on his life. Three of them we know about. We think somebody tried to abduct his two sons. We don't know why all this is happening. It's possible Miss Beyerly might have some information that would help us put a stop to it."

"You police?"

"No, but I've worked with them in the past. I'm a private investigator. But I'm not doing this as a job in the ordinary sense. I've known the man who's been threatened since we were in high school together. He's a good friend. He's in trouble. So I thought I'd do what I could to help him. I'd guess the people around here probably do that sort of thing for friends, too, same as they do in Seattle or San Francisco or Sydney, Australia."

"Sure we do. But what sort of information you think Miss Beyerly, living the kind of reclusive life out here that she does, might have that could help your friend in Seattle?"

"Like I said, it's a long story. I'd rather explain the rest of it to her."

He cleared his throat and stared at his boots some. "I don't want to appear to be asking questions about things that aren't any of my business, Mr. Bragg. It's just that Miss Beyerly isn't all that outgoing. Before she agrees to talk to you—if she does agree to, and I frankly couldn't tell you whether she might feel up to it or not—she would want to know more about what she'd be getting herself into. And if I can't tell her these things I'm asking you when I go inside, she'll just send me back out again to ask them then. I'm really trying to save us all a little time, is all."

"I see. Well, thank you for that. You can tell Miss Beyerly I think she met my friend a few years ago. His name is Benny Bartlett. He's a writer, and he told me he talked to several members of her family at one time. And something one of them told him just might be a clue as to whatever is happening to him these days. Miss Beyerly might be the one who has the information that could lead me to the people threatening to kill my friend. She might be able to help me solve a mystery."

The older man was watching me closely. He was trying to decide whether or not I was shucking him. He'd be telling himself that just because he might be living in a rural area, it didn't make him any sort of dummy. But even I knew that. And the creases in his face suggested he'd been to a place or two besides horse-ranch country.

"I'll go tell her what you said," he told me. "I'd ask you to come inside to wait, but Miss Beyerly doesn't like strangers in the house unless she's approved of them ahead of time."

"That's fine. I understand."

I watched him go inside then, and turned around and went on back to lean against my car and tried to look as sincere and concerned as I knew how. Maybe I'd be under a little visual inspection from behind one of the upstairs curtains. I'd told the ranchhand just before he went into the house that I understood, but that wasn't really true. I didn't understand. I was beginning to think the rich and reclusive Miss Beyerly might be a little whacky.

I spent the next five minutes or so staring around at the surrounding countryside and the bleak skies overhead, watched a couple of chestnut horses romping around in a distant field, and listened to somebody hammering a piece of metal out somewhere in back of the house. The man I'd spoken with finally opened the front door and waved me in.

"She'll see you, but she's in the middle of something right now," he told me. "You can go wait in the living room there. She'll be down as soon as she can."

He showed me into a large room off the entranceway that had windows across the front and along a portion of one side and was filled with Danish modern furniture and paintings on the walls depicting the roping and riding of ranch life. I settled down on one end of a white leather sofa and the man with the seamed face went back outside. A couple of minutes later, a round-faced Indian woman of fifty or so, wearing Levi's and a red-and-green-and-black checked workshirt identical to the one worn by the man who'd ushered me in, came into the room and asked if I'd care for any coffee or tea. I told her no. She nodded her head as if it were the answer she had expected and left the room.

Twenty minutes later I still was waiting for Miss Beyerly to put in an appearance. I was about ready to try hunting up the Indian maid or my pal from outside when I heard conversation from another part of the ground floor and a clatter of dishes. A minute later a very ordinary looking woman in her early thirties came to the doorway and said, "Mr. Bragg? I'm Barbara Beyerly."

I got to my feet and nodded. "Thank you for seeing me, Miss Beyerly. I'm sure your days are busy, running something as large as the ranch here."

"My days aren't all that busy," she told me. She hadn't made a move from the doorway. She stood leaning against one of the doorjambs in a semi-slouch with her arms folded. She was wearing a pair of Levi's, like the people she had working around her, but instead of the lumberjack shirt, she wore a long-sleeved red knit sweater over a white silk blouse. She was a lean-figured woman whose shoulder-length dark brown hair was braided in two plaits. She had an unremarkable face, with dead-looking blue-gray eyes and a mouth that might have been handed down through the years like an old heirloom.

"ID," she said.

"You want to see my ID?"

"Yes. Some identification, please. I don't know you from Adam."

"No, ma'am." I took out my wallet and crossed to show her the photostat of my investigator's license and my driver's license.

"You told Dolph you were from San Francisco. This driver's license says you live somewhere called Sausalito."

"That's just across the Golden Gate Bridge from San Francisco," I told her. "My office is in downtown San Francisco."

She made a humming sound and handed back the ID. "Whiskey," she said.

"I beg your pardon?"

"I asked if you wanted some whiskey. Rhoda said you didn't want any coffee or tea. I read mystery stories, you know, not that that has all that much to do with it. It just does seem to me that a person in the line of work you are in, dealing with the sort of people you must deal with on a more or less regular basis, that chances are you'd prefer whiskey to coffee or tea. Or gin, perhaps."

"Well it's kind of you to ask, but I really don't care for anything right now. I seldom drink this early in the day, even when I'm not working."

"Seldom. When?"

"What?"

She uncurled a finger and pointed to the sofa behind me. "Go and sit down again. I'll join you in a minute. After I've had a chance to size you up. I said when. You said you seldom drink this early in the day. When do you drink this early in the day?"

"Sometimes when I'm off on vacation somewhere. Or maybe at a brunch, with friends. Sometimes on a Sunday I'll have a Bloody Mary or two while I'm watching football on television."

"Football," she said in a way that implied clear disapproval. Then she turned her head and shouted over her shoulder. "Rhoda!"

Rhoda shouted back to her from the rear of the house.

"Bloody Marys, a pair of them," she called. She turned back to me. "Today will be one of the days you drink this early in the day."

I shrugged. "Yes, ma'am."

"The reason is, I couldn't possibly carry on any sort of conversation with a complete stranger from San Francisco via Seattle without a little giddyup out of the bottle under my belt. And if I sat around doing that without company joining in, I might get the reputation that I'm a solitary daytime drinker. And I have enough reputations to bear up under as it is without acquiring another."

I leaned back into the sofa. She stared at me some more.

"Married?"

I was beginning to catch on to her ways. "No, Miss Beyerly, I'm not married. Was one time in the past."

"When?"

"About a dozen years ago."

"I've never been married," she told me, "and I don't expect I ever will be, now. I think if you have a strong mind and if you don't get all caught up during that surge of sexual excitement when you're young, you're apt to not get married."

"Living alone has its advantages," I agreed. "Once you get used to it."

"Right on."

She stepped back out of the doorway as the Indian woman named Rhoda came in bearing a tray that had not two but four generous-size Bloody Marys on it. She placed the tray on a coffee table in front of the sofa, nodded to me and then to the Beyerly woman, and left the room.

Miss Beyerly came over to take one of the drinks off the table and carried it over to one of the Danish modern chairs. She sat down and took a good, long swallow of the drink.

"Drink up," she told me.

I drank. It was a good drink. It wasn't the first time the Indian woman had been asked to pour a Bloody Mary or four.

"President," she said.

"Precedent?"

"Our president in the nation's capital. What do you think of him?"

"I'm not all that impressed by him. But maybe I'm too hard to please. I haven't been overly impressed by a lot of people we've sent to the White House. What do you think of him?"

"It doesn't matter what I think of him. Can't do anything about it anyway." She had two more swallows of the Bloody Mary. That drained the glass, except for the ice. She came across the room to get another. When she was settled down back in the chair again, she winked at me.

"I've got a secret."

I winked back. "I'll bet you've got a lot of secrets, Miss Beyerly. Most of the women I know seem to."

"You can call me Barbara."

"Thank you. Do you want me to ask you what your secret is, Barbara?"

"Not just now. Later, maybe. Out in the loft."

I shifted my position on the sofa. "The loft?"

"Yes. I'll show it to you later if things go right between the two of us."

"Well, I want you to feel comfortable with me, Miss Beyerly, or Barbara, rather. But I was hoping I'd get a chance to ask a few questions of my own. I'm really here to try to help a friend out of a lot of trouble he seems to have gotten himself into."

"Yes, I know. Dolph told me. Benny Bartlett. We can get to him a little bit later. When was the last time you slept with a woman?"

"Last night."

"I knew it. You look a little gaunt around the eyes. Who was she, some prostitute you picked up in Seattle?"

"No, as a matter of fact it was my ex-wife."

She nearly fell out of the Danish modern chair. She choked on her drink and some of the vodka and tomato juice blew out of one corner of her plain old mouth and stained the collar of the white silk blouse she wore under the red sweater.

"That's rich," she told me when she'd gotten herself under control again. "Is that the truth?"

"It really happened."

"How? How did it come about?"

"I'd rather not say."

"But you will, because you want some information from me. And I think I know what information you need. Because I have an active mind, and I think I solved your mystery. I remember back when your friend was around planning to write a story about us all. And when Dolph told me what you wanted to talk about, I sat down upstairs and thought about it. That's what I was doing while you were waiting for me down here. And I think I know what you need to know. I think I might know who's causing your friend all his trouble. But I lead a pretty solitary life, Mr. Bragg. What's your first name again?"

"Pete."

"Yes, Pete. And I think it's only fair for people to exchange things. You want information I can give you, and in turn I'd like a little entertainment. And I think the story of how you and your ex-wife ended up in bed again, along with all the gory details, would be very entertaining indeed. And maybe after that I'll just go on out to the kitchen and get us a bottle of bourbon and we can take it on up to the loft, where I like to just kick back and get a little drunk and look out at the horses. It's in a barn out back. Been my favorite spot around here since I was a little girl. And that's where I'll tell you about my family. Tell you the things I think you want to know. But first you have to tell me about how you and your ex came to crawl into bed together. And about what all you did there."

My hunch had been right. She was nuts. But very serious nuts. So I took a swig of the Bloody Mary and told her tales about Lorna.

## Chapter 15

She lapped it up like a puppy with a bowl full of warm milk, this woman in her early thirties who ran a fifty-acre horse ranch, or at least was able to hire others to run it for her. A little fire came into her eyes when I described the dancing around on the carpet Lorna and I had done the evening before, my hands beneath the sweater, discovering that my ex-wife wasn't wearing a bra, and what that led to. I let her anticipate some of it; tried to take her breath away, as near as I could. I figure if you're going to go out onstage you ought to at least be able to keep up with the animal acts. I thought she'd swoon when I quoted the Robert Louis Stevenson lines.

I probably made up as much as I remembered. I hadn't, the night before, known that questions were going to be asked later. And then I spun my little fairy tale a trifle too far. I told her when it was all over, "we went downstairs and had a shower then went on back up and went to sleep."

"Hogwash."

"I beg your pardon?"

"I said hogwash. You took a shower together?"

"That's right. She has a large shower stall. Sort of a double."

"And you're trying to tell me you didn't soap each other up and start to get excited all over again?"

We hadn't actually taken a shower together. Why, during my feeble-minded accounting, had I said we did? Not enough sleep the night before, I guess.

"Come on," she said. "Tell me. All of it."

And so I spun it out some more, telling her the things I thought she wanted to hear. It was hard. I pretended I was the court jester and if I didn't put on a good show I'd lose my head. I didn't feel terribly good about what I was doing, for a number of reasons. And I finally came to a stuttering stop with my hands locked in front of me, staring at the carpet. I just couldn't think of anything more to tell her.

"What's the matter?" she asked. "Are you ashamed of what you did?"

"No, I'm not ashamed of what I did. Not what I did last night, at least."

"What then?"

"I am a little ashamed of myself for letting somebody make me tell her about it. It's not fair to Lorna, at the very least."

"Pish," she said, getting to her feet. "I've been made to feel shame my entire life. And now you know what it's like, Bragg." She stood looking out the windows, one hand alongside her face. "Well, maybe now I can tell you about my family. Wait here while I get a bottle."

I heaved a sigh and finished the last of my own Bloody Marys. I was beginning to think I might not make it back to Seattle that afternoon.

True to her word, she came back from the kitchen with a full bottle of bourbon and a couple of glasses and a canister of ice cubes. She handed me the ice and the glasses and led me around back to a barn. I didn't know just what she had in mind, but I figured it wouldn't be any tougher than the act it followed.

A wooden stairway led up to the loft, where she had herself a comfortable perch. There was loose fresh straw on the floor and some bales to lean up against and a couple of wooden doors that opened inward, giving a nice view of horses grazing across distant hills.

I politely declined the whiskey when she started pouring, but she ignored me and put some cubes in a glass and poured generously.

"Drink," she told me, handing over the glass.

So I drank. And then she began telling me about her family and what was going on around the time Benny had come up to interview them for the *People* magazine story.

"We all were leading a pretty smug and comfortable life back then," she told me. "Papa had retired from active participation in the bank down in Everett, and he and Mama had just gotten back from an extensive tour of Europe. I mean extensive. Eight months, they were gone. Papa was making plans to head on down to Kentucky to see about getting some special breeding stock for his string of ponies. Mama was entertaining her sister Flo, down visiting from Victoria, and I was spending my time between working the horses in shows and such and carrying on halfhearted liaisons with a couple of different fellows in town. I was about coming to the conclusion I liked the horses far better than I liked the fellows, mostly because I had the feeling I could trust the horses but I never was sure about the fellows. I happen to realize that I am a plain-looking woman and that when a fellow looks at me he isn't looking at Barbara Beyerly the girl with a face that looks like squash, but rather is looking at the Beyerly Bar-4 Horse Ranch and Breeding Farm. Or at what they knew would be at least a one-third interest of it down the road."

She put down her glass and thumped a hay bale beside her. "You know, Bragg, that's something I never worked out until after Mama moved up to live with Aunt Flo, after the tragedy and then Papa dying and all. My mama didn't let me forget for a single day that I wasn't what you'd call pretty. She didn't do it in a vicious way, but my God, how would you like to have somebody telling you all the time, 'Well now, Barbara, you just can't let your looks get you down. Looks aren't everything, honey. You've got a good brain and a winning personality, and that's what's going to count in the long run.'

"Ye gods," she continued, "I should have strangled that woman in her sleep. That's just a terrible thing to keep telling a little kid."

She took a swallow of the bourbon. I had some of my own.

"But then my sister, Beverly, that fall," she said, leaning back. "Beverly was in love. God, she just glowed like a sapphire." She thought about it for a moment, a little smile on her mouth. "Did I show you a picture of her? No I didn't, did I?"

She sat up and pulled a man's wallet from her hip pocket and flipped it open. She showed me a photo of a girl in her graduation cap and gown. The resemblance to her sister was there, in fact I couldn't see her as looking much prettier than the girl beside me.

"Roger Hampton was his name. He was a cousin of one of the girls Beverly knew down at Reed College in Portland. She met him down there, then he came up here that summer looking for some part-time work, and I must say he was very ingratiating. Handsome. A good horseman, polo player. Almost professional-caliber tennis player. Smooth dancer, smooth talker. And he and Bev seemed to hit it off big. I don't know, maybe they'd been seeing some of each other before down in Portland. That summer they were together nearly every spare moment they had. I'd never seen Bev so happy, and Roger seemed just as daffy about her."

She made a little snort. "They were having sex together. I know because I accidentally rode up on them down in the meadow one afternoon when they were in the middle of things. It didn't embarrass them at all. They just waved and called hello and I clip-clopped on past.

"Then," she continued, a little more quietly, "the two of them became secretive. Bev had taken to giving him things. Roger never seemed to have very much money of his own. Bev gave him her Porsche one afternoon. It was two years old and Bev said she was tired of it. She just brought out the title and registration and signed it over to him. Papa wasn't exactly pleased about that, but there wasn't much he could do about it. She was of age and had what you could call a pretty handsome bank account in her own right. That was from Mama's side of the family. And now maybe you can see where this is all leading." She stopped talking and sipped at her drink. She was right. I was beginning to see where it was leading.

"Roger had been away for a few days. Bev wouldn't tell us where he'd gone. That was a part of the secrecy that had been building between them. And then along about the middle of the week, Beverly got a letter from Roger. It was a—what do you call the counterpart of a Dear John letter?"

"I don't know."

"Well, that's what it was. Roger had written to tell her he'd found somebody else and he wouldn't be coming back to the ranch here. Bev never showed that letter to any of us, so we don't really know what all he might have said. But it left my sister Bev in a state of paralysis.

"For four days it was like having a vacant-eyed zombie for a sister. Then on Saturday, while I was out riding, she went into my bedroom and put a little diamond brooch on my dresser. It was something I'd admired for as long as she'd had it. There wasn't any note or anything, just the brooch. And then she drove into town, to the yacht harbor where we kept a little twenty-two-foot runabout berthed in a boathouse. She hung herself that afternoon, from a rafter in the boathouse. They didn't find her body for two days."

She drank some of her bourbon.

"Later, we found out from the bank in town where my sister had her accounts that Bev had given a cashier's check for twenty thousand dollars to Roger just before he left town for the last time. The people at the bank said Bev told them only that it was for a business venture she and Roger were going into."

Barbara Beyerly reached over to where she'd put the bottle of bourbon and refilled her glass. She looked across at me. I finished what was left in it and held it out to her. She poured and recapped the bottle.

"That was when the family began to come unglued, you might say. Papa hired somebody like you to try to find Roger—to exact some sort of retribution—but nothing came of it. Roger's cousin didn't know where he was. It turned out Roger had sold the Porsche in Seattle. The cashier's check was cashed there as well, a couple of days before Bev got the letter. Papa's health began to fail then and just continued to plummet until he died, fourteen months later. Mama became a reclusive neurotic and began imagining things. Her sister Flo was the only one who seemed able to calm her. Flo finally talked Mama into moving in with her. And I took up the bottle and I haven't let go since," she concluded lamely.

It was several moments before she spoke again. "It turns out Roger apparently has made a living at this sort of thing. The detective Papa hired found out he'd gotten a lot of money out of a girl down in Santa Barbara before he came up here."

She was silent another moment before she glanced across at me. "The end."

"You mean that's it?"

"That's it. One family blown away. Isn't that enough?"

"It's enough suffering, God knows, for all of you to have to put up with. But what I meant is, I don't see the connection to my friend Benny in this."

"Your friend Benny took pictures of us all that summer. The family and the ranch and some of the horses and Roger Hampton. When Roger learned about that, what they were for, he got very upset. He wanted Beverly to get them back, the ones of him, at least. Bev told me later it was the only thing they ever argued about."

"Did your sister ever take photos of Roger? Do you have any now?"

"Bev had some. She burned them between the time she got his letter and went down to the boathouse."

I mulled it over. It made a kind of sense, the way things had been going. At least it was a possibility that Roger was behind the threats to Benny.

"The photos Benny took up here have been stolen from his files," I told her, "along with the information he'd been gathering. But if Roger Hampton is the one doing all this, why would he have waited until now to do it?"

"Maybe he's been away, duping women in other parts of the country, been moving around. Maybe just now he's back around here and onto a good thing in Seattle. There must be some gullible women in Seattle, the same as anywhere else. Maybe Roger's going to be showing up in the society pages. Maybe your friend could ruin the next scheme he's planning."

"But Benny didn't know anything about all this. He still doesn't. All he knows is that your sister died. That was enough to kill the story. He didn't know that your sister hung herself or the rest of it."

Barbara shrugged. "I just assumed he would have found out about it. And I'm sure Roger assumes the same thing."

I left Barbara Beyerly soon after that, sitting up in the loft with the bottle of whiskey, or what was left of it, staring out over her ranch. I'd been planning to try to pump up her ego a little before I left, telling her I didn't see all that much difference between her own appearance and that of her sister. But the day wasn't right for that sort of thing. My heart wouldn't have been in it. I was too tired and I'd had too much to drink and the story she'd told me was a little too depressing. I couldn't have given it my best shot, and even my best shot wouldn't have been a lasting impression. She needed a little professional therapy and I suspected she was bright enough to have figured that out.

On my way back into Bellingham, I decided I was ready for a little therapy myself. It was after five o'clock. I checked into a motel and caught up on my sleep.

# Chapter 16

It was raining the next morning. It rained continually during my drive back to Seattle and it didn't stop when I reached there. But I told myself you couldn't think about it like you were somebody from California, where it probably wasn't raining. You had to think of it like somebody from eastern Colorado. Instead of thinking that it probably wasn't raining in California, you had to think that it probably was snowing in eastern Colorado— or soon would be, as soon as this storm out of the Gulf of Alaska moved inland. If you didn't want your mind to cramp up, you had to pretend you were from eastern Colorado. At least when you were trying to work in Seattle.

From the north end of town, I phoned Mary Ellen's studio. Zither answered.

"Where have you been?" she asked once I'd introduced myself.

"Up north. Still trying to put together the pieces of Benny's puzzle."

"How is it going?"

"Slowly. Yesterday afternoon I had to cotton up to a woman who's had a lot of misfortune befall her the past couple of years. The only way she'd talk was over a bottle. It was slow going, and I decided to check into a motel up there to sleep it off."

"With the woman?"

"No. Just with myself and the sad story she had to tell me. It wasn't very pleasant."

"How was it with your ex the other evening? Was that pleasant?"

"I guess Mary Ellen told you about that."

"Blabbed all about it. We sat around drinking white wine and speculating about it last evening. We wondered about how it might have gone between you and your ex-wife. Of course neither one of us has ever met your ex-wife. We don't know whether she might be sweet or sour. But we decided, finally, that she couldn't be too sour. Not in your eyes, at least, if you decided to spend the night with her."

I sagged against the side of the telephone booth. I was beginning to feel worn down, and it wasn't even noon yet.

"Something else we decided," Zither continued. "We came to the conclusion that it was pretty unfair. Not necessarily on the part of you or your ex-wife. We were sure you had a lot of old memories to talk over. But just the circumstances, we decided, were unfair. That a gent should blow into town, single, nice-looking, pretty smart, and instead of picking up the hankie of a new feminine admirer, finds it necessary to cuddle up with his ex-goddamn-wife. That's what we decided. Here's Mary Ellen."

"How are things going, Bragg?" asked Mary Ellen.

"Give me a minute to wipe off the blood, will you?"

"You don't rate a minute to wipe off the blood. What is it you want?"

"A number where I can reach Benny."

She gave it to me. "He's registered under the name Bo Rinkle," she told me, then changed the subject. "Zither isn't standing here any longer. She went on back upstairs after she handed me the phone. I hope you don't mind if I think of you in terms of an old Seattle expression from now on."

"What expression?"

"Shitheel," she said, and hung up.

I put more coins in the phone and dialed the number she'd given me and asked the switchboard operator to put me through to Bo Rinkle. Benny answered on the first ring.

"What did Dolly and the kids decide to do?"

"They decided to come join me at the new hideout."

"What hideout?"

"It's a motel called Easy Aces over in the Montlake district."

"I don't hear any chatter in the background. They shouldn't be out walking the streets."

"They're not. Not down here, at least. One long afternoon and evening with the four of us in just one big room arguing over what we were going to watch on television was too much. They pulled out this morning for Sequim."

"It's better that way."

"You bet it is. I can watch any damn thing I want now. I thought I'd give the soaps a peek this afternoon. Wanna come watch with me?"

"No. The soaps seem to be what I've been living the past couple of days."

"How so?"

I told him about the visit with Barbara Beyerly. Then I told him about my conversation with Mary Ellen. "She of course told Zither I'd spent the night with Lorna.

I'm sort of attracted to Zither, but I figure I can kiss all that good-bye."

"Too many brands in the fire, pal."

"It's always been that way with me in Seattle. I don't understand it. I never get into situations like this in San Francisco."

"Maybe it's the weather," Benny told me. "You want to make sure you'll have somebody to warm your toes against."

We talked some more about Roger Hampton and what Benny's impressions had been of the boy.

"If what the sister told you is true, the boy did a great job of faking it," Benny said. "I thought those kids were really in love with each other."

"What did he look like?"

"He was about six feet tall. Slender. Athletic looking. Had dark blond hair that he wore in sort of a modified boot camp cut. Don't remember just how old he was, but at the time I knew, and I thought to myself he looked a lot younger than his real age. I think he was six or eight years older than the Beyerly girl. But you don't think he's really behind this, do you?"

"Why shouldn't I think it?"

"The voice on the phone, for one. The kid didn't have a voice anywheres near that deep. And you said there were a couple of bozos you chased after they tossed the bomb through my window. And the drawing Timmy and Al came up with. It didn't look anything like Hampton."

"He doesn't have to be doing it all by himself, Benny. If he's got a chance to get his hands on enough money, he can hire others. Just like any other business. When you're not watching the soaps, take a look at the local newscasts. And get both daily papers. His face might show up in one or the other. Maybe that's what's behind it. Maybe Hampton is going to be in the spotlight and he doesn't want you to see him and spoil whatever he's up to. That was the Beyerly woman's suggestion. He'll be using a different name, though. Those missing photos seem to be a key here. Barbara Beyerly said Hampton was very upset when he learned the pictures you'd been taking might show up in *People* magazine."

"Hmmm. Would it do any good to give copies of them to the cops, you think?"

"Copies of what?"

"The photos. I keep negatives of a lot of the stuff I shoot. In this case, the *People* magazine folks paid me for expenses I'd racked up in the course of trying to do the story. I billed them for the photos, so I figure technically they belong to the magazine. If they should ever want them for some reason, I can send them a batch."

"Benny, you're a genius."

"Why so?"

"Showing Hampton's photos to the cops might not do much good, but showing them around town could."

"Around where?"

"Wherever somebody planning to snooker a rich woman out of a bunch of money might put in an appearance. Did you save the negative of the other photo that was taken from your files? The ferroconcrete man?"

"Waldo Derington? I doubt it. I had to eat the expenses on that one. There'd be no reason."

"Okay, where are the Beyerly negatives?"

He told me they were in a metal file cabinet out home in his garage. "Where will you be staying in case I see this Hampton kid's puss somewhere?"

"I'm not sure. I spent last night in a motel up in Bellingham. During the day we can try to keep in touch through Mary Ellen. When I get a place for the night, I'll phone you. And please ask Mary Ellen to be civil enough to pass our messages back and forth. Tell her it's for your sake."

"What do you mean, civil? She likes you, Pete."

"That was before she learned I spent the night with Lorna. She just called me a shitheel a few minutes ago."

"I'll give her a call. What is it with you and Lorna, by the way?"

"If I knew that, I'd know what to tell Zither the next time I saw her."

Benny laughed. "Keep your chin up, pal."

"Yeah. Be talking to you, Bo."

I drove over to Benny's place and let myself in the back door with the key he'd given me. I went to the file cabinet in the garage and found the envelope with the Beyerly name on it. There didn't seem to be anything with Derington's name on it. Before leaving there, I got out my AT&T card and punched a lot of numbers into the phone in the kitchen. When Ceejay answered, I told her it was me and asked if there'd been any messages of note.

"Several," she told me. "Morrisey has a new client in a peck of trouble. The client's wife was strangled in the bathtub and the cops think he did it. Client has an alibi, but it's paper-thin. Morrisey wants you to find the man the client was with at the time the cops say the woman was murdered. He's somebody named Bob who lives in the Gilroy area. Morrisey wants to know how soon you can get on it."

"Tell him within a few days. I hope. What else?"

"You had a query from George Thompson. Wanted to know how you're doing on some sort of background check you're supposed to be running."

"Call him back and tell him I'm waiting to get answers from sources back East. I should have them by the first of next week, or rather you should, Ceejay. You might keep an eye open for letters from the New York state police and a law firm called Smithers and

Wevern. They should have the information Thompson needs."

"Will do. And you had a couple of checks come in that I photocopied and banked."

"Thank you."

"And Allison called."

"Oh? Is she in town?"

"No, she called down from Barracks Cove. Said she'd been thinking about you. She said she had the intuitive feeling your personal life was troubled. She tried phoning your apartment. I told her you were up in Seattle. She was a little surprised you hadn't called to let her know you were going away."

"I guess when Benny phoned me with his SOS I got a little distracted thinking about the old hometown."

"Was she right?"

"What do you mean?"

"Allison's intuition. Was it right? Is your personal life in a turmoil?"

"Yes, but I don't want to talk about it to anybody right now."

"Are you messing up again, Peter?"

There were times, this being one of them, when Ceejay's voice took on the tone not of an employee addressing one of her employers, but rather of a hard-nosed schoolmarm who'd caught me smoking in the cloakroom.

"Frankly, Ceejay, I don't know what I'm doing. It's just something about Seattle. It keeps me off balance."

"Is Lorna a part of it?"

I nearly dropped the receiver. "How do you know about her?"

"A woman who said her name was Lorna also phoned this morning. She said she was calling from Seattle and had been trying to get in touch with you. She wanted to know if I had a phone number for you. Who is she?"

I didn't answer right away. Ceejay was more than a

secretary and office manager. In some ways she was my conscience. And I didn't know what to tell her. She knew I'd been married once, but I'd never gone into the gory details, as Barbara Beyerly would have put it.

"You are messing up, aren't you, Bragg."

Not a question; a statement.

"Someday we'll talk about it, Ceejay, and you can tell me where I went wrong, every step of the way."

"Maybe you'd better try doing whatever has to be done up there and get on back home."

"I'm trying, Ceejay. I'm trying." I gave her Mary Ellen's number for daytime messages and told her I'd phone our answering service and leave them a night-time number when I had one.

I also called the World Investigation office in San Francisco. Turk Connell had heard back from their office in Vancouver to do with Waldo Derington, the man who'd dreamed of building luxurious houseboats on ferroconcrete hulls. Turk pretty much confirmed Benny's account. He said the firm had gone bankrupt despite some pretty hefty down payments that had been made by people who thought they were commissioning the construction of swank dwellings on the water. There was some grumbling at the time, Turk said, because Derington hadn't left behind any extensive accounting of where the money had gone. The crestfallen builder had carried most of it around in his head, and he'd left town and hadn't been seen since. It didn't surprise me. Who ever heard of floating concrete?

I thanked Turk and hung up, but didn't let go of the receiver. I went back and forth in my mind some about whether to make the next call, but I finally dialed Lorna's number at work.

"I'm glad you phoned," she told me. "I was just leaving for a luncheon appointment. I missed you last night."

Now I regretted making the call. "I spent the night in Bellingham."

"Oh? With whom?"

"A few dozen other people. At a motel."

"Nobody in particular, then."

She was trying to make it sound teasing, but she wasn't too successful at it. "Nobody at all."

"Such a waste. What are your plans for this evening?"

"I don't have any. I'm working on the Benny thing. It might carry on into the night."

"Oh. I was hoping we could meet for a drink after work."

"Any special reason?"

"No, no special reason. But I thought maybe you could give me a lift home. I cabbed in this morning. It was pouring out."

I hesitated.

"Well, I don't want to be a burden, Peter..."

"No, that's okay. What the hell, I ought to be able to take a break. I'll try to pick you up sometime between five and six."

She made a kissing sound before she hung up. Ceejay was right, or almost so. If I wasn't messing up, I was on the very edge of it. But I tried to put Lorna and Zither and all the gang out of my mind. I went through the Yellow Pages until I found the address of a professional photography outfit over in the Wallingford district. That wasn't far from where I'd gone to high school.

I drove over there and waited around while they processed the negatives and showed me a contact sheet. I pointed out the photos I wanted copies made up of and a half hour later I had them in hand. Then I began going around to the places rich women and their handsome young squires might go.

# Chapter 17

I didn't have any luck with the people I talked with at the University Yacht Club, the Seattle Town Club in West Seattle, or the Chinook Tennis Club in the Magnolia district. None of them recognized the blond young man in the photos I showed them, even when I asked that they try to imagine him with a moustache or a different hair style.

But a bartender named George in a well-appointed saloon at the East End Golf and Country Club, just outside the city of Bellevue on the east shore of Lake Washington, spotted him in a minute. He said the man's name was Kirby and that he was the swain of one Marietta Narcoff, who came from a very well off family and shot an eighteen-hole round of golf in the mid-eighties. George said Marietta and Kirby had been an item for about the past two months. They were nearly always together, which annoyed George a bit because George used to enjoy flirting with Marietta Narcoff himself, whenever she came into the bar, before she took up with the man he knew as Kirby.

These days, George's free drinks and winks and flirty conversation with Marietta had to be limited to those times when Kirby excused himself and went to the men's room. He said Marietta Narcoff, though well moneyed, was a democratic sort of woman. She wasn't the least bit above flirting with the help at the club. In the way that bartenders have after you've shot the breeze with them for a while, he managed to convey the impression that Marietta Narcoff was a woman who was not above flirting with any man who might appeal to her.

George said Marietta Narcoff's family had made its money in the Pacific Northwest timber industry and owned half the port of Coos Bay, Oregon. The main family residence was a big old stone faced place up on Capitol Hill. But they had getaway retreats as well, over in the Palouse country of eastern Washington, up in the Snoqualmie ski country, and one over on Hood Canal somewhere. Marietta herself, George told me, had investments in this and that and lived by herself in an apartment in a downtown building called Luckner Plaza. George knew this, he told me, because she'd let him take her home one night after she'd had a few drinks too many and couldn't remember how to turn on the headlights of her Mercedes. She'd invited him in for a drink at her apartment, and he had held high hopes she might invite him to spend the night, but she'd passed out on the sofa while he'd been telling her some of the gossip going around the bar at the East End Golf and Country Club, and he had decided prudently to just lift her feet onto the sofa, throw a spread over her, turn out the lights, and let himself out.

I asked George if Marietta Narcoff and the man he knew as Kirby might be thinking of getting married sometime down the road and he said he couldn't say, but then who the hell could figure out what the really wealthy thought about anyway. I knew what a few of the really wealthy who lived in California thought about because I'd worked for some of them, but up in Seattle I had to agree with George. I had no idea what they thought. I found it hard to accept that anybody who chose to live in Seattle through all that rain would have that much money to begin with. So that put me at a disadvantage.

I found her name listed in the Seattle telephone directory, which surprised me some. If Marietta Narcoff had the sort of money that George the bartender implied she had, I wouldn't have expected her to have her name in the telephone directory. When I dialed the number, there was no answer. I drove on back into downtown Seattle. It was after four o'clock by then and I tried phoning her again. This time she answered. I introduced myself and told her I had some information she might find of value.

"Information you're selling, Mr. Bragg?"

She had a low, rich voice that sounded as if she got a lot of fun out of life.

"No, not selling, Miss Narcoff. Passing it out free of charge."

"But if you're a private detective, you root up information for a fee, do you not?"

"Ordinarily, I do. But this information I'd give you is incidental to the real job I'm on. Maybe you can give me some information in return. That would be fee enough. And also I'd like you to look at a photograph."

"Do I smell a whiff of attempted blackmail here?"

"No, Miss Narcoff."

"Good, because I never would pay blackmail money for any photographs somebody might have taken of me, no matter how compromising."

"These are perfectly decent photographs," I told her. "A free-lance writer-photographer took them in the course of an assignment. They're family photos. I want to show them to you to see if you can identify somebody in them."

"You do spin an intriguing tale, Mr. Bragg." She paused a moment, and I heard what sounded like the turning of pages. "Are you, by any chance, related to Lorna Bragg?"

I cleared my throat. "She's my ex-wife."

"How droll. I must meet you, then."

She gave me directions to Luckner Plaza, an eight-story building on Third Avenue, west of the *Post Intelligencer* plant. It was a mixed office-and-residential building that had been put up in the past dozen years or so. Marietta Narcoff lived on the top floor in a roomy apartment with burgundy carpeting, comfortable, dark old furniture, and a spectacular view to the west of Elliott Bay and, on a clear day, the snow-capped Olympic Mountains beyond.

Beverly Beyerly had been in her early twenties when she took her own life, and Benny had told me Roger Hampton was six or eight years older but young-looking for his age. I expected Marietta Narcoff to be in her late twenties or early thirties. That had been kind of me. She had, by now, sailed easily into her forties and didn't go out of her way to conceal it. She was a large woman, five feet eight or nine inches tall. She'd gotten a little thick through the hips and had some lines around her eyes and neck, which a good plastic surgeon could have tucked away easily if that sort of thing were important to her. She had long brunette hair, a wide mouth that smiled most of the time, and a look around her eyes that made me feel that she did indeed enjoy a drink now and then. She wore dark slacks and an off-white knit sweater that clearly showed she wasn't wearing a bra, even though her breasts could have used one. That didn't bother her either. She was one of the most completely at ease women I'd ever met. She offered me a drink, which I declined, poured herself a glass of white wine, and settled comfortably in a corner of a long mohair sofa near the chair she'd directed me to and began to grill me.

"When were you and Lorna married?"

"A long time ago."

"Here?"

"We started out here. Broke up in San Francisco."

"Why did you break up?"

"She left town with a musician."

"Do you keep in touch?"

"We ran into each other a few evenings ago for the first time in many years."

"How does she seem to you now?"

"A lot younger than I would have expected."

"Were you civil to each other?"

"Yes, we were civil to each other."

She would have been a good cop. She picked up on something about the way I answered that. "Have you been intimate with each other since you met the other evening?"

I couldn't believe the way things were going. I wondered if she was going after the gory details as Beverly Beyerly had.

"You don't have to answer that," she continued. "It was discourteous of me to ask. But I'm insatiably curious about people. Did either of you remarry?"

"I haven't. Lorna did—a couple of times, she says."

"Lorna remarried? Why does she still call herself Bragg?"

"She isn't married now. She told me she liked my name in combination with her own given name better than she liked the names of the other people she'd married or her own maiden name. So after the last marriage she changed it back to Bragg. It all sounds a little silly to me, but there you are."

"It sounds deeply complex to me."

"I doubt that it is. I don't think Lorna is a deeply complex person. Where did you meet her?"

"She catered my sister's most recent marriage. She's very good at what she does."

"The catering, you mean?"

Marietta Narcoff didn't answer right away but held her wineglass up toward the dim light given off by a floor lamp of Italian marble over beside the windows. The only other light came from a small lamp on a table across the room. She seemed to prefer a deeply shadowed setting. It had started raining again, in peppery little flurries against the tall windows.

"No," she said finally. "I didn't necessarily mean the catering. She could be successful at any number of things. I was speaking more of the way she manages people."

"People working for her, you mean?"

"Those and others. How long were you two married?"

"Several years."

"You should know that better than I, then."

I shrugged. "Maybe I can't, or rather couldn't, see that. Maybe that's why she took off with the horn player."

She guffawed. "I'm sorry. But is that what he was?"

"With the Stan Kenton orchestra."

The guffaw turned into a fruity giggle. "This is terrible of me. But you must see the humor in it yourself or you wouldn't tell me about it."

"I can sort of smile about it now. It didn't seem all that funny at the time."

"Of course not. When one party in a marriage abandons the other ... well, never mind about that. Are you sure you wouldn't care for a drink?"

"No, I'm not so sure any longer. The only thing is, yesterday I was questioning a woman who has a horse ranch up near Bellingham. The only way she'd talk to me was over a bottle. I had enough to drink, so I had to crash at a motel up there overnight."

She got up with a big, generous grin on her wide mouth. "I promise I won't give you that much to drink. What would you like?"

"I'd ask for a martini if we were going to continue talking about my failed marriage. But instead of what I'd like, I'll have a gin and tonic, if you have it."

"I have it. I'll even join you with one."

She went out of the room. I heard her fussing around with ice and things, but it wasn't just in the next room. She had a lot of space to herself. She came back with the drinks. She handed me mine and turned on another lamp on a stand next to my chair, then returned to the sofa.

Now I could see her face better. I had the feeling she was enjoying herself, and I still hadn't really figured out how I was going to tell her that a man who looked half her age was going to try to bilk her out of some money. She, along with the rest of the town, had me a little off center.

"All right," she told me. "I've been nosy enough. Why don't you tell me what you came to tell me."

"You're a mind reader."

"You're getting edgy. I know my men well enough to tell when they're getting edgy. And I don't like men to get nervous around me. I like them too much for that."

"Maybe after the story I have to tell you, you won't like them as much."

"Try me."

So as briefly as I could, I told her about the conversation I'd had the day before with Barbara Beyerly. Then I told her about the troubles Benny had been having and his connection with the Beyerly family. And then I told her what George the bartender had told me, well, some of it anyhow, and took the photo of Roger Hampton out of the envelope I carried it in and asked her if he was the same person she knew as Kirby. She stared at it for a very long moment before replying.

"Yes, that's Buddy. At least that's the name he's using now. Buddy Kirby." She got up and turned on a few more lamps here and there, then sat back down and studied the photo again. "Can there be any mistake about all this?"

"I doubt it. The Beyerly woman wasn't any too happy telling me the story she told me. I don't think it's anything she would have made up, even with a stranger like me. And I've known Benny for a couple of decades or more. He hasn't seen this photo to positively identify it as being the man he knew as Roger Hampton, but he directed me to the negative and this is the only young man who appears in the photos showing the woman who took her own life."

"How old was the woman who took her own life?"

"Twenty-one or -two. Something like that."

She sat in thought for a moment, then got up and went across the room to a buffet against one wall and took a filtertip cigarette from a red laquered box. She returned to the sofa, lit the cigarette, and stared out the windows.

"Well, I'm not twenty-one or -two," she said finally. "And I certainly wouldn't be apt to take my own life over any bends my relationship with the man I know as Buddy Kirby might take. But I'll hand it to you, Bragg. You did prompt me to light up. I'm trying to quit. This is the first cigarette I've had in five days."

"I'm sorry about that. Quitting's tough. I had a terrible case of flu one year. This was when Lorna and I were still married. I was sick enough so I didn't want to smoke or do anything else except maybe die. It was a good start, so I kept at it. Went three and a half months without a cigarette."

She looked across at me. "Then you went back to them?"

I nodded. "The day Lorna left town with the horn player."

"But you're not smoking now?"

"No. About a year and a half after I started up again, a doctor noticed a funny little growth inside my mouth. He told me it was the sort of thing that could turn cancerous. He said he could remove it surgically, but it would just come back again if I kept smoking cigarettes. That was the day I quit, many years ago. For good."

"Good for you. Maybe that's what all of us need. A funny little growth inside the mouth. But then I've never been all that heavy a smoker. Less than a pack a day." She stubbed out the cigarette in a large onyx ashtray beside her. "As for Buddy Kirby, I don't know what to think. It wouldn't surprise me if he were after my money. Some of it, at least. I have to expect that sort of thing. I know it's like robbing the cradle, a woman my age frolicking around with a boy his age."

"My friend told me he's several years older than he looks."

"It doesn't matter. We have a good time together. But there's never been any sort of talk about marriage. I've been quite candid with him. I like his body and his sense of humor. He's good company."

"How did you meet him?"

"Through a friend. I'll have to ask my friend a bit more about him. And I'd like the name of that woman in Bellingham you spoke to. And a telephone number where you can be reached."

I told her about Mary Ellen and gave her the phone number. She couldn't tell me much more about the man she knew as Buddy Kirby. Nor did she have an address for him. Or a phone number.

"You've been running around with this cowboy for two months and you don't know where he lives or have a phone number for him?"

"He calls here every morning around nine, and we talk about our plans for the day. We don't spend all our time together. We don't even see each other every day. He told me he shares an apartment with three other men in West Seattle. He said all of them are sort of in between jobs. Their phone isn't connected right now."

I rolled my eyeballs. Her smile wasn't as generous when I left as it had been when I'd arrived. I'd cut into her fun some. She told me she'd let me know anything else she might learn about her young boyfriend. I thanked her and took the elevator down and drove over to see the woman who a dozen years earlier had left San Francisco on the arm of a horn player and started me back on cigarettes.

# *Chapter 18*————————————

They were holding a late afternoon rally up in the Scandia Farms offices. A secretary told me a business conference was in progress in Gene Olson's office, which was just beyond the reception area and clearly visible beyond a glass partition. Olson and Lorna were in there, along with Marvin Winslow, the cheery-faced chap with the scraggly moustache from Potlatch Bay. Also in there, which caused me to raise an eyebrow, was the bullet-headed man with scowling face who'd been on the phone the day I went up to the Jackson Detective Agency.

The meeting broke up about ten minutes later with a lot of hand shaking and good-natured banter. As they filed out, the Jackson operative and I locked eyes a moment without exchanging any greetings. Winslow tipped his bowler hat to me and went out with the Jackson man. Olson and I exchanged hellos, and Lorna tugged me off down a short hallway to her own office.

"I seem to have done about all I can do for one day,"
I told her. "How about some dinner before I take you
home?"

"I'd love it."

I helped her into the forest-green tweed jacket that
matched her skirt. She also wore a dark orange-colored
silk blouse. The jacket and a cameo brooch that clasped
the blouse at her throat suggested a certain demureness.
It was a little hard to tell what sort of role Lorna was
into from day to day. She had on a pale shade of
lipstick that matched her blouse and highlighted the
burnished color of her hair. She was one fine-looking
woman, my ex-wife. She watched me staring at her and
gave me a different kind of smile.

Are you starving?" she asked.

"Not really."

"Then I'd like to show you something."

We went down to the garage, where I'd left the car.
"Where are we going?"

"I want you to see the Potlatch Bay site, out along the
ship canal. We had a few last-minute details to iron out.
Monday, we and the others coming into the project are
signing the leases. We're having a big luncheon at the
Olympic Hotel. Inviting the press and everything."

I drove us out to Elliott Avenue and headed north,
toward Ballard. It was raining harder now, drumming
down on the car roof. Lorna scrunched over closer and
rested one hand on my leg.

"Did you know that the stumpy fellow with the sour
puss who was in Olson's office with Winslow is with a
private detective agency here in town?"

"Mr. Brand. Yes, I know. He's the one who ran the
credit check on us."

"Credit check? That doesn't sound like the sort of
work he would do. What do you need a credit check
for?"

"Financing for the Potlatch project. Interest rates are

just blistering these days. If you'd been to your friendly local banker asking for a loan recently, you might have noticed."

"So who does the Jackson man work for?"

"Potlatch. They're tapped into a money source."

"The developer provides his own financing? That sounds a little different."

"You have to be creative in order to borrow big sums these days. Potlatch found some sources in Hong Kong, some of those people anxious to liquidate and get out of there before the Chinese take over. That's why we're getting a break on the interest rates. They're willing to take less just to get their money working over here. Seattle First Trust is acting as agent for the fund transfer. We'll pay an advance fee for the loan, but we're getting the money at such a bargain-basement rate that Gene and I even considered asking for a larger loan than we needed, just so we could invest in Treasury bonds. It could almost be like a no-interest loan if we managed that."

"So why don't you?"

"The Potlatch people discourage it. They have other projects they want to finance with the same money source.

"Oh God, Peter, this rain. You know what I'd like to do?"

"No, what?"

She gave my leg a squeeze. "Look. Up ahead there, on the right."

Up ahead there on the right was a two-story U-shaped structure that called itself the See Fair Motel. It was a little play on Seafair, what they called an annual summer celebration of parades, hydroplane races, and general carrying on.

"It even has a vacancy sign," Lorna giggled. "Let's go there. For a quickie."

"Right now? Are you nuts?"

"No, I'm not nuts. I've reason to celebrate this day. It's pouring rain, and that alone is enough to make me want to get under some sheets. And on top of that it's getting so everytime I'm around you I just want to climb out of my clothes. Do it. Turn in."

She reached as if to turn the steering wheel herself. Maybe she had the right idea. We never used to do that sort of spontaneous thing when we lived together. I parked in front of the office. There was a small market next door.

"You register," Lorna told me, ducking her head to get out of the car. "I'll get some champagne."

I had to wait for the clerk to finish processing another man's registration. I handed over my American Express card and began filling out the registration slip. I was signing the Amex tag when the door opened behind me.

"Hurry up," Lorna told me. "You can finish that later if you're not done yet."

"I'm done," I told her. The clerk handed over our key with a straight face.

"It's an upper on the south wing," he told me.

I joined Lorna. She ran up the outer concrete stairs ahead of me. She was standing, shivering at the room door when I reached it.

"You're such a slowpoke," she told me.

I unlocked the door. Lorna had her moves down. She stepped inside the room, turned on an overhead light, crossed to the wall thermostat, and turned up the heat. She carried the bag of goods she'd bought at the market into the bathroom. She came back out with a pair of fat candles inside red glass globes and placed them in front of the dresser mirror. She took a book of motel matches out of an ashtray on the dresser and, after a couple of false starts, managed to get the candles lighted.

A couple of strands of her auburn hair had worked

loose from the clips she was wearing. She turned, blowing at the hair from the corner of her mouth. She crossed back to the door and turned off the light switch, leaving just the flickering glow of the candles in front of the mirror to light things. She headed back toward the bathroom and gave me a wink.

"Get out of your duds, Bragg." That was accompanied by an expression I took to be a leer.

I wasn't really as ready for all this as Lorna was. I crossed to the closet alcove and hung up my jacket. I hesitated a minute longer. I felt as if I should have been other places, doing different things. I took off my shoes and socks and hung up my shirt and trousers. I went over to the bed and pulled out the pillows from beneath an orange spread nearly the color of Lorna's silk blouse and lipstick. I plumped them up against the headboard, then sat on the bed and leaned up against one of the pillows. I looked across the room and briefly considered turning on the evening news, but figured Lorna probably would kill me if I pulled a stunt like that. I sat there wondering if Marietta Narcoff, who looked to be a veteran trouper, and the younger man now calling himself Buddy Kirby had ever done something like this on the spur of the moment. Probably many times over, I decided.

Lorna had partially disrobed in the bathroom. More than partially. She'd taken off her shoes and hosiery, along with the forest-green suit jacket and skirt and the orange blouse and cameo brooch. Beneath all that fine and proper office workaday garb she was wearing some not so workaday underwear. Skimpy, colorful, and frilly, it was, the same umber-orange color as her blouse and lipstick. She carried two glasses of champagne in front of her like an offering. Instead of using the plastic cups the motel provided, she'd bought a couple of champagne glasses at the market next door. She got onto the bed and walked across it on her knees, carefully, so she wouldn't spill the champagne. It fizzled up from the bottom of the hollow glass stems. She stopped beside me with a little gleam in her eye.

"Are you ready for this, Bragg?"

"If I'm not now, I probably will be in the next couple of seconds." Her bare tummy was right in front of my face. I turned my head and kissed her there.

Lorna giggled, then leaned back to sit on her heels and handed me one of the glasses. "To a rainy evening," she told me.

We touched glasses and drank. "You never used to wear that sort of underwear," I told her.

"You never used to take any notice of what sort of underwear I wore."

"No, I suppose I didn't."

"But this you notice."

"It's got my full attention."

"That won't do," she told me, sipping the champagne. "You have to save some of that attention for the thingamajigs underneath."

She made quick little back and forth movements that set the thingamajigs in motion, then tilted her head to one side. "I notice there's been no fashion revolution in the things that you wear next to your own skin."

I was wearing a pair of white boxer-style shorts.

"You look as if you were still in the navy," she told me.

"I didn't think you'd want me in lace."

"I don't mean that. They have some pretty sexy men's briefs these days."

"And there are plenty of guys around San Francisco who wear them," I conceded. "There are others of us who wouldn't be caught dead in them."

"That's old-fashioned thinking," she told me. "That's the kind of thinking you'd expect to find more in Seattle than in San Francisco."

"Yeah well, there's still a lot of Seattle left in me, I

guess. Maybe that's one of the reasons this has been such a hard trip."

"Has it?"

"Yes. Things seem awkward and out of place a lot of the time."

"Not the other night at my place?"

I drained the glass of champagne and looked across at the candles. "No, not the other night at your place."

She gazed steadily at me for several moments. "That's nice to know," she said finally.

She got off the bed and padded back to the bathroom, walking the way she walked when she knew somebody was watching. She came back out with the champagne bottle and refilled our glasses, then got back up on the bed beside me on her knees again. She took a sip of the champagne, then reached across to put down her glass on the nightstand beside me. She took my own glass from me and put it beside the other. Then she leaned over me with fists planted on either side of me and lowered her face until our lips met. She hadn't swallowed the champagne. While we kissed softly, she let a little of it trickle into my mouth.

That led to some kiss. I turned up my palms and lightly cupped her breasts. She leaned down on them hard.

"Take it off for me," she murmured.

I did as she asked. And the rain beat down outside and the candles flickered in front of the mirror and Lorna and I spent a little time out of mind.

# Chapter 19_____

Sometime during the next hour or so I changed my mind. I decided I didn't need to be other places, doing something else. I decided I was just fine right where I was. The two of us probably could have spent the rest of the night there in sound sleep if something as basic as hunger hadn't forced us back out into the rain and the dark. We considered having something delivered to the motel, but none of the junk food we could have gotten that way seemed fitting. I was ready for a steak, I told Lorna. Preferably New York-cut sirloin. Large.

"T-bone," Lorna had said.

"What?"

"Whenever someone's stolen my breath half away, I like to eat a T-bone."

We ate at a restaurant that had T-bone and New York-cut sirloin steaks in addition to an extensive sea-food menu. The restaurant was built on pilings with windows looking out over the Ballard Bridge and Seattle's fishing terminal on Salmon Bay. Trawlers from there ranged from chill Alaskan waters to down off the coasts of Oregon and California. We supped by candlelight at our table, as we'd done other things by candlelight back at the See Fair Motel. Lorna and I found ourselves staring at the candles, then at each other, with little smiles. Her face was still a little flushed-looking as she lifted a napkin to touch the lips repainted the same color as the silk blouse that was fastened chastely at her throat with the cameo brooch.

"I've always felt comparisons among various lovers weren't fair," she said quietly. "But I thought tonight was rather fabulous. Tonight was rockets and shell fire. I mean tonight, Mr. Bragg, you showed your ex-old lady about as fine a time as she's ever known."

"You weren't bad yourself. I had the feeling I was in bed with the chief pagan."

We continued eating in silence until Lorna looked up sharply. "Come home with me tonight."

"I doubt if I'd be much more good to you, lady..."

"I don't mean anything about sex. I just—I don't know. I just want to be more intimate with you, in a whole lot of ways. I want to spend more time with you. I want us to be close. Doesn't that sound right for us?"

I took a breath and exhaled slowly. "I don't know, Lorna. I'm still a little mixed up about all of this. If I really wanted to think about it, I'd probably decide something just the opposite. That maybe we ought to quit while we're ahead. Who knows? Things might all of a sudden turn on us. Old memories or old habit patterns might come around the corner and mess it all up. It could all turn stale and molder on us."

"You're a stinker," was all she said for the remainder of the meal.

When we left the table, Lorna went to the rest room to freshen up. My mind drifted back to business, and I decided to phone Marietta Narcoff. She told me she'd been in touch with the friend who'd introduced her to the man calling himself Buddy Kirby.

"My friend doesn't know him nearly as well as I'd been led to believe," she told me. "I think I'm going to have a few questions for Buddy when he phones in the morning."

"I have a few of my own," I told her. "That's why I called. I'd like to speak to him myself. You can tell him what I do for a living and say I'm working on a case here in Seattle and his name came up in the course of it. Tell him I think he might have some information that could help me. That's all true enough. And tell him you owe me a favor from the past, so you'd like him to talk to me. I'll meet him anywhere, anytime."

She agreed to it and I told her I'd call her around nine-thirty in the morning.

Lorna gave me directions to the Potlatch Bay site, on the north side of the ship canal, between the Ballard business district and the locks that raise and lower ship traffic between the tide levels of Puget Sound and the high fresh-water lakes inland. It was too wet and mucky for us to get out of the car. The headlights showed a large tract of muddy ground with a perimeter cyclone fence. Off in the distance was a long trailer they probably used for their construction office. Some lumber was stacked off to one side and a brightly lighted billboard proclaimed the site as home of Potlatch Bay, SEATTLE's PREMIER RETAIL-ENTERTAINMENT CENTER.

"What's the entertainment part of it?" I asked.

"They're building a theater complex," she told me. "One of those multi-room showhouses with a central projection booth to screen several movies at the same time. There'll be an adjoining showhouse for live productions. They're hoping to get one of the downtown companies to move its operation out here. And there's been some talk of putting in a small amusement park and arcade, with a huge rollaway roof for year-around operation. A mini-Tivoli Gardens, they're calling it."

I continued to stare out into the dark. "Sort of a bleak-looking place."

"Wait until after Monday," Lorna told me. "Let's go find some brandy."

I drove on down toward the locks and pulled into a parking lot beside an ancient frame building that housed a small bar and lunch counter. The place had wooden floors, a cheery collection of locals yucking it up at the bar, and country western music on the jukebox.

"I came in here once about a million years ago," I told Lorna. "Good enough for you?"

"Just so they have brandy. Has it changed much?"

"Not a bit. I think the same people were sitting drinking at the bar, even."

We sat in a corner booth and the bartender came out from behind the bar and crossed to us. He had a half-apron around his middle, a mop up rag in his hand, and a toothpick in his mouth. He didn't carry any cognacs, he told me, but he had Korbel brandy and I ordered a couple of snifters of it. Back at the bar he poured hot water into the snifters, let them sit a moment, then emptied the water and poured the brandy. When he brought them over, I paid and gave him a pretty good tip.

"Preheat the glasses and everything, huh?" I asked him.

"Hey," he said, grinning. "This is a class operation, pal."

When he went back to the bar, it seemed Lorna and I had run out of things to gab about. She sat staring at the table and thinking her own thoughts. I thought she was just savoring the past two or three hours we'd spent together. I was wrong.

"You know, Peter," she said, swirling the brandy, "I'm going to say something you might not like."

I glanced at her. The tone of her voice had taken on a raw little edge I noticed got into it when she was talking to the help down at Scandia Farms.

"If it's something I might not like, then why say it? If you want us to stay friends, that is."

"Oh I do. It's just, well, it's for your own good, really."

I thought I'd heard her say that to me for the last time a dozen years earlier. I couldn't believe it. I wasn't angry about it, really. More like morbidly fascinated. And wary. "Okay, so it's for my own good. What is it?"

"I think that despite all the years that have gone by, your new line of work, the scars and lines around your face, I think there's still a little bit of the timid boy in you."

I made a sound partway between a snuff and a snort. It was a brief laugh at the heart of it, and I settled back in my chair, a little more relaxed.

"No you don't, Lorna, not this time. I'm sure I have my faults. And sometimes in my work I can get into situations that raise the hair on the back of my neck, but timid? No, I just don't think that's true. I don't think you could find anybody who'd agree with you on that one."

"Then why won't you come stay with me?"

"Maybe because I figure we'd have more conversations like this one. Not that it would bother me as much as it used to in the past, when you'd open up like this. But what's the use? Who needs it? Why go out of our way to spoil the fun we seem to be having together this time around?"

"Fun? A frantic little roll in the hay and a candlelight dinner? Is that what you like about me these days?"

"Lorna, don't do this. You know that isn't what I mean."

"You could certainly get plenty of both hanging around my place."

"Plus maybe plenty of this sort of thing."

"What's wrong with a little constructive criticism?"

"Nothing's wrong with a little constructive criticism, with the emphasis on constructive. No wait a minute, I take that back. As long as I conduct myself properly, don't embarrass you in front of your friends, and maintain reasonable standards of cleanliness, why do we need any criticism at all? Either one of us?"

"What are you going to do, just live out of a suitcase in the trunk of your car for the rest of the time you're up here?"

"No, I'll find another place. I've just been a little busy lately, is all."

"Didn't you like my performance back at the motel?"

"Is that what it was, a performance? That makes it sound cheap enough. I thought what we were doing was a mutual expression of past love and a newly found closeness."

Somewhere through all that, Lorna's eyes sparked fire and her lips flattened out in a thin, tight line.

"Cheap? Is that what you're calling me now, Peter?"

"No, I just meant..."

"You just said that what we did back at the motel was cheap."

"I did not!"

I found my voice rising loud enough to attract the attention of a couple of the gang at the bar. Lorna's voice was getting a little shrill as well.

"How will you talk about me when you go back to your friends in San Francisco?" she demanded. "Tell them you ran into your ex-wife up there in Seattle? Lorna Bragg, the whore?"

I sat back, slightly flabbergasted. "I don't believe this. Lorna, what I meant—what I was trying to suggest..." But I'd lost the thread of the conversation. I couldn't remember what the hell I'd been trying to say. Certainly not whatever Lorna thought.

"I knew it," Lorna said, boring in. "Well let me tell you something, Peter. I'm not a slut. Or a one-night stand. I think you'd better call me a cab."

"You don't need a cab, Lorna. I'll give you..."

She cut me off, her tone icy. She enunciated her words slowly and distinctly. "Get me a cab, please."

I rolled my shoulders in a shrug and went over to ask the bartender to phone a taxi. He had a direct line to a local cab stand. I went back to the booth and we drank our brandy without exchanging another word. The cabby appeared in the doorway about four minutes later. Lorna got up without another glance in my direction and left.

I just sat there a couple of minutes trying to reconstruct the conversation we'd just had, but it was hopeless. I shook my head and carried the brandy snifters back to the bar. I settled on an end stool and asked for more brandy. The conversation at the bar quieted down some.

An older fellow wearing a hard hat was sitting two stools down from me. A pair of stout, middle-aged women wearing yellow rain slickers sat just beyond him, talking quietly. Around a corner of the bar was a younger fellow in a navy peacoat and wearing a yachting cap, talking to the bartender. They all avoided my eyes in the back-bar mirror. The man in the hard hat had a case of hiccups. He kept making a quiet *erk* sound. He finally turned toward me in a neighborly gesture.

"You'll pardon my saying so, sir, but it sounds to me like you've gotten yourself into some deep shit. Let me *erk* buy you a drink."

"No thanks, friend. And I don't know that I've gotten into it so much as maybe I've just started to climb out of it."

"Good to hear *erk*. Good to hear."

They gently welcomed me into their little conversational family then, the way the regular customers of small bars will if you behave in a civilized manner. Not that I began talking a blue streak with them. We just exchanged tidbits of information.

It's funny, the things you can learn chatting with strangers in a bar that way. It turned out the hard hat man was working on a big apartment project out in the north end of town, not too far from where Benny Bartlett lived. The two women in slickers lived just up the street. They were neighbors, and it was bowling night for their husbands. The younger fellow in the peacoat, who turned out to be nearly totally bald when he removed his yachting cap to scratch his dome, owned a forty-foot cabin cruiser that he kept berthed about a mile away at the Port of Seattle Boat Moorage behind the breakwater they'd built on Shilshole Bay. He made a living with his girl friend, chartering the boat for sports fishing and sightseeing on Puget Sound. And the innkeeper, well, he was afraid he was going to lose his lease when it came up for renewal the following year. He figured that with the new Potlatch Bay project going in just down the road, somebody would offer his landlord a lot more money for the site, planning to put in something a lot more foxy than a little bar and lunch counter. But my neighbor in the hard hat didn't agree. He told the innkeeper he felt his fears were groundless. He said that in his considered opinion—thirty years in the construction business *erk*—somebody was in the process of pulling somebody else's leg. A good hard yank, was the way he put it. He said he'd bet everything he had that the Potlatch Bay project would never be built, that nobody had ever intended for it to be in the first place.

# Chapter 20

I had a hangover the next morning when I phoned
Marietta Narcoff. I had a throbbing in my head that
people over in Spokane could have heard had they
listened closely. I'd spent too long in that little bar down
by the government locks drinking brandy and, in time,
drinking draft beer along with it. Lorna had been a
part of it, of course.

I could only half recall what the man in the hard hat
had been telling people about the Potlatch Bay project,
although I did remember that it seemed to make sense
at the time. I barely remembered to make the phone
call to Marietta Narcoff. She told me her young friend
had turned guarded when she told him about me and
my wanting to meet him. He had balked at that, she
told me, until she had said to her young friend that she
thought he should see me before the two of them spent
any more time playing around together. So he'd finally
agreed to meet me and Marietta that afternoon at a

downtown restaurant and bar not far from Marietta's apartment building.

I'd spent the night in another little motel not far from the See Fair on Elliott Avenue. I'd originally intended to go back to the See Fair since I'd already paid for the room, but my brain had come through in the clutch and told me, No, sap, you go back there with the candles on the dresser and Lorna's scent on the pillow cases and your resolve would turn to mush and you'd drive right on up to Phinney Ridge and beg Lorna to let you in so you could stay there and absorb her abuse for the rest of your stay in Seattle. I still didn't know how she'd managed to turn our conversation in the little bar by the locks into the platter of whips and jingles it had become.

I phoned Benny at his motel and asked how things were going. He said he was bored as hell and lonely for Dolly and the kids. I urged him to stay calm and said I might have some news for him by later that evening. I also telephoned a frosty-voiced Mary Ellen Cutler, who told me she didn't have any messages for me.

Seattle seemed to be between storms right then. There still were some low clouds scudding overhead, but there were patches of blue sky and bursts of sunshine as well. People were out and about with pleased grins on their faces, as if a siege had been lifted.

After breakfast I drove back out to the Potlatch Bay site in Ballard. A gate in the perimeter fence was padlocked from the inside. I hailed the trailer office beyond the fence and a moment later an elderly man came out. I asked to speak to the construction foreman.

"Ain't here. Works starts next week. I'm the watchman."

"Who's the contractor?"

"Can't give that out. They're announcing it on Monday. You a newspaper feller?"

"Nope." I took out a card and wrote Mary Ellen's number on it, then wrapped it inside a $10 bill and handed it through the fence. I asked if he could have any of the contractor's men who showed up phone and leave word where I could reach them.

"It's important," I told him.

"It must be," he told me, pocketing the money and studying the card on his way back to the trailer office.

I still had plenty of time to kill. The balding fellow in the yachting cap had told me his name was Ed Bjorkland and he ran what he called Captain Ed's Charter Service. He'd invited me to stop by and have a look at his boat, so I drove on down to the boat moorage. I found the berth number he'd written on the back of a business card and stood admiring the smart-looking craft tied up there, but when I hailed the boat, nobody answered. I drove on back over to Aurora Avenue and found another motel. I checked in, hung up my clothes, and took a long nap.

The restaurant where Marietta Narcoff, her young friend, and I had agreed to meet at was called the Coachman's Rest. It was a gloomy sort of place, with dark wood furnishings and flickering gas lamps. It occurred to me that Marietta Narcoff, although not vain enough to visit a plastic surgeon, might have decided she presented a better face to the world in the kindness of shadows. She and her friend were there waiting for me in a wood and leather-padded booth along one wall. Marietta was wearing a dark tailored suit with a white blouse. Her friend was the man in the pictures Benny Bartlett had taken up at the Beyerly ranch outside of Bellingham. He'd let his hair grow some and he dressed up a little more than he had in the photos I'd seen. He was wearing gray slacks, a white shirt with thin blue stripes, a dark knit tie, and a navy blue blazer with brass buttons. When Marietta introduced us, he barely acknowledged me. I sat down across from the man going these days by the name of

Kirby and ordered a gin and tonic from a waitress wearing a low-bosomed period gown.

"We've already talked some about the things you told me," Marietta said by way of breaking the ice. Buddy tells me he knew the Beyerly girl. He said they just— fell out of love."

I stared at him for a moment. He was a pretty-looking lad, but there was a decided coldness in his eyes. I didn't like him. Not at all. I decided to jump right in and start punching.

"Who fell out of love?" I asked him.

"We both did."

"Her sister told me differently. Barbara Beyerly said you wrote her sister the equivalent of a Dear John letter and left town with twenty thousand dollars the girl had given you a few days earlier."

"Her sister doesn't know what she's talking about."

"You heard, I suppose, that Beverly Beyerly hanged herself from the rafters in their boathouse a few days after she got your letter."

"Yes, I heard that," he acknowledged. "One of the reasons I was beginning to feel distant from Bev was that she'd been showing some unusual behavior patterns toward the end. She was very neurotic. Not nearly as mature as Marietta here." He said that last with a longing look at the older woman he was chasing after.

"Did it occur to you," I asked, "that it might be the gentlemanly thing to do to return the twenty thousand dollars to the family after you heard of the girl's death?"

"Why should I have? Bev wanted me to have that money to start a business with and have a chance to make something of myself. Even if things were coming to an end between us. Some people have that sort of confidence and trust in others, even after the infatuation ends. And the family certainly didn't need any more money."

"What business did you go into?"

"I opened a used car dealership. It failed after a few months. I had cash flow problems."

"Where did you open the dealership?"

"I don't think that's any of your business."

"Benny Bartlett."

He blinked, but his face stayed a blank.

"The name mean anything to you?"

"No."

"He's a free-lance writer. He was doing a story on the Beyerly family the summer you were up there. Took some photos of you and Bev together. Barbara Beyerly told me you and her sister had a little fight over that when you learned what they were for, that you wanted her to get the photos back."

"That's ridiculous."

"It's what her sister told me."

"Look. Her sister's nearly as nutty as Beverly was. I don't know why she told you those things, but they're just not true."

"Do you remember Bartlett, who was doing the story?"

"Yeah, I remember him. A guy who wore glasses."

"Seen him recently?"

"No, I haven't seen him. I haven't been back to Bellingham since Bev died."

"He doesn't live in Bellingham. He lives in Seattle."

He shrugged. "So what?"

"Somebody's been harassing him and his family. With death threats and attempts on his life. I'm here to put a stop to it."

He sat up a little straighter then. "Is that what this is about?" He made a wave of dismissal and got up from the booth. "Come on, Marietta, let's go eat somewhere. I don't know what this jerk's talking about."

"Sit back down a minute," I told him.

"Up yours."

"I said to sit back down a minute."

He almost didn't do it. We stared at each other some. Marietta was keeping out of it. He finally decided that no matter what happened if we went for each other's throats, it would be an embarrassing thing to do in front of his lady friend. He sat.

"Why did you change your name?"

"What difference does it make? Nothing illegal about changing your name."

"Unless you do it for purposes of fraud or a couple of other things."

He was on his feet again. "Come on, Marietta, this is really too much. I said I'd meet him. I've done that. But I don't intend to take any more of this."

"Buddy, why don't you just run ahead without me," Marietta told him. "I have a headache. I think I'll just go on back home when I finish this drink."

He stared at her with a pained expression, wondering if he'd lost her, then mumbled something about phoning her in the morning and left us.

"He doesn't much like you," Marietta observed.

"No."

"Did you find out what you wanted?"

"I don't know. He's lying in his teeth about a few things, but that doesn't mean he's the one who's been bothering my friend."

"You're probably right about the lying. I think he's lied to me in the past also."

"Why did you take up with him in the first place?"

"He amuses me—when he's in a better mood than he was in front of you. But I'm glad you came along and told me what you did about him. I suspected a part of his motivation, I think. Now I know. I'll just make him be a little more attentive in the future."

"You intend to keep seeing him?"

"So long as he continues to amuse me."

"Then what?"

"I'll quit answering the telephone at nine o'clock every morning."

"What if he approaches you all pouty and fuming at the East End club?"

"I'll take him aside and tell him quietly that I've developed the most terrible rash. That my doctor diagnoses it as flaring genital herpes."

"Yeah, I guess that would make him back off a ways."

"Really, Mr. Bragg. This old girl's been in and out of the barn and around the corral a few times. You needn't worry about me around the likes of Buddy Kirby. Oh, what was it you said his name was up in Bellingham?"

"Roger Hampton."

"Yes." She took a small address booklet out of her purse and wrote the name on an inside cover. "I want to remember that. I think when I've decided that my relationship with Buddy has reached the home stretch, I'll just start calling him Roger." She giggled like a young girl.

"Miss Narcoff..."

"Oh for crying out loud, call me Marietta."

"Okay, I'm Pete."

"Nice to meet you, Pete."

"The same. This is to do with something entirely different. I was wondering if you might know somebody with Seattle First Trust. A vice-president or some other kind of company officer."

"No I don't. But I'm sure my banker does. Why?"

"I'm a little curious about a deal they're supposed to be putting together. I'd like to be able to ask them some questions. Probably the sort of questions they wouldn't want to answer for a complete stranger."

"I see. Don't worry about it. I'll call Bill Shakey Monday morning. He's my main money man, and anything but what his name would imply. If he doesn't know somebody at First Trust, he'll know somebody else who does. I'll vouch for you and you can get in touch with him later in the day."

She looked up the phone number of her main money man in the little address book and I copied it down. She offered to buy me dinner, but I told her I had more work to do.

"Then let's try to get together another time before you go back to San Francisco. I'd like to know more about your work. I've never been friends with a private detective."

"It's a date," I told her. "If not this time, then the next time I'm through town. I've never been friends with a really rich old broad."

From a pay phone in the restaurant lobby I called Mary Ellen Cutler. No messages. Click. Thank you, Mary Ellen Cutler. I stood at the phone thinking for a minute. I was beginning to feel maybe I was chasing after more wild geese than one man should try for. But finally I tried to call Lorna at Scandia Farms. The girl who answered told me she was in conference. I left my name and said I was on my way over there.

My ex probably wouldn't be any happier to see me than I was to see her after that eerie little throwback to the past we'd been through the night before. Because that's what it'd been, I finally realized sometime in the course of the day. It had been a long time ago and I didn't see the pattern right away. I didn't even know if I could expand on it, but it was one of the things I used to brood about and try to make sense of back in my Sausalito apartment after Lorna and I had split up. It was an alternating pattern—an overwhelming outburst of passion and affection, then a quick turnaround with the sharp tongue and the critical eye, almost as if she felt sudden shame over such a display of love.

I parked in the basement garage and went on up to the second-floor Scandia office. The conference was still going on in Gene Olson's office. This time Olson and Lorna were in there with Thackery, the Seahawks official, and another man I hadn't seen before.

"I understand there are some very delicate negotiations going on in there," the receptionist told me.

Lorna looked up just then and saw me. She said something to the others and came out of the office with a questioning look. She didn't say anything right away, but led me down the short corridor toward her own office, and when she spoke it was in a low enough voice so she wouldn't be overheard by the receptionist.

"Peter? I'm a little surprised to see you here. If it's about last night..."

"No, Lorna, it's not about last night. At least it isn't anything personal. It's just some information I've heard that might be of concern to you and Gene Olson."

Her face tightened up. "It's nothing to do with the Seahawks, I hope."

"No, no."

She relaxed some. "Thank God. But then, I really shouldn't take the time right now. We're so very close on this Seahawks contract. Could you phone me later, at home?"

"Sure, no problem. Go on back in there and slay 'em."

"Thanks." She touched my arm and hurried back down the corridor. I went on into Lorna's office and phoned Benny.

"Tell me you've cracked it," Benny pleaded. "Tell me you've found and broken the bad guys so I can get the hell out of here. I want out of this dump. I wanna go home."

"Can't do all that yet, Benny. The Hampton boy is up to mischief, but I'd say odds are against his being behind your troubles. I just had a bristling little conversation with him."

"Yeah? What's he up to now?"

"He's changed his name and he's chasing after an older moneyed woman in town here."

"Jesus Christ, how does he do it? He looked like a high school kid when I saw him."

"He's let his hair grow some since you knew him. The moneyed woman finds him amusing. But she's a smart lady, and she was fascinated by the things I had to tell her about Roger Hampton. He'll be wasting his time if he keeps chasing after her in earnest."

"So where does all that leave me?"

"I'm not sure. Look, how about if I pick up some cheeseburgers and bring them by. We can visit for a while."

"Oh, Pete, that'd be great."

"Okay, sit tight."

I hung up and took the elevator back down to the basement garage and went over and unlocked the rental car. Later it would occur to me I was spending too much time worrying about Benny. I'd been poking into enough queer events so I should have been paying a little more attention to myself.

I sensed it just as I started to climb in behind the wheel, but I was in an awkward position and couldn't move quickly enough. Somebody cracked me on the back of the skull with an object that was blunt enough to do the job. It was as if every light in the world had been turned up to maximum with a universal rheostat. And then they all went out.

# Chapter 21——————

They brought me around to where I was partially conscious by throwing what felt like a bucket of water on my head. Sometime in the course of things, I realized they must have had to pour more than one bucket of water over me to bring me around. The top of me was soaked to the skin. We weren't in the parking garage but outdoors somewhere. They'd put a blindfold across my eyes and had jammed what felt like an inch-thick piece of manila line between my jaws and tied it behind my head. It served as a very effective gag. I could only grunt and gurgle—if I'd had anything to gurgle about. I didn't. They didn't want to talk to me.

They'd thrown the water over me so I'd be conscious enough to savor the beating they gave me. I did do some grunting in the course of it all. In addition to putting the blindfold over my eyes and sticking the rope in my mouth, they'd wired my wrists together behind my back.

What went on then went on for an awfully long time. There were at least two of them, maybe three. They started with my face and head and worked down. One of them, wearing gloves, used his fists. One of them had some sort of blunt object, probably whatever they'd whacked me on the head with back at the parking garage. I was on the ground when they'd thrown the water over me to bring me around, and I stayed down the whole time. They kicked and punched and banged. I hunched up as tightly as I could and tried to stay tucked in a fetal position, but this was all pretty useless. I suppose I did it more to keep my body friends with my brain than anything else. I wanted my body to know I was trying, the best I could with my brain, to lessen the impact of what we were going through.

I passed out at least twice more that I remember. Both times they probably left me alone for a bit so they could get a little rest themselves—this was hard, tough work they were doing—before they refilled the water bucket or whatever and brought me around again so they could continue the exercise.

And this was a really dragged out performance. I'm sure it didn't go on for as long as it seemed, but thinking back later, they must have spent twenty to thirty minutes actually beating on me. All in all, including the time it must have taken them to drive to wherever we were at and the time they spent resting while I was unconscious, it could have been more than a couple of hours. It seemed like half the night. And I thought to myself at one point, Why don't they just finish it? Why don't they just put a bullet through my head and go on home to the wife or girl friend or whatever? Why waste this much time?

The last time I passed out while they were still there was when somebody rolled me onto my back and sat on my knees while somebody else smashed a shoe down into my groin.

By the time I came to again, I could tell I'd won, finally. I'd worn them all out. They used another bucket of water to bring me around just so they could say something to me. My groin throbbed with pain, but then so did the rest of me. They hadn't played favorites, these men.

"Listen, slob," somebody told me. "This is your last warning. Go back to San Francisco. If we have to come after you again, next time it'll be with an axe. We'll start with your left leg. At the ankle."

I think they left after that. I passed out again.

It was raining when I came around again. I was lying with my legs in the tucked position, the left side of my face in a depression that was starting to fill with water. I stayed just like that for probably another ten minutes, just listening to things around me, or trying to listen beyond the continual buzz and ring in my ears. I heard a couple of jetliners go overhead. I could hear tires hissing after a while, along a wet roadway somewhere off in the distance. I heard a fog horn, and then I could hear water lapping against something not too far off.

I tested my legs then, started to straighten them some, but it sent a sharp pain through my stomach. I didn't know what that meant. Nothing good, I was sure. I thought of the funny slogan on a T-shirt my lady friend Allison down in California was fond of wearing. It said, "When the Going Gets Tough, the Tough Go Shopping." It was time for me to go shopping.

I tried just one leg this time. Oh so gently. I moved my right leg just an inch or two, then returned it just the same distance. Stretch inches; tuck inches. Down, up. Slowly. Like trying to unlock the brake pads that have become frozen to the wheel drum of a car that's been left outside during a rain storm. Stretch, tuck. Stretch, tuck. At least I didn't get that same sheet of pain that had ripped through my stomach earlier.

Good, Bragg. You're recovering already. Stretch, tuck. Stretch, tuck.

It was maybe another twenty minutes before I worked myself up into a sitting position. Things went blindingly fast after that. I finally realized they'd left the ends of the wires binding my hands out enough so I could work them with my fingers. They wouldn't have let me do that while they were beating up on me. Probably, they would have broken my fingers if I'd tried. But now that they weren't standing over me, pummeling and gasping to catch their breath, it was a snap. It didn't take more than five or ten minutes.

I gingerly felt at the wrists where the wire had bound them. It reminded me of what true pain is like. Pure pain. I almost fainted. For several more minutes I just sat there, shoulders slumped. Then I thought to dip the wrists in a nearby puddle of rain water. It helped. I left them soaking until the pain diminished, then pushed myself into a kneeling position. I didn't try touching the wire wounds on my wrists again. My wrists had told me they didn't want that. Instead, I tried raising my hands to get at the blindfold tied across my eyes. I tried this slowly. Good thing. My right arm went for it, but my left balked. My left shoulder didn't want me raising my left hand more than about halfway up my chest. So right arm and hand had to do the lion's share of the work. I finally managed to get an old rag off the back of my head and down from my face. I blinked into the night but couldn't see anything at first. It was starting to rain a little harder. The fog horn was still going, a mile or more off from wherever I was.

A couple of things began to come into focus, but it was slit-eyed focus. I finally reasoned it out. That would be from having a puffed up face everywhere the man wearing the gloves had hit me, on the cheek and mouth and around the eyes. As near as I could tell, I was alongside some sort of warehouse or industrial plant along the edge of a bay or lake. Bay, probably, from the sound of the foghorn. I could see lights reflected off water, just beyond the back of the building I was next to. Light in the distance had a bluish cast to it. Probably some sort of industrial vapor lamps.

I must have been bleeding from the inside of my mouth still. I swallowed some of it and started to choke. It caused a bit of panic to well up in me until I realized I was able to cough out fluid around the rope. Once again my right arm started to make the salute of the slow people, laboring to bring my hand up behind my head to work on the rope gag. As a comradely gesture, I tried moving the left hand up again too, but the shoulder said, No thanks, pal.

I couldn't do a thing about the rope. Not with just one hand, anyhow. The knot they'd tied was wet and tight. Well, I told myself, that's okay. All I had to do was get to my feet and get out of there and go find the road where I heard that traffic and flag down a passing car with my good right arm. Hell, it's nearly every day you see a bloodied, sopping wet man with a hank of rope in his mouth hitching a ride.

I had to stop everything and just rest again. Every move felt as if I were doing it underwater. There was a drag coefficient I'd never experienced before. I'd been beat up in the past. Not often, but enough. But never, ever had it been anything like this. My mind didn't even want to be bothered right then wondering who might have done it to me or what chance I might have somewhere down the road, say in a year or two, to exact some sort of revenge. My mind right then was dwelling on one very simple aim. Survival. I concentrated on my sense of direction. When I got to my feet, I had to make sure I stumbled away from the water. If I inadvertently fell into the water right then, I would drown. I couldn't move enough of me to avoid that. What a way to go.

With that thought I scared myself enough so I got on my hands and knees and crawled away from the sound of water and toward the sound of traffic. I crawled until I couldn't move any further, but had to sit and rest some more. I spotted some dark blobs silhouetted off to one side. When I felt strong enough, I dragged myself over to them. They were old packing crates. Big things. I raised my right hand and grabbed an edge, pulled myself up until, lo and behold, I was on my feet.

I felt like singing. Look, Ma, it can walk. Only I didn't walk much right then. I leaned against the packing crate and breathed in and out as best I could through a clogged nose and a roped mouth. I found my handkerchief in my hip pocket and got it out to dab at my nose and around my mouth. No pain there. They were both too numb.

I tucked away the handkerchief and wondered what else they'd left me. Surprisingly, most everything. Spare change in my front left pocket. Wallet on my left hip. Keys and a small pocket knife in my front right. The shoulder holster was empty, of course. They'd taken my .45. I couldn't remember where I'd left the .38. Either in the car or back at the motel.

I made a movement that brought back that pain to my stomach muscles. I hoped there wasn't anything inside there ripped and bleeding.

I leaned back on the packing crate and lifted my face to the rain. I'd quit caring about how long all this was taking. As long as I could move, as limited as those moves were right then, I'd get somewhere better. I leaned forward, bracing my hands on my thighs. My right hand felt the keys in my pocket. Keys and knife. Finally, my brain made the connection.

I dug into the pocket and brought out the knife. I unclasped the blade, then felt around my head and face for a place where I could cut through the rope

without stabbing myself through to the brain. I decided
finally to just start sawing in from the back of my neck.
The knife was reasonably sharp, and after penetrating
the outer fibers of the rope, it went pretty quickly.
When I felt the blade was getting close to skin, I
jammed the rope back into my mouth as far as I could.
It was enough so I could then slip the knife blade
between the back of my neck and the uncut section of
rope, sawing in sharp outward strokes. In a couple of
seconds it parted.

I spat out the rope and my jaws screamed. I couldn't
close my mouth. Part of that was because of the cramped
open position my jaws had been in, the other was from
the beating they'd given me around the mouth.

I put away the knife, then felt around on the ground
until I found the rope gag again. I put one of the
severed ends back between my teeth, using it the way a
boxer or football player uses a mouth guard. I stood
straight then and did a little tentative stretching, this
way and that, shuffling my feet, and finally I pushed off
the packing crate and made for the sound of traffic.

It was more of a shamble than it was a walk. But I
kept at it, a steady pitching and rolling pace. I found a
pocked and rutted road leading from the building I'd
been near to the sound of the distant traffic. After a
long trudge, I found the road emptied out onto a city
street. Overhead was a viaduct. That's where the traffic
I'd heard was. The lower-level street I was on gave
access to various industrial activities. It was all dark and
deserted at this time of night.

At least I felt I knew where I was now. The viaduct
looked like the elevated roadway that runs between an
area just south of downtown Seattle out to Alki Point
and West Seattle. Probably, I was near Harbor Island,
at the south end of Elliott Bay. There were shipyards
on Harbor Island, and somewhere nearby there once
had been a steel mill I'd worked at one summer. Also,

somewhere in this area, there had been an old wooden trestle carrying streetcar tracks to West Seattle. I'd been taken over that trestle on a streetcar one time when I was a very young boy. I'd bawled then, terrified at what seemed such a dizzying height. Take me up high enough today and I damn near bawl again.

I started walking east. I went about a quarter-mile before I found an outdoor telephone booth. The light in the booth was out, but there was just enough light filtering in from a nearby building for me to look up the phone number of a local cab company. I took the rope out of my mouth and dialed the number.

When the dispatcher answered, I learned I couldn't talk well enough to be understood. The dispatcher tried to get the information from me, but all I could do was croak back at him. Finally, he hung up. After he hung up I realized I didn't have an address I could have given him even if I'd been able to make myself understood. I started walking again.

And now I began thinking about just where it was I planned to go next. Ordinarily, I would have made my way somehow back to the motel out on Aurora Avenue that I'd checked into earlier in the day. But I didn't have any idea where the people who'd beaten up on me might have picked up my trail. They might know about the motel. Still, I argued back to myself, the motel was where my suitcase was. And I remembered that inside the locked suitcase was where I'd left the .38. I'd quit carrying that in the car when I began carrying the .45 in the shoulder holster. But I was a long way from the motel. Cab. Talk. I had to practice talking.

I took the rope end out of my mouth again and began moving my jaws. It wasn't as painful as it had been earlier, but I didn't seem to have very good muscular control over my mouth. It felt about the way it does when you've been anesthetized by a dentist. My tongue was thick. I couldn't feel the roof of my mouth.

I made a couple of noises in my throat and began to practice talking. I recited the words to songs and made up grocery lists and practiced what I would tell Ceejay down at the office in San Francisco the next time I phone in. I babbled, but I kept at it until a wave of nausea and lightheadedness hit me so strongly I had to sit down on the curb and lower my head to my knees until it passed. It took a while. It was about then I knew I was going to have to get in somewhere off the street. I wasn't going to make it to that motel at the north end of Seattle. Somebody would have to come get me. And I doubted that my speech had improved enough to summon a cab. I was able to articulate a little better than I'd been able to earlier, but probably I still would sound either too drunk or crazed for any hackie to want to pick me up.

So, I asked myself, head still down between my knees, what alternatives did I have? Call the cops? No, they'd take me to a hospital and the people at the hospital would put me under for three days. I didn't want to be unconscious for three days.

Benny? No, I'd need a doctor in and out, and until I knew where Benny's troubles originated, I didn't want to draw unnecessary attention to where he was holed up.

Lorna? After a lot of thought, I decided no. They might know that Lorna Bragg was my ex-wife. They might have somebody swing by the Phinney Ridge condo. I didn't want them tearing up her place. And there were other reasons.

Mary Ellen Cutler, or Zither? Not bloody likely.

Who, then? Marietta Narcoff.

I struggled to my feet and went looking for another phone booth. When I found one, I crossed to read the street signs at a nearby intersection. Then I looked up Marietta's number and dialed.

Her phone rang twenty times before I gave up. My

watch, which had come through the beating in a lot better shape than I had, told me it was a little before 11 P.M. So. I had to go back up the ladder of people I knew in Seattle. Mary Ellen Cutler wouldn't be in her studio this time of night. Zither might. I looked through the pages of names and numbers I'd written in my notepad since coming to Seattle. I found her number and dialed. She answered on the second ring.

I tried to tell her who it was, but my mouth still didn't work right. I couldn't say Peter, and Bragg came out sounding something like Bogg.

"Who is it?" she asked. "I can't understand you. I'm going to hang up if you don't tell me who this is."

My mind, such as it was, raced. "Shitheel," I blurted.

"Bragg? This is Peter Bragg?"

"Yes. I'm hurt. Need help. You have a car?"

"No, no car, but I'll get a cab. Where are you?"

I told her the names of the intersecting streets. She said she'd get to me as soon as she could. I hung up and thanked my lucky stars.

# *Chapter 22* ───────────

The night went on for a couple of more hours, into
Saturday morning. Zither got me back to her place and
made up a bed for me on the sofa in her living
quarters, looking out over the Alaskan Way viaduct and
the piers beyond. She and the cab driver had been
properly subdued when they saw the shape I was in,
but then Zither pulled herself together and showed she
had a good head on her shoulders. She didn't know any
practicing physicians who made midnight house calls,
but she did know a physician and professor of medicine
at the University of Washington Medical Center. He
didn't ordinarily make house calls either, nor did he
particularly care to be called out on a Friday midnight,
but Zither had told me she and the doc had dated at
one time and still were pretty good friends. She was
able to talk him into coming down to have a startled
look at me.

He told me he'd rather have me go into a hospital for

some X-rays, but I told him there were reasons why I couldn't do that. So he cleaned me up as best he could, swabbed me with this and that, taped my rib cage, gave Zither a couple of prescriptions she was to get filled the next day, and left me some pain pills. I gave him a business card, asked him to be discreet, and told him to bill my office.

"You bet I will," he assured me, snapping shut his bag and stepping out through the beaded curtains accompanied by Zither. Earlier, while I'd been waiting for the doctor to arrive, I'd phoned Benny at his motel and told him why I hadn't brought over the burgers. Now, while Zither was seeing the doc to the door, I made another call, waking Turk Connell, head of the World Investigations office in San Francisco. I apologized for the hour, then told him briefly what had been going on. I'd used my mouth enough by this time to be practically intelligible. I asked him to have one of the men in their Seattle office get my car out of the parking garage the next morning and return it to the rental outfit and to check me and my gear out of the motel on Aurora. I told him to have the man drop my stuff off at Zither's studio and gave him the address.

"But have him do some loop-the-loops first to make sure nobody's tailing him. I don't want those people coming in here after me."

"I'll tell him," Turk said in the middle of a yawn. "You want some of our people up there to give you a hand? Sounds like you could use it."

"Maybe. Make sure they know my name, so they can jump if I call them."

And then I slept.

I thought that with a sound night's rest I should have been able to get up about midday Saturday. It didn't work out that way. I could barely lift my head, let alone swing my feet off the edge of the sofa. Between stints of work out in her studio, Zither fed me soup and pain pills and some other anti-infection agents she'd gotten that morning with her doctor friend's prescriptions. I slept most of the time, but it wasn't a comfortable sleep. A lot of it was in that fuzzy twilight stage between sleep and wakefulness. I dreamt about the beating.

Sometime in the course of the day a local World investigator dropped off my suitcase. I went through it and dug out the .38 and put it on the carpet next to the sofa. Zither watched somberly but said nothing.

It must have been about seven o'clock that evening when I went back into a deep, deep slumber and pretty much stayed that way until the next morning. Zither was sitting up in bed looking through the Sunday paper and drinking a cup of coffee. She looked over at me.

"How do you feel?"

I moaned a little. On top of everything else, I was feeling bed sore. "No church for me this morning."

"Want some coffee?"

"Maybe. Give it a minute." I rolled my head around some and tried stretching my limbs. I hurt like a blister, but at least things didn't refuse to move. Even my left shoulder was working again. I sat up and clamped my hands to the small of my back where a couple of shooting pains shot.

Zither threw aside the covers and got up quickly to come over and kneel beside me. She was wearing a black T-shirt and black lacy underpants that emphasized the alabaster cast to her skin.

"You should get out in the sun more, you know that?" I asked her.

She made as if to hit my arm, but drew back her hand just before making contact. "Just never mind what I should do. Try to concentrate on what you should do. How about the coffee?"

"Sure, okay. I don't suppose you'd have some bourbon to put into it?"

"I don't, but Mary Ellen has some downstairs I can get."

She bounced up and went back up on the bed platform and got a pair of jeans off a wall hook and stepped into them.

"Is she here Sundays?" I asked.

"Most Sundays, and she is today. Got here about an hour ago. She stopped by yesterday, too, but you were asleep. She said you were about the sorriest-looking shitheel she'd ever seen. I told her that was how you'd described yourself on the phone the night before, so I'd know who it was calling. It put her into a fit of laughter."

"I suppose it would. Well, maybe she's right," I said, gingerly swinging my legs over the side of the sofa and rubbing my face. "Maybe that's exactly what I am. It's hard to explain about Lorna. My ex-wife."

She came back down off the platform. "Let's not talk about your ex-wife, huh? According to Benny, you two spent a lot of years together. I can understand how . . . things might have gone. I only wish you'd gotten that all out of the way before I met you."

"Yeah, me too. At least I think it finally is all out of the way, if it means anything."

"Don't, Pete. Let's not get into that just now. You're here because Mary Ellen and Benny and I are all good friends. Benny's in trouble, and you're trying to help him. That's why you're here."

"Yeah, well. Thanks."

"I'll get the bourbon."

I phoned Benny while she was gone. He said that the night before he'd put on his false whiskers and wig and contact lenses and gone out to a couple of bars. He said it'd been Dolly's idea and to a certain extent it had worked. He didn't have cabin fever the way he had in recent days. But he didn't know how much longer he could hold out that way. I told him to keep his chin up, that I had a couple of ideas but it would take a day or two to put them into operation.

Zither came back in with the bottle of bourbon while I was finishing the conversation with Benny. She poured me some coffee and whiskey and brought it over to me.

"What are the couple of ideas?" she asked after I'd hung up. "Or can you say?"

"I can't say because I really don't have any. I'm just trying to keep his spirits up. I still think, more and more, that something's going to happen around here, and when it does, Benny's the one who's going to be able to figure out what it's all about. Waiting for that to happen is the toughest part of this whole thing."

"Seems to me that what happened to you Friday night would be the toughest part."

"No, that only strengthens the hunch I have. Whoever's doing this must know by now I'm up here to help Benny. He's still the key to things."

The phone rang. Zither answered it, then handed me the receiver. "Benny again."

"Yeah, Benny?"

"Pete, I forgot to tell you. When I talked to Dolly last night, she said Lorna had phoned her up in Sequim. She was asking if Dolly knew where you were. She said she'd expected to hear from you Friday night, or yesterday at the latest."

"Does Dolly know where I am?"

"No. I just told her you were lying low for a couple of days. I didn't tell her where."

"Good. I don't want anybody else knowing. It's bad enough that you and Mary Ellen and even Zither here have to know. Thanks, Benny. I'll be in touch."

I hung up and stared at the far wall for a moment.

"Do I hear the sound of large thoughts gonging around?" Zither asked.

"I don't know," I told her finally. "It's really just a small one, but it might have a little meat on it." I braced my hands on my knees and started to get up. "Ow!" The pain dropped me back to the sofa. Zither watched with a stricken look on her face.

"Better go easy there, partner."

I grunted, then rolled slowly off the sofa onto my hands and knees on the carpet. I rested there a minute, then raised my left knee. I stretched my back some more, then slowly was able to push myself partway erect, and finally heaved all the way up onto my feet. I hurt in some new places.

"Congratulations," said Zither.

I looked out the windows. The streets had dried during the day I'd spent mostly passed out, but now more clouds were cruising in low again, looking for a good place to dump on people. I looked over at Zither. She was pouring more bourbon and coffee into my cup. She came over and handed it to me.

"I need a pool," I told her. "A swimming pool where there won't be a lot of people standing around staring at my black and blue marks."

"I don't know any of those."

"Somewhere in or near this town there has to be a private swimming pool owned by a man or woman willing to let me use it yet able to keep his or her mouth shut." I had a sip of the coffee, then turned with a ragged grin. "Would you like to go swimming with me? It's an outdoor pool, but it'll be heated."

"I don't know. Where is it?"

"At the home of a retired high-ranking mafioso living over on Mercer Island."

Her eyes widened. "I wouldn't miss it for the world."

I hadn't realized just how ragged had been the grin I gave Zither until I gingerly ran my electric razor over my face while staring into her bathroom mirror. It was the first time I'd seen my face since the beating. I looked like a purple and black gargoyle and wondered how Zither could have stood sleeping in the same room

with me. I would have given myself nightmares. But it
was a little tonic to me at the same time. My face and
head didn't feel nearly as rotten as they looked. It made
me think things were going to start looking up. And
they did.

When I phoned and told Bomber Hogan what had
been going on, he not only invited me over to use his
outdoor pool, but insisted on sending a car with a
couple of his men to pick me up. I asked if it would be
okay to bring along the young woman who'd risked
giving me shelter since the attack.

"She doesn't get outdoors enough," I told him.

"What the hell," said Bomber. "Bring her along. We
can make it a party."

And he did his best to do just that. He and his blond
girl friend, Kathy, were standing at the front door to
greet us. When Bomber got a look at my face, he
turned Kathy around and sent her back inside with a
pat on the fanny.

I got into the pool soon after we got there. Zither
joined me, wearing a one-piece black swimsuit. She got
out about ten minutes later, when it began to rain. I
stayed in the water. I always enjoyed swimming in the
rain, and the exercise was doing its job. I could feel the
knots and kinks leaving my muscles and the pain sub-
siding. By the time I climbed back out, I almost had a
spring to my step.

After I'd toweled off, Bomber had a surprise for me.
He'd called in his personal physician to take a look at
me. The physician took his look, then insisted I accom-
pany him to his clinic over in Bellevue, where he had
an X-ray machine. He wanted a look at the ribs. He
found a couple of hairline fractures but nothing worse
than that.

He drove me back across the East Channel Bridge
onto Mercer Island and down to Bomber Hogan's
place. While I'd been gone, Zither had been charming

the pants off everybody in sight by sketching them in pencil. Bomber wanted us to stay for dinner, but I was beginning to flag.

"I hate to swim and run," I told him.

"Never mind. You look lucky to be standing on your feet. You know, I've taken part in a beating or two my own self, God forgive me, but I never seen anything like what happened to you. If you ever find out who did it, let me know, huh? My guys could maybe learn something."

He insisted that we at least have a drink before leaving, so I told him I'd have a gin and tonic. Zither said a glass of white wine would be pleasant. That was the word she used—*pleasant*. You'd think we were in the home of royalty.

We were seated in the sprawling study where Bomber and I had talked the first time I'd visited him. Zither and Kathy were chatting over in one corner. Bomber was at the bar fixing drinks. I got up and hobbled on over to him to ask if his sources had anything more to say about the funny money movements he'd told me about earlier.

"Oh yeah, I almost forgot about that. Your friend who's in trouble, does he have anything to do with this big Potlatch Bay project going on over in the city?"

"No, not that I know about. But there's somebody else I know who's involved in that. Or plans to be."

"Yeah? Who's that?"

"My ex-wife."

Bomber turned with the gin bottle in his hand and looked across the study to where Zither was talking to Kathy. "Her?"

"No. Somebody else."

Bomber shrugged and turned back to the drinks he was mixing. "You're a man with many corners to his life."

"Too many, almost. What did you hear about Potlatch Bay?"

"Not a whole lot. Just that that's where the funny money movements might be going on. Are you on friendly terms with your ex-wife?"

"Depends on the day of the week."

"Heh-heh. Yeah," he said a little sadly. "I know just what you mean. Well, you might suggest to her that somebody maybe ought to check a little closer into the backgrounds of everybody involved in that thing. I'm not saying everything isn't legit, but maybe somebody should hoist the caution flag. At least that's what the people I know said."

"I'll pass it along. Bomber, I'm afraid I'm getting deeply into your debt."

"Don't worry about it. I'm out of the business, mostly."

The same two men who'd picked us up drove us back to Zither's place. They hadn't spoken much on the drive over, but they'd been among the people Zither had sketched while I was being examined by the doctor in Bellevue and now they opened up a little. They were chatting between themselves. One of them mentioned some physical problem his father was having back in Cleveland. Then they began talking about the chances of the Seahawks making it to the playoffs that year. The one drink I'd had back at Bomber's had nearly set me on my ear. I settled back and dozed.

When we got back to Western Avenue, the driver cruised around the neighborhood some before letting us out, making sure nobody was keeping a watch on the place. They asked if I needed help getting inside.

"No thanks, I can make it. You guys have been a comfort. Thank your boss again for me, okay?"

"No problem," said the lean fellow, whose father was having physical problems back in Cleveland.

Like I'd told them, I could make it, but I had to stop

and rest a couple of times on my way up the stairs. Zither hovered around a little nervously.

"You really ought to be in a hospital, you know that."

"No. I'm doing just fine."

I thought about what she had said as she was unlocking the door to her studio.

"I'll be getting out of your hair tomorrow," I told her.

She flung open the door and turned to me. "That isn't what I meant. And for your information, I don't want you getting out of my hair."

She tugged me inside by the sleeve. I made my way back to her living quarters and took off my jacket—the back-up one I'd had in my suitcase, not the one I'd been drenched and beat up in. I stretched out on the sofa and tried to bring a little order to my slightly gin-woozy mind. I could try phoning Lorna and tell her I'd been hearing some curious things about Potlatch Bay. Where did you hear these things? she would ask. From a hard hat bar mate out in Ballard and a retired hood on Mercer Island, I would tell her. And what curious things had they to say? she would ask. They weren't too specific about any of that, I would reply. No, I told myself. I wouldn't try to phone Lorna. Maybe after I talked with somebody at Seattle First Trust tomorrow. Maybe then.

I rolled over and stared at the back of the sofa. Still off balance, that's what I was. Off balance in Seattle. Maybe that's how it would be for me in Seattle forevermore. How could you feel that way about the town you'd grown up in? Why did I feel like such a hulking alien here these days? Superfluous, that's what I felt. In Seattle I was superfluous in the lives of everybody I knew. Benny and Dolly. Lorna. I couldn't seem to do what any of them wanted of me.

Zither? Well, she didn't really want anything of me. She just wanted to paint me without my clothes on. As a young man, it would have shocked me. But after the life I'd been living the past few years, that was pretty tame stuff. I heard her over at the sink doing something and rolled back around on the sofa.

"Hey, Zither?"

She turned toward me, her eyes ready for trouble. "Yes?"

"You're all right."

She blinked a couple of times. I dozed.

# Chapter 23

I looked and felt a lot better the next morning. Anybody who knew about that sort of thing could still tell I'd taken quite a beating in recent days, but the facial swelling had gone down enough so at least I could walk the streets without scaring the horses and children.

I thanked Zither for the hospitalization. She told me she'd be happy to have me stay on. I thanked her, but told her it would be better for me to find my own accommodations. It wasn't that I felt I'd have to sing lustily for my supper if I stayed at her studio, the way I would have felt if I'd moved in with Lorna. There was just something that made me shy away. A part of my mind told me I was being noble, that my staying at the studio would put Zither in jeopardy, that the men who'd beaten me might find me there and hurt the girl as well. But a different part of my mind said something else. *Timid*. That's the word Lorna had used. I wondered.

I took a taxi to a downtown car rental agency and got

myself another compact car. Marietta Narcoff had called her main money man, Bill Shakey, and told him to be expecting a call from me. Shakey in turn gave me the number of a man named Clausen at Seattle First Trust. I phoned Clausen. He told me his morning was clear and to stop by anytime. I went over and chatted with him about First Trust's role in the Potlatch Bay financial picture. It turned out the role wasn't all that major. First Trust had been approached by the Potlatch developers and asked to handle the transfer of funds from a bank in Hong Kong. It was mostly minor paperwork, for which First Trust would get a fee. Like trimming your fingernails, almost. First Trust wasn't really guaranteeing anybody anything despite the impression Lorna had given. First Trust was just going to handle the cash flow when the cash started flowing. It hadn't yet.

From a pay phone in the vault-ceilinged bank lobby I tried to call Lorna, but she and Gene Olson had already left for the luncheon and press conference at the Olympic Hotel. I put some more coins into the phone and dialed Benny Bartlett.

"Boy, am I glad to hear from you," he told me.

"Why? What's up?"

"I'm up. I mean, I've been up since six-thirty this morning. I'm packed and as good as checked out. I have to get out of this place. I gotta rejoin mankind."

"Benny, there are reasons for you to keep your head down, remember?"

"I remember. There also are reasons for me to get out of here. Mental health comes to mind. If nothing else, I'm going up and join Dolly and the kids in Sequim. Seriously, Pete."

I thought for a moment. Maybe he was right. We really hadn't accomplished much by his hiding around town. I'd been busy on my wild goose chases and getting beat up. Benny read the newspapers and watched television and we were still as much in the dark today as we'd been more than a week earlier, when I first hit town. Some private detective.

"Okay, Benny, maybe you're right. But let's meet and talk about it. Right now I want to go see Lorna. She's at a Potlatch Bay luncheon at the Olympic Hotel. Why don't you meet me there?"

"I'm practically walking through the front door."

I drove on up to the hotel and left my car in the garage where Gregory "Pappy" Boyington used to park cars in the days after this country was bombed into World War II. Boyington and some other hot-shot military flyers had been induced into resigning their commissions prior to this country's entering the war and joining up with Claire Chennault's Flying Tigers in Southeast Asia. There was a secret document held by the brass in Washington that stated in the event this country did go to war, these men would be allowed to quit the American Volunteer Group and be readmitted to their old service branch. But after Pearl Harbor, nobody seemed to remember that understanding. So far as Chennault was concerned, his flyers were to be inducted into the air corps for the duration of the war. Boyington said to hell with that, he was a marine and he was going to fight as one. He came back to this country and began lobbying for his reinstatement into the marine corps. He had family in the Seattle area and was told to go there and wait while his request was being processed. It took a while before he was sent back to the Pacific Theater of Operations, where he indeed did fight as a marine. He was nearly broke at the time, so while waiting to hear from Washington, he parked cars at the Olympic Hotel garage in Seattle.

In the hotel lobby, I found a placard listing the day's events and the name of the room where the Potlatch Bay luncheon was scheduled. I went on up there. Tables had been set for about fifty people. Another table had been set up to one side, where various people

could sit and say a few remarks to the media. Micro-
phones had been set up, and camera crews were
positioning their light racks nearby. Lorna and Gene
Olson were standing off to one side talking to some
other people. There was another man there I recognized as being from the Jackson Detective Agency. He
was the hatchet-faced fellow with slicked down hair
who had been banging cabinet drawers open and closed
when I'd gone up to introduce myself to old Grady
Jackson. He recognized me in turn.

A couple of minutes later the two men from Potlatch
Bay Lorna had introduced me to, Marvin Winslow and
Bruce Sherman, came through a nearby door and
settled down at the table the cameras and lights were
focused on. I made my way through knots of people.
Three-legged stands had been set up behind the table.
Architectural renderings of the Potlatch project were
displayed on them. Now a man I recognized as Seattle's
mayor joined Sherman and the cherubic-faced Winslow
at the press table. Still-photo cameramen were flashing
pictures. Reporters were asking questions, and the trio
at the table were boasting about the Potlatch development.

A tap on my shoulder drew my attention away from
the love feast going on in front of the cameras. It was
Benny Bartlett, wearing the fake hair, but also his
eyeglasses. He winced when he saw my face.

"You look like hell."

"I know. What happened to the contact lenses?" I
asked him.

"They were beginning to irritate me. It doesn't matter. I'm ready to get out of town anyway, just like
somebody wanted all along. What's going on here?"

"Press conference about the Potlatch Bay deal that
Lorna's firm is going into."

"Oh? That's curious."

"Why?"

"Do you know those birds at the table answering the questions?"

"Sure. The mayor's on the left, a fellow named Marvin Winslow is in the middle, and the other jasper is named Bruce Sherman. Winslow and Sherman are the developers."

"I see," said Benny with a funny sound to his voice.

"What is it, Benny?"

"Something smells. The man you said is named Marvin Winslow. I've met him before. Only then his name was Waldo Derington. He's the fellow who had the scheme to put houseboats on ferroconcrete hulls up in British Columbia."

I looked from Benny to Marvin Winslow then back to Benny. "Are you sure about that?"

"Dead certain, Pete. I spent most of a day with him."

"Wait here," I told him.

The press people were laughing over something Winslow had just said. I started making my way through people and over toward Lorna and the people she was standing by, who were off to one side of the press table. The press conference itself was beginning to break up. Camera lights were going out. Winslow, Sherman, and the mayor were standing shaking hands with people. I finally got over to Lorna and tugged at the sleeve of the navy-blue wool suit she was wearing.

"Oh my God, Peter, your face!" She just gaped a moment, then blinked. "What are you doing here?"

Winslow, beaming and with arms raised, told everybody to seat themselves at the luncheon tables. He said he'd be right back, then he and Bruce Sherman stepped back through the door they'd come through earlier.

"Lorna, something's wrong with this setup. Winslow isn't the man he says he is. He might be an old con man from British Columbia."

She looked as if I'd slapped her. "Peter, I don't believe it. Look at the people here," she said, gesturing around the room. "These are some of the city's shrewdest businessmen."

"Shrewdest."

"Yes."

"I've always associated shrewdness very closely with avarice."

"Well, Peter, let me assure you, this is all very legitimate. You just have to be mistaken about Mr. Winslow."

I looked back over the crowd to where I'd left Benny, but I couldn't find him. "Look, Lorna, it's not my money involved here and what I know about high finance you could stuff in a peanut shell, but I was talking to a First Trust officer earlier today. When is it you're supposed to get these low-interest loans?"

"We sign—or rather just did sign—documents that will channel the development money to the Potlatch Corporation."

"When did you sign the documents?"

"Just before the press conference."

"Then no money has actually changed hands."

"No. Except for the loan fee."

"What's that?"

"Oh really, Peter, this is too much..."

"What's the loan fee?"

"The premium we give Potlatch for making the low-interest loan money available."

"How much of a fee are they asking?"

"It varies, according to the size of the individual business. Ours was rather modest. Ten thousand dollars."

"Was? You've already handed it over?"

"Yes, I told you that. All of us here did."

"Checks?"

"No, cash."

"But that's crazy. Even I know that. Nobody does business with cash outside of the mob."

"Peter, please. This is a special situation. We're all on a tight schedule. They wanted to put the loan fee cash into the local branch of the Hong Kong bank we're dealing with. That gives us immediate release of the construction financing. Building crews will be on the site tomorrow morning."

"How much in all would you guess they got? In loan fees? In cash?"

"I don't know. Maybe a hundred and fifty thousand dollars. Maybe two hundred."

I looked around for Benny again but still couldn't find him. A waiter was setting luncheon trays on a stand over by where I'd left him.

"Peter? What is it?"

"I think the Potlatch people aren't planning to stick around for lunch," I told her.

I went over to the red-jacketed waiter.

"Did you notice a short fellow with a wispy beard and thick eyeglasses here a couple of minutes ago?"

"Why, yes I did. He left—well, actually appeared more to be propelled on the arm of another tall gentleman."

"Tall, with a narrow face and slicked back hair?"

"That's right, sir. They went through that doorway over there."

He pointed to the same door Winslow and Sherman had made their exits through. I trotted on over there and opened the door. It opened onto a short utility hallway. A fire door off it led to a concrete stairway. From the landing I could hear the clop-clop of feet a couple of floors below and what sounded like arguing voices. I couldn't tell if one of the voices was Benny's, but I started down the stairs anyhow. I heard another door open and close. When I got down to it and opened it, I was in the hotel garage. I heard a car door slam off to the right and started toward the sound.

A big dark green Buick screeched around a row of cars and came right at me. I had to leap back to keep from being hit. Bruce Sherman was at the wheel, with

Winslow seated beside him. The man from the Jackson agency was in the back. As they went by, I saw the Jackson man drive a fist down at something or somebody beneath him. It had to be Benny. They hadn't waited for a parking attendant. Neither did I.

# Chapter 24

I almost lost them in heavy traffic on streets around the hotel, but I got a break when they were stopped at a red light. I pulled up to within three cars of them. They drove north, out Dexter Avenue, above the west shoreline of Lake Union. I was trying to weigh my options. I didn't much care about the cash some of the shrewdest businessmen in Seattle fell all over themselves to give to their Canadian friends. I just wanted Benny before he got killed or hurt badly. Dolly and the boys wouldn't like to have their father dead. Nor would they like him to sustain the sort of beating that I had.

Probably, the Potlatch people just wanted Benny out of the way until they'd left town. Probably, the Jackson agency man had been hitting him just to keep him quiet. But then, who knows about men like that? I just wanted to stop it. I began moving up on the Buick. I was going to try to force it over wherever I found a spot where I figured I had a chance to pull it off. I expected the Jackson man would be armed. I had my .38 with six bullets in it on my belt. Spare ammunition was in the suitcase in the trunk of the car. I'd slipped up there.

Bruce Sherman must have seen me drawing closer. The Jackson man turned and stared back at me through the Buick's rear window. He turned for a minute to speak to the men in the front of the car. Then the Jackson man rolled down the window beside him to stick his head and one arm out of the car. There was a pistol in his hand, and it was aimed in my direction.

It didn't seem real somehow. Outside of the movies and TV, I'd never actually seen a man do that or try to do that—hit somebody from a moving car. It was crude and old-fashioned. But then this was Seattle, folks. In addition to being crude and old-fashioned, it also was very effective. I saw a flash from the pistol barrel and hit the brakes. So did several other people driving in front and in back of me. The Jackson man shot again, then pulled his head and arm back inside the Buick and kept an eye on me through the rear window.

The Buick was speeding up now, swinging through traffic. I kept pace as best I could. We zoomed down a moderate grade to where Fremont Avenue crosses the ship canal, but the Buick didn't cross the drawbridge. It turned sharply left onto Nickerson Avenue, which runs along the south bank of the canal.

I made the same turn in their wake, almost colliding with a beer truck. The truck driver and I both had fear on our faces when we whistled past each other. The Buick continued over to 15th Avenue Northwest, then swung right and crossed the Ballard Bridge. I followed at a respectful distance. We came down off the bridge and worked our way through streets that put us onto the main arterial that ran west past the locks and up to the big yacht basins behind the breakwater of Shilshole Bay.

They turned into one of the yacht basin parking lots

and screeched to a stop near one of the long piers running out into the harbor. Winslow and Sherman got out of the car, each of them carrying a couple of briefcases. They began trotting out to the pier. The Jackson man got out of the back and dragged Benny out after him. Benny was staggering, but at least he was conscious and on his feet. He'd lost the fake beard and wig. He still had his eyeglasses, but they were dangling from one ear. He grabbed them off and stuffed them in a pocket. I parked a good fifty yards away from them and just sat behind the wheel. The Jackson man had one hand on the back of Benny's shirt collar. He held his pistol to Benny's head in the other. He gave me a look that dared me to follow them. Then they started on out the pier after the other two men. I turned the car in a tight circle and drove back out of the parking lot and turned north, toward the yacht basin where Captain Ed moored his charter boat.

I ran out to his slip, but this time it was empty. In the slip next to Captain Ed's, a large woman wearing yellow oilskins was hosing down the front deck of a smaller boat. I called to her.

"Any idea where Captain Ed is? Or when he'll be back?"

"He went out early this morning with a fishing party," she told me. "Probably won't get in for another couple of hours."

I looked out over the water for some sign of a boat with Benny and the others on it.

"You got a problem?" she asked.

"Yeah. I wanted to charter Captain Ed's boat."

"What for?"

I looked back at her, wondering if she'd believe me if I told her. She was a muscular woman with a round face and short dark brown hair. She looked as if maybe she could drink and swear right along with the fellows.

"I think some men are planning to go somewhere on

a boat from a basin just south of here. They've got a bunch of money that doesn't belong to them, and they're holding a good friend of mine hostage. I think some of the same men kicked the hell out of me the other evening. I'm kind of mad, and I'm worried about what they might do to my friend. That's why I wanted to charter Captain Ed's boat. I was going to offer him double his normal charter rates if he was willing to risk going after those people."

She stared at me for a couple of moments. "You from around here?"

"Used to be. Now I'm a private detective from San Francisco."

"Show me some ID."

I climbed down onto the boat and showed her my investigator's license. She nodded.

"You want to hire a boat, you can hire this one. It's faster than Captain Ed's, and I'm a better skipper. Same deal as you'd offer Captain Ed. What do you say?"

"I say let's get going."

I don't know much about boats, never much cared to. But it was soon apparent this woman knew about them and was capable around them. She told me her name was Dee and her boat was the *Puget Pan*. She said she was the girl friend Captain Ed had told me helped him with his charter service. Her boat was about twenty feet long and was powered by a big pair of outboard motors. She kept the boat fueled, and within three minutes of the time I'd first called to her, we were pulling out of the slip.

She roared out past the breakwater and made a wide looping circle. She reached back to hand me a pair of navy surplus binoculars and told me to study the other traffic leaving the harbor. Five minutes later, a boat twice the size of the *Puget Pan* purred out from behind the breakwater with the man from the Jackson agency standing by the stern rail scanning the shore.

"That's it," I told Dee. "The black hull with the white housing. Think you can keep it in sight without their knowing we're keeping tabs on 'em?"

"Easiest thing in the world," she told me, putting on power and roaring out into the choppy bay.

She was smart, this lady skipper. She kept us well ahead of the black and white boat, looking over her shoulder to keep track of its course. I stayed down in one corner, pretty much out of sight, in case they had binoculars on the other boat.

"Is this something we should try getting the coast guard in on?" she asked.

"Yeah, maybe. I couldn't prove anything about the money, but as long as my friend's alive, he can sure swear to the abduction."

She steered the craft with one hand while she worked overhead radio switches with the other, then unhooked a microphone and began speaking into it. I couldn't hear her over the noise of the big motors. We were far enough out into the sound by now to be encountering some larger swells. I had to tell my stomach to behave itself. The black and white boat chugged along behind us.

"Any luck?" I shouted when she rehooked the microphone.

She shook her head. "Couldn't raise them. I'll try again."

We stayed on a northwesterly course for six or seven miles, until the black and white boat turned sharply left and curled around the northern point of Bainbridge Island. Dee spun the wheel and turned us in a clockwise circle until the black and white boat was out of sight. She brought us in close to the shoreline before slipping into the same southwesterly channel the black and white boat had taken.

Dee used the contour of the shoreline to keep us out of sight of the boat ahead of us except for brief stretches of open water. We tailed the black and white for nearly twenty minutes before its nose turned toward shore. Through the binoculars, I could see a small wooden dock at the base of a sloping brown cliff. Wooden stairs had been built into the face of the cliff leading to the plateau above.

"Any idea what's up above the pier?" I asked.

"Nope. I've been through this channel lots of times but never been ashore there. What do you want me to do?"

"Try to keep us out of sight until we see what they're up to."

She nuzzled the *Pan* in behind a low jog of shoreline and cut back on the throttle. We watched the black and white craft go into the dock. The Jackson man jumped down and tied some lines.

Winslow and Sherman clambered down quickly, carrying their briefcases. They and the Jackson man began climbing up the stairway dug into the cliff. There wasn't any sign of Benny. I clamped my jaws tight until the three men reached the top of the stairs and moved out of sight.

"Let's hit it," I told Dee, and the double outboards roared into life.

It took us a couple of minutes to reach the dock. Dee brought the boat into a curving slide to just behind the black and white boat. I jumped onto the dock and fastened a line to a metal cleat. Dee cut the motors and followed me onto the dock, fastening another line. I trotted up to the black and white boat and clambered up a short boarding ladder.

Benny was lying, groggy, at the rear of the cabin.

"How you doin', tiger?" I asked him.

He began to chuckle. "Jesus Christ, Pete, what are you doing here?"

"I got another boat. What's going on?"

"They have a plane up there. I faked being unconscious and heard them talking. They're on their way north, to Canada."

"Well, what the hell. So what? Let's go home."

Benny struggled to his feet. "What do you mean, so what? Those are the people who did all those awful things to me, Pete. Or at least had them done to me. I heard them swearing about me showing up at the luncheon. The whole thing was to prevent me seeing and recognizing Waldo Derington before they'd pulled off their scam and left town. We can't let those people get away with that."

"What do you want me to do?"

"Go get 'em. Me and Dolly and Timmy and Al want to see a little justice done around here for a change. Just go get 'em."

I had to grin at him. His priorities were right. I don't think either one of us would give a damn about the money. No skin off our noses. It was the principle of the thing.

"Okay, I'll see what I can do."

Dee came over the railing. "What's going on?"

I briefly explained things. "I'm going to go see if I can stop them."

"Want me to come with you?" Dee asked.

"Let's all go," said Benny.

"I'm good," Dee told me. "I've been in tavern fights."

"No. The two of you wait on the *Pan*. Pull out a ways from the pier. Try raising the coast guard again. If you get them, ask them to call the local sheriff. I don't even know what county we're in."

"Kitsap," said Benny.

"If someone comes back down to the other boat, tail them and try to give the coast guard their position."

"How far offshore should I wait?" Dee asked.

"Far enough so somebody can't hit you with gunfire."

I left the dock and started up the stairway built into the cliff. On the way up, I remembered I'd forgotten to get spare ammunition for the .38 out of my suitcase before I ran out to Captain Ed's slip. Too much going on.

I crouched low going over the top of the cliff. I saw Winslow and Sherman over by a small plane parked a couple of hundred yards off. It looked like a Cessna 172, high wing, single engine, and tricycle landing gear. There were a million of those things around, a good plane to sneak off in.

Winslow and Sherman were pulling out parking chocks and stowing the briefcases. Three other light planes were parked in a row on the far side of the primitive landing field. It looked like somebody's pasture. Probably just a cleared strip of land used by island residents who had their own planes. Between me and the Cessna there was a corrugated metal shed with a windsock flying from a mast atop it. The Jackson agency man was leaning against a corner of the shed watching the two men at the plane. Nobody else seemed to be around. The windsock was blowing in a northwesterly direction, which meant the Canadians would have to taxi up toward me in order to take off into the wind. Now they were climbing into the plane, and a moment later the propeller made a little whine and the motor coughed raggedly to life.

I did know a little bit about planes. If nobody had been out to the field to warm up that particular plane's engine, they'd have to spend the next few minutes doing just that. You can get away with jumping into a car and starting a cold engine and driving off, but you can't do that with an airplane. At least I didn't know any living pilots who ever tried that sort of thing. I took out the revolver and began creeping up toward the shed and the man from the Jackson agency, standing with his back to me.

The sound of the Cessna covered my approach. There are times when you address an opponent and formally demand this and that, and then there are times when you just whack him across the skull with your gun barrel. I whacked the Jackson man with my gun barrel. He was made of tough stuff. He only went down on one knee. I raised a foot and shoved him hard, in the middle of the back. I grabbed him by the collar of the topcoat he was wearing and dragged him across a shallow drainage ditch somebody had been digging and pulled him inside the shed and over to a corner, out of sight.

He was wearing his shoulder holster. I pulled out the .45 automatic he carried, hoping it was the one stolen from me on Friday night, but it wasn't. I put my .38 back into its belt holster.

I heard the airplane engine rev up a couple of times. I looked out in time to see the Cessna turn out onto the strip and begin a taxi toward the upper end. I ducked down beside a workbench as the plane went past the open front of the shed. The men in the plane were looking around, probably wondering where the Jackson man had gone. Bruce Sherman was at the controls. He'd driven the car. Probably, he had operated the boat as well. Universal wheelman. I ducked out of the shed and began trotting after the moving plane.

One of them must have looked back and seen me. Instead of continuing all the way to the end of the strip, Sherman spun the small craft around, shoved the throttle forward, and released the brakes. I ran out further onto the strip, got down on one knee, braced the Jackson man's automatic against my raised leg, and began firing at the Cessna's right wheel.

The .45 banged and bucked twice in my hands, then jammed. I uttered a few colorful words as I threw the weapon aside and clawed out the .38 again. The plane was gathering speed. I concentrated on just the one tire and emptied the revolver as fast as I could cock the hammer and squeeze the trigger. I figured my aim would be shaky enough at the moving target without trying to fire with the gun's double-action mechanism.

The plane roared past. I figured I'd missed with all eight shots, but then it began to wobble and spin sharply right, as if somebody had planted the right wheel into the ground. Sherman pulled back on the throttle, but he'd already lost control. The little plane's tail pitched skyward and the craft spun onto its back. I got up and began running toward it.

The plane's engine had choked to a halt. A hatch was batted open, and first Winslow, then Sherman tumbled awkwardly out of the cabin and crawled away from the plane. They'd been badly shaken up. Winslow was holding his head in his hands and Sherman stretched out on his back, moaning. I turned and went back to the shed.

The Jackson man was about the way I'd left him. I was looking around the workbench for something to bind him up with. I had my back to him when I learned he'd been playing possum. He came up onto his feet with a steel crowbar in his hand and took a vicious swing at my head. I saw movement just in time to duck. The bar missed my head but banged off my right shoulder. He was between me and the workbench now. I couldn't reach anything to defend myself with. There are times you stand and times you run. I ran.

I ran out of the shed and around behind it, the Jackson man stumbling after me. He was still a little whoozy from the whop I'd given him earlier. I could run faster, and what I wanted to do was get all the way around the shed and back to the workbench to find something I could strike back with. A revolver with six empty shell casings in its cylinder wouldn't do the trick. I was nearing the front of the shed again when I tripped and stumbled over a clod of earth. The Jackson man got close enough to take another swipe at me with the bar. It clanged off the shed, just behind my head. Instead of ducking into the workbench, I had to keep running. We went around again. This time I got far enough ahead of the Jackson man to dash into the shed, glance this way and that, then spot the long-handled shovel that must have been used to dig the shallow drainage ditch outside. I smiled inwardly. It was an oddly appropriate Seattle weapon. I'd used one of those as a building laborer, making enough money to put myself through school. Digging ditches, packing lumber, doing what had to be done. I knew all about shovels, and when the Jackson man came panting around the corner, I swung the shovel in a sharp arc, slapping the shovel head into the startled man's groin.

He stopped in his tracks, doubled over. I pulled back the shovel and stabbed it roughly into the man's neck. He yelped and dropped the crowbar. This time I sent the shovel in a roundhouse swing and clanged it off the back of the man's head. He fell to the ground and began to moan.

I picked up the crowbar and threw it toward the rear wall of the shed. I kept the shovel with me as I reached down and began dragging the man one-handed out onto the air strip. I dropped him finally and stood a few feet off to let him catch his breath. When he was able to take a couple of deep, ragged breaths, I stabbed the shovel head viciously into the ground a couple of times, to let him see I knew about shovels.

"Let's talk," I told him.

# Chapter 25

The Jackson man, who said his name was Munch, told me pretty much what I wanted to know before a couple of Kitsap County sheriff's deputies arrived in response to a call from Dee to the coast guard. The Jackson agency had been hired by Derington, alias Winslow, and Sherman to "take care of any problems" that might come up in the course of a business venture they were setting up. The Seattle detectives hadn't been told right out what the Potlatch Bay project was all about, but they had a pretty good idea after they'd been on the job for about two days. And they were the sort of agency willing to look the other way in order to make a couple of bucks.

"We might look like a bunch of thugs—that's the image we want to give—but we're a smart group of men," the shovel-battered man told me.

The Canadians' objective had been exactly what had occurred earlier in the day, to gull those shrewd businessmen Lorna had told me about out of advance fees for the fictional low-interest loans to develop the Potlatch Bay property. On the boat, the two men had crowed about lifting nearly $250,000 from the people at the luncheon. That was a nice return on about $25,000 they'd spent since hitting town to set up the scam. They'd acquired a short-term lease on the Potlatch Bay site, stuck an old trailer office on the property, fenced it and hired a watchman, had some lumber dumped there, put up a few billboard messages around town, and began whistling Dixie to anybody who'd listen to them. There wasn't any cheap money to be had. There was no Hong Kong bank waiting in the wings to be angel for the project.

The harassment campaign against Benny had been to avoid exactly what happened at the Olympic Hotel, Benny spotting Derington. The Canadians wanted Benny out of the way until they'd gotten their money and left town. Benny was the one person who knew Winslow's true identity. There was a danger Benny might see the con man in a newspaper photo or on television.

The Jackson agency had agreed to scare off Benny until the Canadians had what they wanted. The agency had been responsible for all of the violence and threats except for the incident with Benny's car, Munch told me. Derington had spotted Benny running his errands downtown that day. He saw Benny park his car on the hill and disappear up the street. Battering loose the brake lines with a tool from his own car had been a spur-of-the-moment act on Derington's part. When he thought about it later he decided he didn't want to run the risk of a murder charge, so asked the Jackson people to solve the Benny problem. But Munch swore there had been no serious attempt to take Benny's life.

"We missed him purposely when we shot at him at Woodland Park that day," he told me. "If we couldn't have hit him with the thirty-aught-six with a scope on it at that range, we don't deserve to be in the business."

The attempted abduction of Timmy and Al had been just to throw a further scare into Benny, the man told me. He said they had planned to hold the boys for a few hours, then release them with a threatening message to their parents.

"You must have been the one to break that up," Munch said.

"I was. Who were the two men who tried to pick up the boys?"

"Old man Jackson's boys, Tom and Wally. They did most of the rough stuff, plus beat the crap out of you. I was used as escort for today because it was supposed to be a piece of cake. Jesus," he said, rubbing his neck. "Some piece of cake."

"Why did they work me over?"

"You were getting too close for comfort. The watchman at the site called Winslow and said you'd been by asking things."

"How did Tom and Wally know I'd show up at the Scandia garage?"

"Winslow said you were sweet on your ex-wife. He said to keep watch there, and you'd probably show up."

Munch said Wally and Tom also had tossed the bomb into Benny's office but that they'd purposely waited until Benny was away from his desk. They had rightly figured that the phone call to him, without anyone answering on the other end of the line, might scare him out of there. He said Wally was the one who threw the bomb and followed it up with a couple of wild pistol shots.

"That Bartlett's a tough little guy," Munch told me. "We didn't think he'd ever leave town."

"It turned out he didn't."

"Yeah, well. Cut of the deck, I guess."

"Wally and Tom came down to Benny's office all yelling and cursing about the article in *Sound Sounds*. What was that all about?"

"They were just trying to find out if he was still around or not."

"When I was beat up the other night, somebody lifted a pistol I was carrying. Who was that?"

"Wally. He's got it in his desk back at the office. They thought you'd be in the hospital for a week."

I looked down at the two men by the Cessna. Sherman tried once to get to his feet, but finally gave up on it. "Those two were on their way to Canada?" I asked.

"I guess. I wasn't supposed to know that when people came around asking about them and the money. I wasn't supposed to know about anything."

"What were you going to do next?"

"Wait till they were airborne, then take the boat back to where we'd leased it, call Grady Jackson, and tell him the job was done."

"What were you going to do with my friend down on the boat?"

"Leave him on the dock. Let him make his own way home. He didn't know who I was. If he ever found out, it'd be his word against mine. He couldn't prove anything."

"What about me? I knew who you were. Where you were from."

"Yeah, well. We would have had to think of something to do with you."

I stabbed the shovel into the ground beside his ankle.

"I didn't mean anything like that. I didn't expect to see you today at the hotel. Grady just would have had to pay you off somehow."

"And you recognized Benny at the luncheon?"

"Of course. We all knew what he looked like, even with the rug and chin mop. His glasses gave him away."

When the deputies arrived, I went back to the stairs

at the top of the cliff and waved Dee and Benny back into shore. Benny told the deputies enough for them to take the Jackson man in for investigation of a number of things. Benny said he'd give them a complete statement the next day. He wanted to get back to Seattle and put his life back together. The shrewd businessmen in Seattle had acted quickly as well. The Seattle police had a number of complaints they wanted to talk over with the men calling themselves Winslow and Sherman. The deputies got on the radio and asked for a back-up unit to help carry people.

Which, so far as I was concerned, left the Jackson Detective Agency to deal with. I doubted that much in the way of criminal charges would stick against any of them. None of them would admit any of the things their man at the airstrip had told me. And even Munch wouldn't repeat it to law enforcement people. He'd only told me because I pretty well convinced him if he didn't, I was either going to brain him or sever his head with the shovel.

I didn't feel any great need for revenge against any of them, not even Tom and Wally Jackson, who were supposed to have put me into a hospital for a week. They at least hadn't broken any bones, other than the rib damage. They could have broken bones.

But something needed to be done about those people. I thought about it on the cruise back to the boat harbor behind the Shilshole Bay breakwater.

I gave Dee a card and told her to bill my office for the use of the boat and her skippering services. Benny phoned Dolly up in Sequim and told her to come home. I finally made a phone call of my own, to Bomber Hogan. It was a hard decision to make, and one I knew could come back to haunt me someday. I rationalized it by telling myself I wasn't really asking the old hood to do me a favor, but just to give the impression he was doing me a favor.

Bomber and the two men who'd given me and Zither a ride the day before met me out in front of the Jackson Detective Agency building at a little past five o'clock. I'd phoned ahead and told Grady where he could find his employee with the slicked down hair and asked him to stick around the office until I could get there. I told him we had a couple of things to talk about.

The four of us went up the worn stairs and into the office. Both of Grady's sons were waiting as well. They hadn't known I'd have company with me. And from the startled looks on their faces, they recognized Bomber Hogan.

"Hello, boys," he told them. "How do you open this thing?"

Tom came to the front desk and buzzed us through. I asked Bomber to wait up a minute and went over to where Wally stood uncertainly behind his desk.

"I hear you have something of mine," I told him. "A product of the Colt manufacturing company. I lost it the other evening. I understand you found it and have been saving it for me."

He slowly licked his lips, making up his mind, but then he bent and opened a desk drawer. He took out the .45 and handed it to me butt first. I checked. It still had its fully loaded magazine in it.

"Thanks," I told him.

Grady Jackson had heard our voices and now stood in his office doorway. He was as astonished to see Bomber Hogan as his boys had been. Before we went back to his office, one of Bomber's men brought out a camera with a built-in flash assembly. He snapped closeup photos of both Tom and Wally. The brothers blinked dumbly in the flashes of light but didn't move. Then Bomber and his two men and I walked back to Grady's office.

Bomber walked up to the older Jackson and stared at

him a moment without expression. "Hello, Grady," he said at last.

"Hello, Bomber."

Hogan looked into the inner office. He saw just the one visitor's chair and turned to drag in another castered chair from a nearby desk. Grady went in ahead of us.

"You two wait here," Bomber told his men.

They folded their arms and stood staring back at the Jackson boys. Tom and Wally sat down at their desks.

Inside Grady's office, the older Jackson had started around to his chair.

"No, Grady," said Bomber. "You sit here." He indicated the chair he'd wheeled in from the outer office.

Grady hesitated, then came back around his desk without a word and sat in the castered chair. Bomber went around behind the desk and sat in Grady's chair. Bomber was wearing a light gray business suit with a vest. He wore a pale blue shirt with a dark print tie and had a ruffled handkerchief stuck in the top suit coat pocket. He looked quite spiffy, and he sat regarding Grady Jackson very soberly for two, maybe three minutes. Then he opened Grady's desk and searched through drawers until he found a small tape recorder with its spools spinning.

He didn't bother to turn it off. He just swung around in the chair, opened the window behind the desk, and pitched out the recorder into the night. We could all hear it smack into the alley below. Bomber closed the window and turned back around. He cleared his throat.

"I don't want to hurt your boys, Grady."

"What?" Jackson asked sharply.

"I don't want to hurt your boys, Tom and Wally. Probably, they're good boys."

"Yes, they're good boys."

Bomber nodded, and stared for another minute or two at the older man sitting across the desk from him in the castered chair from the next room. Grady had a little tic working in one cheek.

"Maybe a little excessive," Bomber continued. "Tom and Wally. I think they've become a little excessive."

Bomber lapsed into silence again. Grady Jackson stared down at his feet.

"And you," said Bomber.

Grady's head snapped up.

"You've gotten sloppy, I think. You're taking on business I don't think you should. You're taking on the sort of business my people take on. You're crossing a line there, somewhere. You're giving your own profession a bad name. I've been watching it for a long time now."

"Bomber," the older man protested, "we've worked together in the past..."

That made me raise my eyebrows, but then I thought there shouldn't be anything too surprising about that.

"That was in the past," Bomber told him. "Many years ago. I'm in retirement these days. You're an older man than I am, Grady. I think maybe you should be in retirement, too."

Grady opened his mouth as if to say something but then closed it again. He was staring at the edge of his desk, and then a faint shrug lifted his shoulders.

"All right, Bomber, if that's what you want. I'll leave the agency. I'll retire."

"No," Bomber told him. "Not leave the agency. Close down the agency. I think the Jackson agency should go out of business. Give up the license. Take things easy. Let your boys, Tom and Wally, find something else to do."

Bomber made the barest pause. "Before something bad happens to them."

Grady Jackson slowly raised his eyes, dread tugging at slack facial muscles. "Oh no, Bomber. You wouldn't do that."

"Yes I would, Grady. I would have it done. Somebody

from back East, probably. Several somebodies from back East. Some men who would like a trip to the Coast, do a little work, then swing down for a little fun in Las Vegas before going home. Shotguns, I think."

Grady lowered his head to his hands. "Oh God, Bomber, I beg you. No."

"Yes, I think so. If your boys stay in the business, I think so. Shotguns. We'll try to have it happen in their showers, though. Easier to clean up things afterward that way."

We all sat there for quite a long while without speaking. Grady lowered his hands finally. He made another little shrug of his shoulders.

Bomber stared at him a moment longer. "Good," he said then, getting out of the chair. He came around the desk and put one hand on Grady's shoulders. "By the end of the month. You'll tie up the loose ends and farm out the longer-term business and you'll shut down by the end of the month, Grady."

"Yes," said Grady in a bare whisper.

"Good," Bomber said again.

On the sidewalk out in front of the building, Bomber turned to me, stripping the cellophane off a cigar. "Well, what do you think? Did I do okay?"

"You did wonderful. You certainly convinced me."

"Yes, but Grady is a tough old bird. He might change his mind. What then? What if he doesn't shut down?"

"I think he'll shut down, Bomber. But if he doesn't, forget it."

"I could have it done, you know. Just the way I told him. It would cost somebody some money, of course."

"No, Bomber. That's a favor I couldn't ask. I'm already worried about the kindness you've extended me. Worried about phone calls I might get down the road."

He laughed and clapped me on the back. "Don't worry about it. I like you. If there's a phone call down the road, it shouldn't be anything that would upset you. After all, I'm retired now, practically."

# *Chapter 26*

When Bomber and his two men left, I just stood on a nearby street corner and thought about things. It had been dark out since before we went up to see Grady Jackson. It wasn't raining, but there were no stars out, just streetlights, auto headlights, light from nearby buildings. A sharp little breeze had come up and people were scurrying by, heads down, shoulders hunched. Something I'd noticed since coming into Seattle more than a week earlier was that there were a lot of guys walking around town in navy watch caps and carrying paper bags who looked as if they were fresh off the boat.

What I was doing, I knew, was delaying a decision about what to do next. Fly back to San Francisco and home and get to working on saving Morrisey's client from the gas chamber or bum around Seattle for a few more days. I decided I couldn't make that decision yet. I have a friend on the *Chronicle*. Whenever you ask him how are things, even when he's just two minutes away from putting on his hat and going home, he answers, "It still could go either way."

I got my car and drove down to Benny's building on Western Avenue. Benny had been eager to get back to the office as soon as we'd pulled into the boat moorage out in Ballard. Probably, he was still there. Dolly and the kids wouldn't get home until later that night. Or the next day maybe. I decided I'd go see how Benny was settling back in. And then I leveled with myself. What I really wanted to find out was whether or not Zither might still want me to pose for her, with or without my clothes on.

I went into the building and didn't even look down the hallway toward Benny's office. I just went up the stairs and down the hall to Zither's studio. I rapped on the closed door and heard her call out for me to enter.

I went in and closed the door behind me. I didn't see Zither, but then she called from behind the beaded curtain.

"I'll be right out."

I nodded and strolled over to a painting she was working on to see if I could see whatever erotic imagery she was trying to put into it. I made out a hand, but I couldn't tell what it was doing or even whether it was a man's or a woman's. I heard the clicking of the beaded curtain behind me and turned.

She looked gorgeous. She had blossomed from stark black and white. She was wearing a pair of form-fitting white satin lounging slacks and a hot pink blouse. Her long hair was cinched at the back of her neck with a matching pink scarf, and she was wearing eyeliner and lipstick and some other makeup. She also was carrying two glasses of white wine and stopped in her tracks and gave me a wide-eyed look.

"Oh, hi," she said.

I had the feeling I wasn't the ship she'd been waiting

for to pull into the harbor. "Hi. Look, if I'm interrupting something, I'll just..."

"Oh no, that's all right," she told me, crossing and handing me one of the glasses. "I'm expecting Zack, is all. He's the man with the gallery that'll be showing my work next week. We're having dinner this evening to discuss things."

"Sure."

"Benny told Mary Ellen about the day you two spent. Pretty exciting, it sounds."

"All in a day's work," I told her, setting the wine aside.

"So when are you leaving?"

"Soon, I think."

"Will you be coming back?"

"Not for a while, chances are."

"Oh. Too bad."

There was another rap on the hallway door. I picked up the glass of wine and went to the door.

"Pete?" Zither called.

I turned.

"I'm sorry. But I never know what your schedule is."

"Don't fret. I hardly know myself." I opened the door. A tall pleasant-looking chap who looked about half my age was standing there. "You Zack?"

"Yes, sir."

I should have known he would call me sir. He had respect for his elders. I handed him the glass of wine. "This is for you. Have a good evening."

He turned as I stepped past him and started down the hall. "Why, thank you. Thank you very much."

I went down to Benny's office. He was filing things away.

"Mind if I use your phone?" I asked.

"Help yourself."

"When do Dolly and the boys get in?"

"They'll pull in around ten o'clock. We'll probably

stay up half the night drinking champagne and cele-brating. Why don't you join us? Spend the night?"

"No thanks, Benny. This should be a night for family."

"But I told you. That's what you are."

"I know, but..." I dialed around until I found an airline that could put me on a midday flight for home the next day.

Then, without giving myself any more time to think about it, I dialed Lorna's home number. Maybe we could have a farewell toast of some sort. Maybe dinner, even. Depending on how things went, maybe I'd even cancel the phone reservation and spend another couple of days there.

Brad Thackery, the Seahawks fellow, answered the phone for her. I almost hung up then and there, but screwed up enough courage to ask for my ex-wife. Lorna came on the line as high as a kite. She said the Seahawks had signed the contract for Scandia Farms to cater their big post-season bash. She was so excited she didn't even think to mention all the money I'd saved everybody by stopping the two men from taking off for Canada. It was all Go Seahawks time. I told her I'd just called to say good-bye. So we said good-bye and I hung up the phone, uttering another colorful word or two.

"Ball take a bad bounce?" Benny asked.

"The goddamn ball always takes a bad bounce in this town."

"Now, now..."

"No, I swear to God, Benny, Seattle is a jinx for me. It always has been. I've never had a relationship with a woman in this town that went straight and true all the way down the line."

"Have you ever? Anywhere?"

"That's not the point."

Benny broke up in a fit of giggling. He closed the file drawer and came over to punch me on the arm.

"Don't worry about it," he told me.

"Why not worry about it? You know, Benny, I don't think I've grown an inch emotionally since Lorna and I were still married. We're different people now, but you know, our relationship this time was basically the same as it ever was."

"Ah hell, Pete, forget about Lorna. Why don't you pop upstairs and say hello to Zither?"

"I already did. She has a date."

Benny didn't giggle this time. He howled. He was fun to watch, and by the time he got a grip on himself, I was smiling a little myself. Ruefully, perhaps, but smiling. I had to get out of this town, that was all.

Benny and I shook hands and told each other to keep in touch. I drove out north on Aurora Avenue again, looking for a motel where I could spend the night. These were old habits. I drove north instead of south toward the airport, because the north end of town was where I'd grown up, such as it was. And I drove out Aurora instead of Interstate 5 because when I was a kid, Aurora had been the main thoroughfare.

I slept well that night and had a leisurely breakfast at a nearby pancake house, then got back onto Aurora Avenue and headed toward downtown and the airport beyond.

I was looking at all the new buildings down there again, resenting them. Aside from one monster that should have become another Tower of Babel before it was finished, there was one other dark, monolithic thing that always got my attention. It had a sharply sloping top to it, so that at a distance it looked like a huge ship that had been upended, with its sharp prow sticking up into the sky.

I wasn't in any great hurry, and I decided to drive over there and find out just what that monster was. It was on the corner of Fourth Avenue and Blanchard Street. I parked on the street nearby and went up some stairs and into the building lobby. I asked the first man

I saw what the name of the building was. He told me it was the Fourth and Blanchard Building. It figured. I thanked him and went back outside, but before going back to the car, I wandered down to a small plaza beside the building entrance. The sun had come out and a couple of people were sitting there on benches enjoying the break in the weather. And then I stopped.

They weren't people. They were statues. Bronze statues, I supposed. One of them was of an old woman in a cloth coat and hat, bent over a shopping bag. And across from her, on another bench, was the statue of an older man with his topcoat unbuttoned and his bronze hat tossed on the bench beside him. He was staring up at the morning sun with his hands behind his head and a big grin on his face. It was the most astonishing statue I'd ever seen. It captured something about Seattle that was just slam-bam right.

I went back to the car then, pulled away from the curb, and headed for the airport, and I had to ask myself, How could anybody not like a town where they did something that perfect?

# 27 million Americans can't read a bedtime story to a child.

It's because 27 million adults in this country simply can't read.

Functional illiteracy has reached one out of five Americans. It robs them of even the simplest of human pleasures, like reading a fairy tale to a child.

You can change all this by joining the fight against illiteracy. Call the Coalition for Literacy at toll-free **1-800-228-8813** and volunteer.

## Volunteer Against Illiteracy. The only degree you need is a degree of caring.

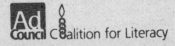

Ad Council Coalition for Literacy

Warner Books is proud to be an active supporter of the Coalition for Literacy.